Murder

COMES TO

Madtree

THE SIXTH
Snoopypuss
MYSTERY

*Pat
Wishing joy
Georgann Prochaska*

Georgann Prochaska

outskirts
press

Cover Photo © 2020 www.gettyimages.com. All rights reserved - used with permission.

Outskirts Press, Inc.
http://www.outskirtspress.com

Paperback ISBN: 978-1-9772-2703-4
Hardback ISBN: 978-1-9772-2715-7

Library of Congress Control Number: 2020908203

Outskirts Press and the "OP" logo are trademarks belonging to Outskirts Press, Inc.

PRINTED IN THE UNITED STATES OF AMERICA

In memory of my dad

List of Characters

Alice Tricklebank and Audrey

Lena and Julian Mueller

Reverend Francis Brandau

Rikki, the photographer

Elizabeth Madtree, owner of the Madtree Apple Orchard Resort

Artie Levitsky, brother of Elizabeth Madtree

Angelo "Frosty" Killian, employee

Mrs. Laura Leigh Penrose, face-painter

Maia, daughter of an apple picker at Madtree

Sylvie Jakubowski, guest

Virgil Deke and his older brother Cyril Deke, guests

Wayne Rasmus, guest

Bernadette and Lester Livingston and Gavin, guests

Pepper Finwall, guest

Wedding Invitation

Lena Vincenti and Julian Mueller

Request the honor of your presence

Saturday, October 24, 2014

At 11:00 a.m.

Elizabeth Madtree's Apple Orchard Resort

(No gifts and no dead bodies, please)

Chapter 1

October 24, 2014

A woman in her fifties, dressed in crisp, tangerine golf wear, waved her arms in wild gestures at two staff members of the Elizabeth Madtree Apple Orchard Resort. All three stood on the front steps of the main building and peered up at the third floor. A lone police car sat askew, off to the right.

Sitting with a congregation of guests in a clearing between two apple orchards, Alice Tricklebank couldn't hear what they said, but she felt their agitation. Her best friend Lena wouldn't be pleased if this performance on the steps detracted from the comfort of her outdoor wedding.

Julian's and Lena's wedding guests checked their watches and cautioned children to stop squirming. A man behind Alice said, "You'd think they've had enough practice to start the ceremony on time. They're both in their sixties, for God's sake. How long are they going to make us wait?"

Alice easily imagined Lena being late to heighten the intensity of her entrance, but Julian, a retired truck driver, liked a schedule. So, what was the delay?

Julian's daughter, who took on the role of best man, stood alone beside the podium, shifting from foot to foot. She tried to smile at guests, but she cringed as she caught glimpses of the inn.

Men and women stood on ladders nearby and picked apples, paying little attention to impatient guests. They leaned toward the trees and twisted as many as three apples at a time before slipping them into the collection bags strapped to their waists. Watching them strain forward made the back of Alice's legs hurt. How did they do it hour after hour, day after day?

For over a year, Lena teased Alice about being her matron of honor, but in the week prior to the improvised ceremony, Lena changed her mind.

"*Matron of honor* sounds too much like you stock toilet paper. You're a witness, not a matron. Besides, I'm a bit superstitious. You were my matron of honor when I married my favorite husband, Charlie. I never expected his death. And—Julian is tired of waiting to get married. He's forced this marriage by making all these slap-dash arrangements. Not that I'm complaining. May as well marry my love monkey." Her eyes sparkled with naughty glee.

Lena often expressed her love for Charlie Sweet, but he had died too soon. Her three other marriages had ended in divorce. Alice had spare details on one of the weddings until the day Lena appeared at her door wearing a wedding band on her finger. "I didn't tell you," Lena had explained twice, "because you'd have tried to talk me out of it. Look at this gold band next to my new sparkly rock. Alice, I was a gorgeous bride."

Julian and the minister, mere blips in the distance, exited the front doors of the inn, squeezed past the tangerine woman, and hustled toward the wedding guests, a cross between a jog and a very fast walk.

From her position behind Lena's sons, grandchildren, and daughters-in-law, Alice kept an eye on the front of the inn. Just before Julian scooted into his place at the altar, Lena and her daughter, Cheryl, finally left the inn and climbed into the long resort tram for their ride to the apple orchard wedding site. A drone with a camera hovered overhead taking pictures of the welcomed day.

Time moved slowly. Alice watched the activity on the front steps.

The tangerine woman appeared to be hysterical as she backed away from two staff members. Her arms reached out to the growing crowd. With a staff member on either side, she was escorted into the building and away from heads that turned with her retreat.

Once the tram arrived, Cheryl steered her mother over the gravel aisle draped in white cloth. Lena took a moment to primp. Cheryl kept one hand on her mother's big hat to prevent it from taking flight. Alice had a perfect view of the minister and Julian who huddled with their backs to the guests.

Lena sang to the congregation, "It's showtime."

The minister, Julian, and his daughter looked grave and uncomfortable in front of their seated family and friends.

This marriage ceremony came after the bride and groom's bumpy start. Until they admitted love for each other, they both had engaged in name calling, and one of Lena's ex-husbands had threatened Julian's life. There also was the time one murder suspect broke Lena's ribs, and another bad guy busted up Julian's hands. Still Alice's two friends had stuck with her through murder investigations and helped with Audrey the bloodhound when Alice was desperate to travel to California for her grandson's graduation. Through it all, they hoped this wedding day would come.

Julian must have become impatient if he took charge of the wedding planning, thought Alice as she took a deep breath. *At last. They'll marry on a beautiful, cool fall day.*

Out of the corner of her eye, Alice saw a determined Limekiln police car pull into the Madtree Resort. No lights flashed. The car moved with purpose but not because of an imminent crisis. Alice experienced enough murder cases to know the difference. Orchard workers intent on filling wooden crates took little notice. The second police car parked next to the first.

Perhaps the tangerine woman became more disorderly once she went inside, thought Alice.

At the inn, the police officer left his car, put on his hat and entered with his hand on his gun.

The minister, Francis Brandau, had a serious demeanor as he leaned to talk privately with Julian, but a snarky smile punctuated his sentences. As he spoke, his eyes darted to look over Julian's shoulder as if he expected any minute an intruder might haul him away from the podium.

Standing almost six feet tall, Francis was imposing. A simple rubber band pulled his two-foot-long white ponytail back from his face. His eyebrows sprouted like uncontrolled black wires, his beard, scruffy. Since neither Lena nor Julian wanted formality, they asked guests to dress for comfort. Francis wore a white clerical collar over his black T-shirt. A creepy tattoo of a snake curled from under his short sleeve and around his forearm. The artist positioned the snake head to rest above his fingers.

To set up this wedding, Julian had apparently twisted his boyhood friend's arm, and Francis became an ordained minister through the Internet.

Alice knew both Lena and Julian were skittish about this marriage, but with the announcement of the wedding, Lena's eyes brightened as she said, "We'll make this work, even with our past. Julian's right. What we need is a relaxed setting."

The orchard was quiet. Early fall yellows had already fallen and deadened footsteps. Late autumn oranges still blazed as they hung onto the branches of nearby maple trees. None of the workers in the orchard seemed to talk or play music. Trees rustled and ladders creaked. Dull rumblings drew wedding guest's attention as apple pickers added their bags of apples to a bigger wooden box.

"I'm waiting," sang Lena standing behind the congregation.

Reverend Francis nodded for Lena's grandson to start the recorded music. Cheryl gave her mother a push toward the make-shift altar of pumpkins and gourds, but Lena, known for her drama, stood behind the audience and waited until the touching song played by a piano and cello finished. With everyone a little nervous, Lena nodded at her grandson, and the song began again. She walked slowly toward Julian, the piano's light notes voicing hopeful determination set against a moody cello of dark complications. Lena's eyes welled up as she focused on Julian, who wiped his hand across his eyes.

The minister's craggy face and hard eyes looked more disgusted than moved by his friend's emotions. He turned one more time to look back at the inn before his mouth set hard as if he might leave this all behind and walk away.

At least Julian's not the one wishing to escape, thought Alice. She tried to focus on her friend, but her eyes were also drawn to quick looks at the inn.

Lena wore a dressy, icy-blue lace dress with a bolero jacket—a rare sedate look for a woman who liked dazzle. A matching Queen-Mum-style hat with a dancing feather covered most of her blonde curls. Although she looked almost weepy with the day, Lena's eye had flirty pizzazz.

Alice checked her own attire—inky blue pants, inky blue shell top, and inky blue duster. But the dark did set off nicely against the orange mums and pumpkins lining the aisle. Her naturally curly gray hair remained uncooperative and bordered on frizzy. Her gray, owl-like eyes always carried wonder. At six feet tall, her choices of monochrome clothing made her stand out like a pillar.

All invited guests knew a lunch and dancing followed the ceremony, but most dressed for the resort's entertainment: miniature golf, the weekend Apple Butter Train ride around the property, the bails of straw forming a scarecrow maze, and the heated Olympic-sized swimming pool.

For the wedding Julian had succumbed to a haircut but chose his signature orange bandana to cover his head. He wore black cargo pants and a white island shirt with elaborate stitching. The short sleeves revealed chilly goosebumps on his heavily tattooed arms.

A third police car, this time from the county, drove down the long lane toward the inn, and as the officer made a turn, the wheels kicked up some dust. He was followed by an ambulance and another police car. Alice twisted in her chair to check out the entrance to the Madtree Orchard and caught Sylvie Jakubowski's eye. The woman in her eighties sat on the groom's side with Julian's other friends from hometown Bottom Ridge. Wearing her typical layered clothing—sweater over sweater over Cuddly Duds—Sylvie winked at Alice as her mouth scrunched up with sour disapproval. Her hat wiggled as she tilted her head in the direction of the police cars, indicating *Get-a-load-of-this*.

Rather too many police cars for a fight at the bar, thought Alice. *Unless the tangerine woman scolded a couple of young guys consuming too much cider. One pushes, the other breaks his nose. A martial arts roundhouse could follow.*

The reverend steepled his fingers before Julian spoke his promised vows. "I loved you from the moment I saw you walk into the Butter Churn Café. I almost couldn't breathe. How could someone as beautiful as you ever love someone like me? I called you *Fatty* because I thought you'd reject me." With a tear in his eye, he choked out, "I promise to do all I can to make you happy in the time we have together. I'm lucky to have you in my life."

Alice felt the sincerity of the touching moment, but she didn't like the tone of Julian's voice. It sounded more appropriate for someone saying goodbye.

Alice corrected her suspicious nature. *Just stop it. They'll be fine.*

Lena's eyes spilled tears as she gazed back at Julian. She began her vows by first joking about murder investigations they had been involved in and her understanding of his nickname, the Octopus Man. She turned to the audience, "A well-deserved nickname. He's a hot surprise." She struck a pose, and the guests chuckled before politely curbing their laughter. Facing Julian, she became serious. "I promise to be by your side and to love you forever. I always know that when darkness comes, my light is Julian."

Women sniffed and dabbed at their eyes with tissues. Men cleared their throats.

Sylvie caught Alice's eye again and held up a note before she bullied other guests with an evil expression and shooing fingers to pass it along in Alice's direction. Virgil, Sylvie's companion also in his eighties, lost his concentration on the service and blinked at Alice. His older brother Cyril, every bit of ninety, punched Virgil's arm. Immediately, both brothers straightened and faced forward. Sylvie rolled her eyes.

Had it been just the previous Christmas that Sylvie and Virgil had been Alice's house guests for another wedding. They had weathered her stairs and kept a protective eye on her. Alice studied Virgil. Without his vigilance, she might have died.

Two more police cars, also from the county, sped in and blocked the driveway in front of the Madtree Inn. Although guests were doing their best to pay attention to Lena and Julian, everyone seemed to fidget with awkward head nods toward the crowd gathering around the police presence. Alice knew if this number of county police cars were on the scene, murder was a sure thing. Soon, the forensic van should appear.

Apple pickers' hands never stopped, yet they managed to cast quick glances in the direction of the police.

Alice noticed Julian's attention waver away from Lena and toward the inn. Reverend Francis Brandau also struggled with eyes forward as he blessed the union.

"All right!" said Francis, his voice gravelly. "Time for the groom to give this young lady a big smack."

The audience clapped as Julian took Lena into his arms and kissed her, a long kiss as if he never wanted to let her go. Alice hoped the crisis at the inn wouldn't ruin Lena's wedding day.

Like a series of misbehaving kids passing Sylvie's note, guests concealed the folded paper in the palm of their hands, and side-glanced at each other and the minister. With the note finally delivered, Alice read, *Police cars, huh? Guess murder follows you everywhere. Don't say this is none of our business. Hope you're ready because this Bottom Ridge posse stands ready to sink our teeth into a good murder investigation, again.*

Chapter 2

Once the wedding party, family members, and selected friends posed for pictures with a backdrop of fruited apple trees, next to the scarecrows in the maze created with bales of hay, and near the miniature golf windmill, Lena called in Alice's direction, "This hat has flattened my hair. Cheryl and I are going to change clothes for the reception to make me sparkle. Wait until you see my reception dress." Lena pushed out her ample derrière and struck a pose with her right arm in the air, her wrist bent.

"Do you want some help?" asked Alice.

"She wants to make an entrance," said Cheryl, shaking her head.

As Alice watched, the crime scene van pulled in. Lena turned. "Did you count the police cars?"

"I did," said Alice.

"So many cars and the van? Go find out who was murdered," ordered Lena. "We might have a case."

Alice grinned at Lena's reaction to murder and echoed Sylvie. "And what if someone says it's none of our business?" She knew the answer her best friend would give.

"Piddle! Then they shouldn't have killed someone on *my* wedding day. We're calling dibs on this investigation. Did you know there is a writer staying at the inn?"

"No. What kind of writer?" asked Alice. It was just like Lena to spin a discussion into an opposite direction.

"For a travel magazine, I think," said Lena. "Everyone was all abuzz at breakfast. No one knows who the writer is, but gossip says the research is for *Everyone Can Magazine*. They are evaluating the inn as a travel destination for people with physical difficulties. What could be more challenging than a murder at a wedding?" Lena gave an impish grin. "Cheryl, come on, we have a wedding show to put on at the lunch. Who knows, maybe I'll be on the magazine cover? Think of the headline: Bride Solves Murder."

With that said, mother and daughter rejected the tram ride back to the inn because it was slowly filling with guests. Instead, the two of them hijacked an electric utility buggy bigger than a golf cart, the back filled with bins of dead leaves and debris. Alice shook her head. Lena always pictured them as real detectives on the front lines of gossip and described their snooping friends with words like *posse, squadron, crew, choir, or brigade*. Lena had even influenced Sylvie to pick-up the investigation bug. Virgil, as an older gentleman, came by his protective nature toward women naturally. In truth, they collected biting secrets or encouraged witnesses to spill what they knew.

So, Lena had begun the collection of gossip. A writer was on the property, but Alice doubted Lena's information about *Everyone Can* being a travel magazine. She remembered it as suggestions for people with physical challenges to adapt. In the distance, Alice watched as Lena grabbed her hat, scrambled out of the green buggy, and fought with the soft breeze tugging at her clothing. She entered the inn without any heads turning in her direction. Everyone focused on the police officer who stood by the front entrance and those who moved in and out.

Wedding guests' attention drifted from the orchard wedding to the resort entertainment. Children stripped off outer clothing to reveal swimsuits before they plunged into the bath-like water of the pool. Julian's male friends traipsed off to the outdoor bar to sample hard cider. Only a few of the older adults caught the lure of the investigation outside of the inn.

Alone, Alice completed her walk over bare dirt, gravel, and sidewalks and joined the other guests who had wandered to the police crime scene tape. Forensics had just brought out the first evidence collection in small bags and weaved their way through the crowd to a van.

Cyril's face registered disapproval as Sylvie stood with the curious and waved a hanky to catch the eye of anyone with law enforcement. Virgil held tight to his persona of an observant, older gentleman, but Alice noticed he wasn't particularly interested in the police. He studied the crowd. Had he heard the rumor about the writer? Alice's own curiosity made her scan the cluster. Who in the crowd might fit the stereotype of a writer? Which one a killer?

Whatever am I going to do with these three who see themselves as an extension of law enforcement? thought Alice. Her sense of responsibility kicked her with worry for Virgil and Sylvie but particularly Cyril, who leaned heavily on his walker.

She felt torn by the events. Standing outside at a police line almost never yielded useful information. The looky-loos wanted stories for dinner conversation. The by-standers who knew details might not even realize they had valuable nuggets of truth.

Too soon to lurk, thought Alice as she made a twisted face of frustration and studied the Madtree resort.

The older part of the inn started as a white farmhouse with a wide front porch. Once the Madtree family took over the property, they added a three-story annex of rooms at the back of the house. The white painted inn stood in stunning contrast to the russet-colored outbuildings. To the northeast of the inn, one barn processed apples for shipping. Another held the country store. A third pressed apples for cloudy sweet cider and experimented with the harder stuff. The aroma of apples dominated the property with a tangy sweetness.

Every year workers at the resort created the scarecrow maze near the pool. Miniature golf sat closer to the county road and enticed families to stop. The tracks for the child-size Apple-Butter Train circled the entire property, but the train only ran on weekends when the Limekiln Locomotive Club could man the entertainment.

Beyond the entertainment areas, clustered a camp of russet-colored cabins for the few families of seasonal pickers. Alice knew men without families lived off the property. In the distance, Alice saw a few small children stand with an older woman to watch the activity of guests and police.

Alice felt lonely. For over a year, her bloodhound Audrey had been her constant companion. Not to have her dog by her side was a disappointment. Alice's hand patted her thigh, almost expecting a bloodhound to offer comfort or to insist they check out the children who waited for bone-weary parents to leave the orchard and head home.

Audrey waited at home, entertaining her next-door neighbors Gretchen and a new friend Wells. Alice imagined both laughing as Audrey and Wells' dog Cooper raced the yard. She pulled out her phone. Maybe Wells had sent pictures? But there were no pictures of dogs at play.

As Lena's best friend, Alice wanted to be in the room as Lena prepared for her big reveal at the reception. Lena took splash and spectacle seriously, and Alice willingly accepted her role as the first to applaud and shout *Wow*. However, what was she supposed to do while Lena dressed? Realistically, she was no help at all. Lena's glam style contrasted with Alice's utilitarian eye.

If Audrey had been allowed on the grounds, maybe the bloodhound's nose could detect a scent out of place. Of course, collecting scents often motivated Audrey to slam her nose into crotches—for most targets, an embarrassing surprise. The Limekiln officers knew Audrey well, and might call upon her skills in a day or so, but Alice knew it was too early for them to have enough evidence to engage a hound.

Sylvie, Virgil, and Cyril continued to stand behind the crime scene tape with other guests of the inn. The woman in her tangerine shirt, shorts, and even socks, returned to the porch and claimed the crowd's attention with what she knew about the murder of a man in a suite on the third floor.

"His room is just above our room," she said with her eyes wide open, her voice breathy. "We didn't know! We didn't hear a shot or a scream. Nothing. An officer came to our room and asked if we were all right and if we had heard anything. We didn't know the guy was murdered last night! Right above us. Housekeeping found him this morning. Can you imagine a murder at an apple resort?"

A tall-ish man in his middle sixties, holding a putter, stood five steps behind the woman who ranted. Wisps of thin hair were combed forward and plastered to his brow. His shoulders slumped and his cheeks blushed embarrassment even as he gave a sheepish grin. As Alice scooted closer to him, the tangerine woman turned to nod at the man and began her story again for the newbies who joined the onlookers. Alice heard the man with the putter whisper to another, "She'll be at this for hours." He retreated toward the outdoor bar with a posture of being beleaguered.

Alice checked her watch. She had forty-five minutes until the official wedding lunch, and without Audrey, she didn't exactly know who to target first for gossip or how to break the ice with these particular strangers.

What to do? Where to start? I hate waiting. A man is killed in the middle of the night and no one hears it? No one heard a scuffle? Not the tangerine woman or her husband?

Alice couldn't see a killer skulking off the property in the dark of night. *That would be too cinematic, too clumsy.* Her experience with murder investigations told her killers stuck around, felt smart, and relished the benefits of the chaos he or she had created.

The killer could be in this crowd.

Alice looked at the age of those gathered. No children—they were off playing. No young parents—also off, watching children at play. A few couples hung around and listened to the tangerine woman, but most shifted their weight from foot to foot. They would soon leave. Virgil dragged a bench into the shade for an older woman so she could sit in comfort. Cyril had already found a table and chair in a shady spot under a big maple.

Well, probably no killers in this specific crowd, thought Alice.

Chapter 3

A crush of who, what, when, why murder questions niggled at the back of Alice's mind until Elizabeth Madtree herself grabbed Alice's arm with such strength that Alice thought she might sport bruising by morning.

"My office."

Elizabeth was an elegant woman, several inches shorter than Alice's six-foot height but also thin and willowy. Elizabeth claimed she wasn't yet fifty. On this wedding day, she severely swiped her straight black hair behind her ears. She wore black pants, a crisp white shirt, and a long black jacket showing four-inch white cuffs. Gold-toned, chunky chains hung around her neck and jangled as she moved. Her signature candy-apple red lipstick needed a touch-up.

"Alice, you have to help me."

"Me?" asked Alice. "What do you need?"

Alice's nose was still slightly out of joint from Elizabeth's previous rejection of Audrey being the ring bearer at Lena's wedding.

"With a murder investigation?" guessed Alice.

Elizabeth nodded.

Alice only knew Elizabeth through her children. Several years prior, she had taught the two Madtree sons. Both college-educated and now with families of their own, they had entered the family apple business. Rod ran the cider making and Christopher, marketing.

"The county police are here, and Lieutenant Unzicker from Limekiln is heading up the investigation. Our resort only has one security officer, Old Nelson. We've never had anything disagreeable like murder. Look around. Madtree is the Grant Wood of apple orchards."

Alice hoped Elizabeth wasn't picturing American Gothic's crusty, stern farmer with a pitchfork or his plain sister in an apron.

"We work at keeping the resort homey." Her voice crackled as if issuing an order. "Quiet. Wholesome! We have Story Time for children on weekends. Nothing bleak has ever, ever happened until this murder. Anyone of any age or ability can come here."

"Maybe if you—" attempted Alice, hoping to prompt Elizabeth to share early facts of the murder.

"Alice, this timing is so bad for business. This month we have a journalist on the property to review our accessibility. Do you know how important that is? Our support generally comes from surrounding communities, but to grow we need to be a destination. Christopher said we need a bigger profile online. Young families need to give us positive online reviews. Naming us as a cooperative destination for people who have a disability could be magic for us. We don't have enough acres to be big enough for a roller coaster or a high-tech light show to draw in the enormous crowds. But I want to pass on to my sons and grandchildren a business that will be something they can be proud of. Now this—no one wants to sleep where a man has been murdered. No one wants to read a review about murder at an inn."

Alice chose not to disagree even though she knew many people sought out hotels or resorts with a hint of a ghost roaming the stairs.

"Elizabeth, what can I do to help?"

"You don't have your dog with you?" Elizabeth stood straighter, as if annoyed at the inconvenience of no bloodhound at the ready.

"No, Elizabeth, you said your resort doesn't allow for any kind of dog on the property."

"Oh, that's for pets," she said with a wave of dismissal. "Audrey's a service animal. Of course, she can stay." As if speaking to a reporter, Elizabeth said, "All service dogs are accepted. I'll set you two up in a room at the far end of the annex for as long as this investigation takes. That way you can walk her without disturbing guests. She doesn't bark, does she?"

"She's a hound, so there are times she expresses excitement," said Alice. "Mostly she's quiet and adorable. Generally, people don't mind even if she howls."

Elizabeth's forehead wrinkled with concern, and she bit the corner of her mouth.

"Could guests be allergic to her?"

"People have allergies, Elizabeth. Do you have guests allergic to apple butter?"

Elizabeth blinked at the indignity of the thought. "Apple allergies are overblown. Now are you going to bring your dog or not?"

Alice felt her own hackles rise with Elizabeth's lack of dog experience and insistence that Alice do her bidding.

The orchard owner's face clouded as she seemed to struggle. "Despite her howling, I want her *here*."

"Are you waiting for the police to make a suggestion for a search by a sniffer dog," asked Alice. "Or do you need our help finding someone specific?"

"Maybe someone specific." Elizabeth turned cautious, her voice attempted nonchalance. Her eyes checked out a fold in her cuff. "I don't know yet. I think it's better to be prepared."

"That's very kind of you to offer a room," said Alice, "but I have a few of Lena's wedding guests staying with me from out-of-town. Long-time friends of Julian. I don't believe they can afford rooms here, and it's too late to find other lodging. They're elderly with a tight budget. Besides, none of them drives anymore."

Elizabeth's face reddened. *She's used to having her own way*, thought Alice.

"You have to be here. You simply have to. So does Audrey." Elizabeth's eyes blinked desperation. "Alice, I need someone I can trust to be discreet."

"I'm sorry, but I can't stay," said Alice.

She reminded Elizabeth of the three elderly houseguests who were unable to drive and waited for her promises to them to finally dawn on Elizabeth. When the commitment didn't make sense to the younger woman, Alice continued with a plan.

"Let's try the next best thing. Audrey and I will be here early every morning. It means, however, I'll need to bring my houseguests with me. I can't impose on my neighbors to entertain them. And trust me, now that they know of a murder, Sylvie, Virgil, and Cyril won't let me leave the house without them."

Elizabeth's brow wrinkled as her fist briefly covered her lips. "Sorry, plan B won't work. You must be on the property. I'll comp them too. Three guests? Will a suite do?"

Startled at Elizabeth's generosity and insistence, Alice thanked her. A suite was a lovely idea. She knew climbing the stairs at her house was challenging for Sylvie and Virgil. And she had seen Sylvie's eyes light up when she spotted the amenities at the resort.

"Why don't you tell me what you need from Audrey? Start with the murder. Who was killed and when? So far no one in the crowd in front of the inn claimed hearing any gunshots."

"According to our registration clerk," began Elizabeth, "the victim is a large man from Copperleaf Village . . . Wayne Rasmus. He was staying on the third floor in the Winesap Suite. He was . . . well . . . he wasn't exactly stabbed." She pronounced *stabbed* as if it were a riddle Alice needed to solve, a riddle Elizabeth wasn't ready to put into words. Alice decided to wait until Elizabeth could get past her fright.

Alice stopped herself from asking, *The town of Copperleaf has a prison, right?* Was the dead guy on the third floor a prisoner, a guard, or simply a resident of the town?

Elizabeth paused to take a breath before continuing with spare details. Alice listened as she described police actions and questions. As far as Elizabeth knew, the murder happened the previous night or very early in the morning. One of the housekeeping staff found Rasmus when she entered the room around 9:45. She notified the office who then called the police.

"Have you told the police about the time?"

Elizabeth's palm flattened on her forehead. "I'm sure someone has. I personally haven't told the police anything. This morning I was in a meeting with my sons. Our numbers for the month are down. Registration talked to the police."

To Alice, Elizabeth had one of those guilt faces. "But you know the murder was discovered before ten?"

Elizabeth nodded.

Alice recalled the first Limekiln officer pulling into the resort a little before 11:00 a.m., followed by the second police car. County officers might experience delay in driving to a crime scene in rural areas, but Limekiln officers usually managed to be somewhere in fifteen minutes.

So, backing up the timeline from their arrival put the call from the resort to the police at 10:30. We have almost a missing hour, thought Alice. *That is, if Elizabeth is correct about the 9:45.*

"The police have asked for a list of all my employees and guests, in addition to anyone who visited the property yesterday or registered for activities today. I have a clerk going through all reservations and credit card receipts." Elizabeth's shoulders rose and then sagged. "My secretary is gathering histories from personnel files. Alice, I need this to be over quickly before too much police meddling scares away guests. I heard Lieutenant Unzicker has asked Rikki, Lena's wedding photographer, to supply footage from her drone's camera. I don't understand why. Afterall, the murder happened on the third floor. What possible clue can he get from a drone?"

"I'm sure they're looking at guests for telling behaviors. Do you have security cameras?"

"Yes. Unzicker has asked for those pictures also."

"Other than Lena's wedding, what other events are going on?"

"Today, we have a birthday party with children in the miniature golf area. Many of those family members came in yesterday. Lena's family arrived two days ago for the wedding. Again, according to registration, Wayne Rasmus's girlfriend set up their reservation and said he was coming to reunite with an old friend. I'm not aware of that man staying on our property. Rasmus arrived two days ago." Elizabeth made a sour face. "The girlfriend just arrived this morning when we were reporting the . . . body . . . to the police. She demanded to see him, but we knew the police would want to see the room first. Telling her there was an unfortunate event didn't stop her from carrying on about her rights." Elizabeth rolled her eyes. "Alice, I try not to judge, but really!" Her hands made wide circles in the air. "She's not our typical guest."

"You object to them not being married?"

"No. I don't care. It's just . . . I don't know the word to describe her. *Chip on her shoulder, loud, bad-tempered, rude, pushy*—none of those words cut it. Let me use one of my grandmother's terms. She's a tart."

"Oh." Alice understood the reference and pictured a woman who probably wore too much makeup or clothing too revealing. A woman used to the world judging her. She wondered if Elizabeth worried about the girlfriend's picture appearing in *Everybody Can Magazine*. At another time, she might have argued with Elizabeth's notion of wholesome: a woman with heavily painted eyebrows or ample cleavage apparently threatened Elizabeth's concept of wholesome, but men getting sloppy while bingeing in the hard cider room was okay? Alice rammed down her defense of women for a later time. Elizabeth didn't need a lecture with a murder on her property.

"It's October, Alice. We have many day-tripper families with young children to explore our special events like Story Time." Elizabeth wrung her hands. "This is all so bad. Autumn is our peak season with Halloween and Thanksgiving coming up. Murder could terminate our seasonal guests for years."

"Elizabeth, it may not be as devastating as you think. Lieutenant Unzicker will handle this *discreetly*."

"He better. The Southern Midwest Beekeepers arrive at the end of next week for a workshop. I don't want people who care about dying bees to think they are networking at a murder site."

"There are enough guests still around for the police to interview, and you have surveillance tapes to give clues. Now, why do you think you need Audrey?"

Elizabeth took a deep breath and stiffened her spine. "Well, okay, but not a word to the police unless they bring it up. One of my valued employees missed work for the last two days and hasn't shown up today."

"What's his name?"

Elizabeth looked frightened. "I'd rather not say. He mostly drives the tram to the activities.

"Give me his name."

"Everyone calls him Frosty."

"He works with the children?" asked Alice.

"Yes, but when we buy sides of beef and pork from local farmers, he cuts and trims them for the kitchen." Elizabeth bit her lip. "I've watched him work. He's very . . . efficient with a knife. Do you see what I'm saying?"

"Not quite. You're worried the police will focus on him as a person of interest because he's missing, and he cuts meat?"

"He uses his own set of knives." Elizabeth's words were measured.

"Are they also missing?"

"Afraid so. He keeps them in a leather wrap, and they are never far from his sight." Elizabeth took a deep breath before explaining.

Some staff regarded Frosty as distant and odd. A few in the kitchen gave him plenty of room as he sliced fat from the meat. According to fellow workers, Frosty might relish his work a little too much. Under his fingers, fat flew into appropriate bins, scraps for soup into others, and cherished steaks, chops and roasts readied for the chef. Frosty unnerved kitchen workers with stories of his agility and skill with a blade. He is delightful with the children, but with adults, I think he wanted . . . wanted . . ."

"To put on a performance for respect," concluded Alice.

"Exactly. He's short. Much older than any of our kitchen staff. In his sixties. Oh, Alice, if my secretary gives the list of employees to the police and they see that Frosty is missing work without an explanation—well, you can imagine. Despite his kitchen zealousness, he's lovely when he entertains the children as he drives the tram to Story Time. I don't want your Lieutenant Unzicker to jump to conclusions and think Frosty had something to do with this murder."

"I can't imagine Lieutenant Unzicker not following the evidence. How exactly was Rasmus killed?"

"Um, well, like I said . . . not precisely stabbed." Elizabeth's eyes widened as she drew her index finger over her throat and cast her attention to a window. Alice saw shame in Elizabeth's eyes.

Had she hired a killer to work with children? A killer capable of slashing a man's throat? Another scenario, however, popped into Alice's mind—was the employee another victim as yet not found?

Part of Alice's process evaluated weapons which tended to pair with motives. Guns were easy to use and readily available. They were compatible with impulse, explosive anger, and fear. A motive could be complicated. But the use of a knife to cut someone's throat, was a more cerebral weapon. An intentional weapon. There would be no hysterics from a killer. One swipe and done. More than a gun, a knife needed confidence that came with practice. A killer using a blade plotted this kind of murder to be decisive. His motive: most likely revenge and hatred.

ORDER J. P. McDunn's BOOKS ONLINE

Build Me Up, Buttercup

J. P. McDunn

What's Best for Bindy

J. P. McDunn

jpmcdunn@gmail.com

523 ION

RB Roku
Live T

"Just because someone works with a knife doesn't mean he's a killer," said Alice. "Did Frosty seem angry?"

"I wouldn't say angry, but not cheerful." Elizabeth squirmed. Her finger touched the corner of her mouth as if she knew her lipstick wasn't right.

"Lieutenant Unzicker won't let simple connections dictate his investigation. Did Frosty have any contact with the victim?"

"How would I know?"

Alice took her tone as expressing a possibility.

"You want Audrey to find Frosty?"

Uncharacteristic of her status as owner of Madtree, Elizabeth's posture crouched like a supplicant, "Please. Can you go get her now?"

"And miss Lena's reception?" Alice's voice pitched higher. "No, I'd never hear the end of it from Lena. Besides, if Audrey follows Frosty's scent, Lieutenant Unzicker would spot us trailing and demand an explanation. That would put a spotlight on Frosty's disappearance. I believe you want this to be quiet."

"I do! I do!"

"Let me ask Lieutenant Unzicker if he needs Audrey to do a search. We'll try to make it his idea. And I'll ask around to see what the gossip is. Then tomorrow morning if the murder is not solved, I'll be here with Audrey and my houseguests."

"Do you think I can get away with leaving Frosty's name off my list of employees?"

"Bad idea."

"What if I leave off his address? I could list his address as unknown or homeless."

"Still a bad idea. Do you know where he lives?" Alice couldn't believe Elizabeth would allow a respected employee to be homeless.

"He refused a picker's cabin when we offered it and favors one of our utility trailers on the far side of the orchard. He's fixed it up to his taste, but it's not exactly up to housing code. He's been there for over three years and seems content."

"Elizabeth, presume your other employees will tell the police about him."

"Even if I ask them not to?"

"It will slip out. Things like that always do."

"I suppose." Her voice softened with concern. "I sent someone from the kitchen to check on Frosty yesterday when he didn't show up again. He wasn't at the trailer. I have no idea where he is. This has never happened before."

"Do you think harm has come to him?" asked Alice almost as a whisper. "Could he be another victim?"

"Harm? Like another murder?" Elizabeth shuddered before she sat down. "No, no, no! Alice, we can't have two murders on the property. Think of the scandal."

Elizabeth's excitable side flared, and she popped out of her chair only to sit down again. She scooted her chair away from Alice.

"We'll be ruined if there is another dead body. My sons have chosen this orchard as their career. All these people who rely on the orchard for jobs." Again, Elizabeth's fist covered her mouth.

"It's just a curious thought," said Alice. "Probably he's okay because if something had happened to him, housekeeping or the apple pickers would have found him by now. Yes?"

"I suppose," said Elizabeth with no confidence.

"The police will do their preliminary investigation, and I'll talk to Lieutenant Unzicker either before or after Lena's reception. We won't worry until we know more."

"It will be just my luck if the writer is here," said Elizabeth. "He probably hates apples or is allergic to hay. If he writes about the murder, I'm ruined."

"Elizabeth . . ." Alice bit down on her lips. "Could the murdered man be the writer?"

"No. Don't even joke! Please no." The elegant woman shook her head and couldn't seem to stop. "If I just knew what he or she looked like . . . if I knew if the writer is disabled."

Alice asked, "Give me more details about Frosty."

"Like I said, he's a hard-luck guy in his sixties, really short—maybe five-two or shorter—no fat on him, very muscular. Quiet. Shaved head. And he's insistent that everything be clean. Frosty wipes down the tram's seats with a kitchen cleaner after each run. On property he wears shirts with our apple logo; otherwise, his wardrobe is dreadful, Army fatigues. But clean fatigues. Alice, he came highly recommended. I know Frosty's got attitude, but he's been so sincere in his work. During his time off, he's like a recluse. I can't, can't, can't imagine him killing anyone."

"Are you *sure* it's not possible he's a suspect?"

Elizabeth bit her lip.

"Do you have a photograph of him in your employee file?"

A headshake from Elizabeth.

"Contact information for family?"

Elizabeth's face stiffened. "I don't know him all that well. I may not have vetted him the same way as other staff. But he has become necessary to our operations." Her voice challenged, "He's respected by someone I respect. I will not have this murder add to his difficulties or stain the reputation of my family or orchard. Frosty's a veteran. How is that going to look if I allow him to be harassed?"

"The police are going to ask you for information even if it's not in his file. Who is he close to? Has anyone mentioned the type of knife that was used in the murder? Was it a kitchen knife like for boning fish or a serrated knife for bread?"

"Why?" Elizabeth's back went ramrod straight.

"Because a blade used in the kitchen might point to Frosty. But if it were a diver's knife or a carpenter's knife, the police might focus on someone else."

"The weapon wasn't from my kitchen . . . I don't think. The police haven't asked about that. I don't know the kind of knife."

"But Frosty keeps his own knives, right?"

Elizabeth nodded.

"Pardon me for asking this. Do you have a special tie to Frosty?"

One eyebrow raised with shock and annoyance. "Me? No! Been married once. Not again!"

Alice turned to leave, but Elizabeth fiercely grabbed her arm again. "I haven't been in the room, but the poor housekeeper who found Rasmus is majorly upset. She said the knife must have been very sharp because the wound didn't look big. The blood pool was . . . just under the body . . . maybe a bit more." Her fingers splayed and made circles in the air around her neck. "She said it wasn't all over like in the movies. Alice, I want no blowback on my orchard from this murder. You and your dog have to help me find Frosty."

Chapter 4

Alice checked her watch: time for wedding guests to celebrate Lena and Julian's wedding. She peeked through a window and scanned the outdoors for her houseguests, but they were no longer in the scattering of people gathered at the crime scene tape. No one she knew stood outside. No drone buzzed in the sky to capture the younger wedding guests yearning for more time in the swimming pool or playing miniature golf. No tangerine woman entertained guests on the front steps of the inn.

Hurrying to the dining room, Alice hoped she wasn't late for Lena's big entrance. Dashing down a hallway, Julian, Reverend Francis, and another man headed in her direction. Julian had changed his island shirt from white to black. He had added a sparkly golden tie but still wore his usual bandana on his head.

The third man stood about five feet eight inches. His body type reminded Alice of a barrel-chested wrestling coach, only older. His jowls drooped as he held his head forward and struggled to keep his balance for this burst of speed. His burgundy sport coat with a Madtree logo hung on his body like an over-sized blanket.

"She's going to kill me. Am I late?" asked Julian when he reached Alice's side.

"I don't think we're late," said Alice. "I'm sure before Lena makes her entrance, Cheryl will orchestrate the moment to be sure all eyes are on the door. Aren't you entering with her?"

"No. I'm supposed to be inside the dining room to greet her and take her hand. Then Francis announces us as Mr. and Mrs. Have you talked to Unzicker yet?"

"No. Why?" asked Alice.

"No reason. Just thought he'd pull you aside by now." Julian cast his eyes down the hallway before eyeing Francis, almost as if he pressed for help.

"Maybe we can talk inside the dining room when you have a moment," said Alice.

"Maybe," said Julian. "Magpie will probably keep me pretty busy."

Alice grimaced at Julian's choice of nicknames for Lena. Why did he feel the need to pick on her valued collections as if a waste?

She entered the dining room, but Francis drew Julian and the other man aside and whispered to them. The one who Alice didn't know returned the way he came.

The large dining room sported flowers of orange and gold for the reception. Five round tables with white tablecloths, gold trimmed plates, and black napkins clustered to one side, leaving half the room empty. A young DJ finished setting up his equipment for playing music and positioned a spotlight to cover the entrance. A small buffet table with appetizers already had nervous parents filling plates with sliced apples spread with peanut butter and pizza triangles for hungry children anxious to eat and go play. Older children, particularly boys with pencil-thin bodies, whose shirts escaped their too-big trousers, mounded tiny-bite appetizers onto plates and found chairs along the side of the room for the required privacy from adults. As older guests entered, the DJ lowered the volume on the background music. The sounds of the Bee Gees' "How Deep is Your Love" temporarily erased the Madtree Resort as a murder site.

Still wearing his white clerical collar over his black shirt, Reverend Francis closed the doors behind him and checked his phone. His face lit up, and he signaled the music to stop. Julian moved into place and waited. When the doors opened, the DJ hit the Star Wars theme and the spotlight. Framed by the doorway, Lena stood in a gauzy golden flapper sheath with no waistline, but her marshmallow curves refused to be hidden, and the daring plunging neckline revealed soft, spotted flesh. The dress reached mid-calf with an irregular handkerchief hem. Lena smiled and waved as she struck various suggestive poses. Her hands pointed out the embroidered beading with sparkles like fire. A ribbon of glittery flowers across her forehead helped to lift her blonde curls and allow them to cascade down to her shoulders. Tenting her fingers under her chin, she looked toward the ceiling and batted her extra-long black eyelashes.

Alice had to grin at her best friend. How many times had Lena said, *"No way anyone is going to mistake me for the mother of the bride"*? Her fear wasn't likely to happen. All the guests were family and friends. And in the doorway, she was stunning.

Alice loved her best friend's moment of being unafraid to marry again.

The DJ put on the Captain and Tennille's "Love Will Keep Us Together." Lena waltzed through the room and swiped her fingers in the air as she greeted guests at each table. From the far side of the room, she swirled toward her new husband.

"Oh, Julian," called Lena.

Alice thought Julian walked to Lena's side like a serious mope before he took her hand. Francis introduced the newly married couple, and Rikki snapped a stream of pictures. Lena was buoyant as friends clinked glasses, waiting for the couple to kiss. Julian walked next to her like a prop. Alice knew something was very wrong. Whatever bothered Julian before, still disturbed him, but he took Lena into his arms and the music changed to Beyoncé singing "At Last." The spotlight hit the couple, and Lena sang along while dancing in the glittery lights of her golden dress.

"We are in heaven," she sang, "For you are mine, at last."

Alice wiped a tear from her cheek and hoped Lieutenant Unzicker, who stood at the entrance, hadn't noticed her soft moment. His head tilt indicated he wanted Alice to join him in the hallway.

Chapter 5

"I want to see you before I leave," said Lieutenant Robert Unzicker.

The man Alice knew as *Bobby* had been in Alice's senior English class many years ago. She'd helped him weather the loss of his father and the remarriage of his mother. Their friendship grew as Bobby joined the police force in Limekiln, married, and became a father of two boys. Alice had a reputation of snooping into situations that were none of her concern, but fortunately, Bobby found it more humorous than annoying.

"You're taking off already?" Alice's thoughts went to Elizabeth. Had Bobby zeroed in on Frosty?

"Hardly. I knew I could find you here virtually alone, with everyone occupied with lunch." He escorted her away from the dining room doors and down a quiet hallway. He kept his voice low. "We've interviewed all the critical observers . . . at least for the first round. We talked with the victim's lady friend who arrived this morning, or so she says." His chin rose as his expression turned grave. "Now we piece together forensics before we go back to specific guests and staff a second time. I'm still waiting for lists from the resort's office. We need to study tapes. Usual stuff—so don't ask. Elizabeth tells me you're staying on the property tonight."

"Not tonight," said Alice, "but I'll be here tomorrow along with Sylvie, Virgil, and his older brother Cyril. Elizabeth offered rooms for all of us. She thinks we can be useful. Audrey, of course. I can't ask dog-sitters to spend the night and literally sleep with a hound in the same bed. And yes, I know I spoil her. Do you see a need for a sniffer dog?"

"Not yet." Hollows deepened in his cheeks as he leaned into his professional stance. "I'm assigning two officers to be here tonight. More for apprehensive guests than continuing an investigation. I can't have them demanding to leave until after we ask a few more questions. They might know something, and the murderer could still be on the property. Frankly, for this case, if I need a bloodhound, I'd rather use Jim Kennedy's dogs."

"Why?" Alice felt the sting of rejection.

"Because I know what Audrey means to you. I don't want either of you hurt."

"You think it's that bad?"

Unzicker nodded. "Look, the victim is your height and pretty big. Method of killing was precise. Before you get onto your high horse, I know a woman could have done it, but this guy is big, and the murder doesn't smack of a woman's technique. The killer needed practice and skill."

Alice was ready to argue with his assumption of rejecting a female killer.

"Was there a skirmish?"

"None."

"When I talked to Elizabeth, she mentioned a small blood pool," said Alice.

"Let's say it was compact."

"No blood splatter on walls?"

"Three tiny droplets on an upright chair."

Although he was probably right about the killer's skill with a knife being true of men, Alice felt weary as Unzicker bought into the hierarchy of crimes committed by men versus those of women. Alice had always found a woman could be just as evil as any man. But she had to admit, women often took a sneakier approach—poison . . . setting a fire . . . bashing a guy on the head as he slept. Without a struggle, could a woman with a knife have taken on a big brute of a guy? She'd have to be mighty strong and big herself, and Alice hadn't noticed any women of that description on the property of the resort.

"Is he big and meaty like a retired uncle or more like a man-beast?" asked Alice. She hoped her tone cut the tension.

Unzicker shook his head and worked to stifle a smile. "In the saggy man-beast category. One that no longer works out. A few too many burgers and beer. Know what I mean?"

"He wasn't stabbed?" asked Alice even as she recalled Elizabeth's finger slicing across her throat.

Unzicker recalled his professional code and tightened his facial muscles even more. His eyes narrowed. "You know, I never mentioned the weapon was a knife. Who told you about the weapon?"

"Oh!" Alice couldn't lie. "Elizabeth's very worried about her business reputation, particularly with a writer on the property. She might have let a few details slip. I'm guessing housekeeping mentioned to her the small blood pool and the wound . . . because of clean up later."

Unzicker gave a respectful smile. "I don't know what Elizabeth has in mind for you. Is there any way I can talk you out of participation? I'd like you to stand down. I know it's a big ask, and I'm not ordering you to let this slide. This murder isn't like others you've elbowed your way into. Please walk away. The killer wasn't messy. We all know general anatomy, but this guy had a surgical efficiency—he knew exactly where to find the carotid artery and how deep he needed to cut."

Elbowed my way into? Huh? Alice felt her shoulders lower but at the same time felt scolded. Did Unzicker regard her mental gymnastics of puzzling through all the evidence as bush league? She felt a twinge of self-doubt. Maybe some investigations didn't depend on the gossip of what innocent observers saw.

No, that's not true at all, thought Alice. *People know morsels of truth. Maybe tidbits. Specks of insight that when smooshed together create a mosaic portrait of the villain.*

"Elizabeth has made arrangements for me and my house guests to move in tomorrow. She hasn't asked Audrey to search out the murderer, nor would I know how to use Audrey with all these distractions at the resort." She edited out the word that was on her lips—*yet.* "I think it's more for reassurance than anything else."

"I'll accept that for now," said Unzicker. "I know I can't keep you from asking questions of strangers or making guesses. I feel this one is going to be bad. You know to be careful. Let me know the instant pertinent information crosses your path. There's danger here. How about meeting me tomorrow afternoon to share that thing you and Lena do with gossip." His face appeared to struggle with additional information.

"Hmmm!" In the past, Unzicker held back information to protect her from danger, but she felt a certain buoyancy. She loved the way Bobby trusted her and wanted to protect her. "I'll see what we learn. Just so you know, I saw Sylvie and Virgil work the crowd at the crime tape line. They seem thrilled by another murder. Lena will be focused on the wedding gathering until her children leave tomorrow morning. Then she may bring all her energy into the investigation. She's not pleased the murder happened on her wedding day. So, helping to find a killer might satisfy Lena's taste for revenge. And Julian—I can't imagine what's going on with Julian. I think this new reality as a husband to Lena has discombobulated him."

"Ah, Julian . . ." Unzicker looked away and shook his head. One hand went to his hip. Alice recalled his posture—he had the same rigid stance as an angry teen considering hitting his new stepfather. What had Julian done to rile Unzicker?

"What's up with Julian?" questioned Alice.

"We've only known Julian for what? A little over a year? His friends, not at all."

"Is Julian in danger?"

Unzicker ignored her question. "I'll approach Virgil. See if I can get him to back off this case." He walked her back to the entrance and glanced through the dining room door as it opened. A mother with a child scurried toward the bathrooms down the hall. "Isn't this a bit much for a fifth wedding?" asked Unzicker.

"Compared to her other weddings, probably toned-down, but I missed two of them. For number three, I was out of state. For four, Lena made a quick trip to Vegas. The funny thing—after Lena talked about this one being another destination wedding, Julian seems to have put it together. Only fifty guests and mostly family."

Unzicker's eyes had a hard look of assessment. He bit his lip as he scanned the dining room guests. "Julian doesn't look happy." Alice felt uncomfortable.

"He'll be happier tonight. I imagine Lena has plans."

"I guess," said the lieutenant. "Before I leave, I do have a question for you. How well do you know the minister?"

"Met him for the first time before the service. It was hi-bye. Why do you ask?"

"Okay." He took her arm and walked farther back down the hallway. "I want you to keep this confidential. Did Julian mention that Reverend Francis carries a concealed weapon?" His voice was close to a whisper.

"Francis?" Alice quickly lowered her volume, but her voice squeaked in shock. "A gun? No, I didn't notice." A parade of questions crossed Alice's mind. *Francis carrying a gun?* Her hand went to her throat as her pulse throbbed. True, Francis wasn't a career minister, and he did have a rough look with his bristly eyebrows and snake tattoo, but Alice couldn't picture him being armed. Perhaps he was the cause of Julian's strange, nervous behavior.

"Not a gun," said Unzicker. "Before the wedding, Julian and Francis approached the first Limekiln officer as he was initially collecting information about the murder. Francis felt it necessary to tell him about the knife he carries, strapped to his ankle." Unzicker's breathing changed as if he were uncomfortable. "Julian also told him that he too wears a blade, but not today."

"I saw a car pull in about twenty or thirty minutes before the scheduled wedding." Alice had a hard time imagining the timeline.

"The manager spoke to the officer first," said Unzicker. "Francis interrupted their conversation about the murder to explain his knife."

"That's why the start of the wedding was disorganized and delayed," concluded Alice.

"With the surrender of the knife, the officer allowed the wedding to go forward, figuring we could always pull him in later if we needed to. He noticed Francis's blade was nicked."

"I take it the murder weapon wasn't nicked."

"No. Once we saw the wound, we ruled out Francis's weapon."

"Why on God's green earth would either Julian or Francis carry a knife on any day? Particularly on a wedding day?" Alice couldn't believe it. She wanted to bop Julian on the head.

"You tell me. Both men said knives are with them most of the time. I have to say, I've never noticed Julian carrying any kind of weapon."

"Me, either," said Alice feeling confused. "Why would he do that?"

"To his credit, Francis readily relinquished the knife for forensic testing," said Unzicker. "He said he'd heard about the murder and wanted us to check him off the list of suspects."

"Francis knew the murder weapon was a knife?"

Unzicker nodded.

Alice felt slow to understand the moments before the wedding when the shock of the murder made responses quick. Feeling details fall like sand through her fingers, Alice tried to slot events into a timeline. The murder took place in the early a.m. Elizabeth said housekeeping found the body at 9:45. Unzicker told of Francis turning over his knife to the first officer before the scheduled wedding at 11:00. Was it a coincidence? Deep in the pit of her stomach, Alice knew. How did Francis . . . and Julian know the murder weapon before the police arrived?

"What do you know about Arthur Levitsky?" asked Unzicker.

"Arthur Levitsky? I don't know him at all. By any chance, is he the pudgy guy in the sport coat with the Madtree logo? I saw him follow Julian toward the dining room." Unzicker nodded as he watched the hallway for listeners. Alice continued, "I haven't been introduced. Tell me he doesn't wear a knife on his ankle."

Unzicker shook his head. "No, he doesn't. But all three men are in their middle sixties. Levitsky does reservations for the inn and manages special events. He worked with Julian on setting up the wedding, and the three men, Artie, Julian, and Francis, casually mentioned being in Vietnam in the late sixties-early seventies."

"How is Vietnam relevant to the murder?" asked Alice.

"I don't know yet. Not a detail I would've considered, but they brought it up. This early on—a telling detail to mention. Another siren call that identifies the three know something."

Alice felt her mouth go dry. What ham-handed scenario was Julian playing at? And why?

"Our victim is also an old guy in his sixties," said Unzicker.

"Also once in Vietnam?"

Unzicker shook his head. "We don't have details on that."

"I don't know what to say," said Alice. "But you aren't seriously thinking Francis or Julian could be the murderer?" Alice's fingertips patted her thigh, expecting a warm, comforting wet nose of a bloodhound to push into her palm. Her hand curled into a fist. She pictured Julian's muscular build, but probably too short. Francis, however, had the height and muscle. Alice wanted to rule him out because of his attitude was more in tune with mocking the world not stabbing at it.

"Maybe their information was nervous oversharing," stated Unzicker, "or maybe they're setting up clues to send us down the wrong path. I won't pull punches if Julian wastes our time. A knife is one helluva coincidence that we now need to check out. If this is Julian being . . . *cute*, he'll pay a price."

"I can't stand coincidences," said Alice feeling guilty for no real reason.

"Do you see why I asked you to let us do our job?" Alice nodded without making eye contact. "If it were any other detective, Julian and his friends might be questioned at the station—today—for obstruction. Alice, I can't allow them to mislead our investigation by using up time while we eliminate them as suspects. For right now, we've got interesting facts in need of a big picture. You know to keep all of this to yourself? Say nothing to Julian . . . or Lena."

"I understand. I can't imagine Julian—" Unzicker held up his palm, and Alice paused as the mother and child walked back through the hallway toward the dining room. "You're right. None of us have known Julian for very long, and we know nothing about Francis. I promise not to spill any beans. I take it if the knife was strapped to his ankle that it wasn't a kitchen variety knife."

Unzicker's face remained blank. "You're asking about a kitchen knife?"

Alice squirmed as her face flushed. She had let *kitchen* slip. Unzicker didn't know about Frosty's disappearance or his job in the kitchen of carving slabs of meat. *Oh well*, she hoped she only let one small nugget of information out of the bag.

"Why do you ask?" Unzicker's eyes took on a coldness but his mouth, amused.

"Showstopper, isn't it? The buddy of a guy, whom we both respect, arrives wearing a knife for the wedding. A victim turns up with his throat cut," said Alice. "One sees a crazy chef on television dramas all the time, but very rarely is the temperamental food artist a murderer."

"Temperamental kitchen worker? Might have known you'd have the latest tittle-tattle. Before I go home, I might take another crack at

Elizabeth Madtree," said Unzicker, his eyes narrowing. "Make sure she knows the severity of working behind my back. We need an employee list ASAP. To ease your mind a little, Francis's blade was old military and not maintained to be as sharp as the murder weapon. But that he had it at all, tells me he knows more than he said." Unzicker raised one eyebrow. "See you tomorrow, Alice. Nice to know you don't intend to *butt* into this investigation tonight. Remember: play this one safe. We don't know who to trust."

Chapter 6

Alice returned to the dining room and stood with her back to the wall before finding her assigned place at a table. She wondered how much about Julian she still didn't know. He had been generous with help and kind to Lena, but her best friend had a weakness for bad boys as husbands. So far as she could see, Julian didn't yell at Lena, didn't intend malice if he embarrassed her, didn't point out faults to demean her, didn't strike her, or break fingers as one husband had. But Alice still didn't like the jabbing nicknames Julian sometimes chose for Lena. Calling her Fatty because of her weight or Magpie because of her many collections still caused Alice's jaw to tighten. Lena's response? "He doesn't mean anything by it." Alice hoped her best friend hadn't fallen for a conman-murderer, one so slick he had even fooled her.

Guests had finished with appetizers and clinked glasses with forks or knives, and the newly married couple responded with deep kisses. Or rather, Lena kissed her new husband sincerely while Julian continued to look embarrassed.

Before the main course arrived, Alice rose to check on her houseguests at a different table. Returning from the washroom, Cyril parked his walker and sidled close to Alice. "I told that one," he said pointing at Lena, "that she's insane to get married in an apple orchard. No good can come from a fifth wedding like this one. She didn't seem to know about the apple curse."

Ninety-year-old Cyril was in great shape for his age even though his body stooped forward and moved slowly. Like his younger brother Virgil, his white hair was sparse and soft. Pliable wrinkles covered his face. He dressed in a shiny blue suit with overly large lapels, a white shirt, and subdued striped tie. A fresh application of polish tried to hide the cracks and scuffs on his leather shoes. In his hand he held one of the resort's apple-naming quizzes.

"Apple curse?" asked Alice. "I don't think I know about a curse."

"Plain unlucky. You don't know, then you don't study the Bible. Adam and Eve? Apples temptation? Apples and betrayal? From what Julian told me, Lena's first four marriages didn't turn out so good. I tried to tell him it's nutty to think anything will change. He's in for a bad ride. Julian shouldn't have picked an apple orchard for a wedding. No surprise to me we have a murder on our hands. Apples brew and compound trouble. Mind what I'm saying."

Alice knew arguing with this elderly man about Bible stories was never a good idea. So, she chose to talk about Elizabeth's display of all things abundant in the fall. Outside the dining room's wall of windows stood a farm wagon loaded with harvested squash, pumpkins, gourds, and dried ears of corn. Beyond the walkways, children played tag while their parents waited in line for the scarecrow maze or for a ride in the open-car train circling the property. A clown gestured wildly in front of a sign announcing a bushel of apples would be rewarded to anyone who named all twelve varieties of apples picked from the Madtree orchard.

"My favorite apple is the Golden Delicious," said Alice as she looked at his quiz. "Although some apple names are entertaining like the Sheep Nose Apple.

"Names of apples? What about Crab Apples, Red Flesh Apples, Blush June, Limber-twigs, Scarlet Surprise Apples, and Pink Ladies. Every one of them speaks to infidelity."

"Oh, look," said Alice tiring of an argument she couldn't win.

"Guests have finished their salad and the waitstaff is bringing out a plated lunch. We don't want to miss the sliced pork with rye bread and apple stuffing. Have you seen the dessert table?"

Cyril turned and repositioned his walker. His nose inhaled deeply. "I do like me a good pork roast. And those pies look like they got a buttery crust. Smells like the pork has some garlic, and that pie's probably stuffed with cinnamon-coated apples." With that, the tennis balls on the tips of his walker made a soft shush as Cyril first pushed toward the dessert table before taking his seat and tucking the napkin under his chin.

Chapter 7

On the drive home from the wedding reception with Cyril next to her and Sylvie and Virgil in the back, Alice elaborated on Elizabeth's offer of rooms for all of them to stay at the resort. If they agreed, the three elderly friends were to share a king-bed suite with a pull-out couch that opened into a queen. The suite had two full bathrooms, and the guests had access to all the entertainment and both restaurants.

"Yippie!" said Sylvie. "What's not to like? No offense, but I'm not enjoying your stairs, and Audrey comes to our closed bedroom door at night and softly woofs. It keeps me awake with worry. First time she did it, I thought you might be dead."

"Scratches at my bedroom door downstairs," said Cyril. "What does Audrey want in the middle of the night? I thought maybe the house was on fire. You never know about a strange house. When I opened the door, your dog brought me a sock."

"Tell that dear woman we don't need a suite," said Virgil. "It's too grand for us. A double bed is enough for me and Sylvie as long as there's a couch for Cyril."

"Wait a minute," said Cyril. "Who said I want to share a bathroom with you two."

"I don't think we have room for negotiations," said Alice. "October is the resort's busy season because of the harvest and Halloween. Elizabeth indicated a suite was the only room available." Alice kept her eyes on the road and her voice even as she hoped they wouldn't detect her embellishments. "Just think, while you're on the property, you can enjoy all the activities. No cleaning. Dine whenever you want. A siesta before dinner."

"Who pays for the food?" said Cyril. "That kitchen put out a big spread for the wedding."

"Elizabeth promised to take care of everything," answered Alice. "Since the murder happened, she wants all the guests to feel safe by having Audrey on the property—and all of us, of course, to help solve the crime."

"It has been years since we stayed some place really nice," said Virgil.

"It's our payment in kind for helping Alice solve the murder." Excitement filled Sylvie's voice.

"Can I run the train? I was once a conductor on the B & O Railroad," said Cyril. "Remember Virgil when Dad took us to New York on the *Capitol Limited?*"

"That's way in the past," added Virgil, "Do you really think you can crimp your body to sit atop a child's train? Besides, that train only runs on weekends. We'll have the murder wrapped up by then."

Sounding like a peacemaker, Sylvie said, "Cyril, we don't want to impose on our employer at a time when Alice needs us. Our job is to keep her safe. Like the last time, right Virg?"

Alice could feel everyone nodding, as a lump took hold of her stomach. She pictured a parade: Audrey leading the way, herself, possibly Lena and Julian behind her, and trailing far behind, her posse of friends—one with a walker. *What have I created?*

When Sylvie and Virgil had visited at Christmas, Virgil accepted the responsibility of being a police informant. Luckily for her, Virgil was excellent at eavesdropping.

Alice gripped the steering wheel of her dowager Lincoln. Maybe the old girl would get a flat tire before morning, and she wouldn't have to return to the resort.

"It's settled then," said Virgil. "We accept Elizabeth's offer."

"I heard a rumor," said Sylvie, "that some big-time reporter is doing a story about the guests at the resort. Virg, maybe you and I can be famous. How are you at miniature golf?" Sylvie cut short her witchy laugh that sounded like a cackle.

No one else answered, and Alice allowed silence to follow. The road was dark with few shadows until the clouds broke and the sky sparkled with stars against navy blue. Her heart continued to thump at the thought of these three helpers.

"It was a lovely wedding," said Sylvie. "That Lena's a pip, but she did look beautiful as a 1920s flapper."

"Too many curves to be a true flapper," said Cyril. "Those babes were skinny."

"Now, brother, she wanted to have a bit of fun. I noticed she got you out on the floor to dance."

Out of the corner of her eye, Alice watched Cyril's shoulders puff up. "I was being polite to Julian's girl."

"You know," said Alice, "of the two times we have worked together, I never asked you what Julian was like as a boy in Bottom Ridge."

"He played sports. I coached him for a while," said Cyril. "He wasn't as wild as he pretends."

"He doesn't deserve that nickname of Octopus Man?" asked Alice.

"That he deserves," answered Sylvie. "But I think the girls hung around him to catch the eye of that wonderful Summers' boy."

"Riley Summers. Now there's a name from the past," said Cyril.

"You also knew Riley?" asked Alice.

"Don't want to speak ill of the dead," answered Cyril, "but he had a stranglehold on every young person in town. They'd do anything he said."

"He wasn't that bad," said Sylvie with authority in her voice. "He was a good kid, and when he passed, we missed him."

"Why'd he sign-up for Vietnam?" Cyril turned in the front seat to face his brother behind him. "Why'd he get himself killed?" He turned back to face the windshield. "Those boys were loyal to a fault. I had enough of faraway wars. Lost many friends in my lifetime."

"I know," said Virgil with a weariness in his voice. "We all took the death of our boys hard."

"And we were only friends and neighbors," said Sylvie. "Look what Riley's death did to his father. Broke his heart. His sister, too. Too much death."

Alice tried to move the conversation away from loss. "Was Artie one of Julian's friends?" Silence caused her to repeat the name. "Arthur Levitsky?"

"Don't know him," said Sylvie.

"No. He never lived in Bottom Ridge," said Virgil. "Why?"

"Just curious," said Alice.

"Isn't that something about the timing of the wedding," said Sylvie. "A wedding complete with a murder investigation." Sylvie cackled again.

"Curious coincidence," said Alice.

"Alice Tricklebank, the short time I've known you . . . shoot! You don't believe in coincidences any more than I do," said Sylvie. "But isn't it odd that a girl like Lena would agree to a rural setting for her wedding?"

Virgil spoke up. "Julian said Lena had trouble choosing a place, that's for sure, so he stepped in and chose the resort because it's close to home. He made all the resort arrangements. She just had to show up."

"She's the type that wants something dramatic to remember," said Sylvie. "Julian told us she first wanted September in Vermont, then November in Colorado." Sylvie gave a deep sigh. "Hawaii caught her eye for December. None of us could attend if they traipsed off on a wild destination wedding."

"I think Julian worried she was getting cold feet," said Virgil, "and he wanted the thing settled. You know, after he came home from Vietnam, he was always a mite nervous. He didn't like things left up in the air. Probably came from his medic experiences. I think after all these years he's more settled with Lena, but if a thing needs deciding, Julian takes charge."

"He once told me the men who came home from Vietnam had changed," said Alice, eager to seed conversation.

"For every war, I imagine that's true of all soldiers," said Virgil. "All our Bottom Ridge boys did—not necessarily a bad change—many of our boys stood up. Julian certainly became more serious, and in many ways that was good."

"When Lena and I were in Bottom Ridge," said Alice, "I thought he wanted us to think he was a bad boy."

"Well, of course he did," said Sylvie. "How was he going to attract Lena's eye? And Virg, don't give me that look. Anyone who sees her walk knows what interests her."

"I feared our boys would come back broken," said Cyril. "I didn't want to see it, so I moved out of Bottom Ridge."

"Broken?" fired up Sylvie. "Nobody was broken. Maybe bruised or moody but not broken. You moved out because Mary Rose turned you down twice and wouldn't marry you. The war had nothing to do with it."

The three houseguests all argued at once about their perspectives of war still claiming lives . . . or not. Eventually all three salted their comments with digs about Mary Rose.

Sylvie changed the direction by saying, "You all know I think Lena is flighty, but she's good for Julian. Keeps him living in the moment."

"The minister, Francis Brandau, is from Bottom Ridge. Right?" asked Alice.

"Talk about boys changing," said Sylvie. "His father would roll over in his grave if he saw him dressed up with a minister's dog collar. His father was a hard drinker like his own father."

"Now, Sylvie," said Virgil, "Francis saw a lot. He was a Marine on the Laos border. Tough for those boys to reenter our real world. Once he was home, Francis continued to be helpful until he headed north for a business in fishing."

"I always thought it would have been better if Julian and Francis could have served in the same unit," said Sylvie. "Friends supporting friends. Probably they were scared at times."

"They were different boys with different kinds of reactions," said Virgil. "They came home with different stories."

Cyril turned to aim his voice at Sylvie and repeated slowly as if to a child. "One was Army in charge of patching up. Other one, a fighting Marine."

"We haven't seen much of him," added Sylvie.

Quiet followed. None of the elderly friends spoke.

"When I visited Bottom Ridge," said Alice, "the nicknames everyone had drove me crazy. Julian was very proud of his nickname. Did Francis have a nickname?"

"Not that I remember," said Sylvie. "Of course, in those days I wasn't privy to the inside jokes of boys."

"Don't you remember? He had a nickname, but it didn't stick until he came home," said Virgil. "He asked us to call him *Gut*. No idea why. When he got home from the war, there wasn't an ounce of fat on him."

Chapter 8

Audrey's happy jumping greeted Alice as she walked through the door. The three houseguests went to bed, but Alice had sloppy dog kisses coming her way. She thanked Wells and Gretchen for entertaining Audrey and petted Cooper, Wells' mixed breed pup. The neighbors left Alice's house and walked home.

Audrey finished eating her dog food, slopped down a bowl of water, and bounded up the stairs. Alice felt sleepy and followed. In bed, Audrey took her customary position sleeping diagonally with her head on Alice's foot. Alice fell asleep in seconds but awoke ten minutes later with her mind working on the pickers in the apple orchard. She slipped from the bed and pulled a book of Robert Frost's poetry from her shelf. Quietly, she settled under the sheet with her foot again becoming a dog pillow. Turning to "After Apple-Picking," Alice read the lines that haunted her.

"My instep arch not only keeps the ache,
It keeps the pressure of a ladder-round."

Funny thing about memory, she thought, *brain memory can be unreliable but body memory—spot on.*

She recalled long road trips with Baer and their two children. Those nights in a motel room, the hours spent watching the roadside sweep by didn't stop. In the dark with her eyes closed, Alice continued to feel the aching sensation of driving down the road. Probably the apple pickers also felt the pressure of the ladder step even as they walked home to their dinner. Now that she was older, her body memory caused her to lurch with each sensation of tripping and falling. After all these years, a stumble jolted her heart into racing. Our bodies remember the ache from the past. So, what ache do Julian and Francis remember?

With eyes wide open, Alice pinched her lip. *Why did Julian choose the Madtree Apple Orchard Resort for the wedding? Because he was impatient and the inn convenient? Nah. I can't believe it.*

Alice couldn't see Julian as a cider drinker or as someone who enjoyed a round of miniature golf or scarecrows decorated by children. The heated swimming pool, however, did seem a big draw for the grandchildren even though the air was cool.

Ache of the past echoed in her mind.

Why did Francis carry a knife strapped to his ankle? Can't be a coincidence.

To Alice it felt like he must have learned about the murder prior to the wedding. Housekeeping must have passed the information of the murder along to Artie Levitsky in his apple logo sports jacket . . . then Artie to Francis and Julian? But for Francis to have a knife at his fingertips, either it belonged to someone else or he'd brought it from home. And why did he find it necessary to relinquish it to the police? The timing bothered Alice.

She closed her eyes tightly to shut out the fear that Unzicker's speculation was correct. She didn't want to consider Julian or one of his friends being involved with the murder. For all of his controlled swagger, did Francis fear an assault of some kind? But this was an apple orchard resort—what threat could they have assumed?

Her fingers found Audrey's furry ribs rising and falling with each deep breath. She could almost imagine Julian and the guys getting tipsy at a bachelor party and being enticed by the enchantment of an ancient marriage ritual of protecting the bride from being kidnapped by the lord of the manor. Alice was sure she'd disapprove of their bachelor party jokes. This marriage was Lena's fifth.

Francis was a buddy of Julian from Bottom Ridge—and back in the day, a Marine stationed near Laos. To Alice, Francis appeared to nurture contempt in the way he looked at people as if he were the only one who got the joke. For Artie, Alice still had no information other than his jacket.

She mused with recollections of high school students bonding—wearing similar clothing, or perhaps being extreme fans locked into the support of a band or a sports team. In school lunchrooms, groups of friends claimed a cafeteria table as their own or initiated new members into the group by TPing their house. What drew Julian, Francis, and Artie together? What was their bond?

Of course, the knife could be a bad-news, clumsy joke, chosen with equally bad timing. Guys spoofing a shotgun wedding? But by all accounts, neither Lena nor Julian were getting cold feet and never showed any unease concerning Lena's four previous husbands.

Alice's hand circled figure eights in Audrey's fur, and the dog gave a grumpy gargle in her throat.

"Shhh," whispered Alice. "I'm puzzling."

She had a question for Unzicker. She thought she remembered him saying Francis's knife was government issued. Was it possibly from the Vietnam era? Possibly a Vietnamese war trophy?

Alice allowed her right leg to remain Audrey's pillow as she twisted her body to lie on her side. It was too early to pull information from Unzicker. From Elizabeth? Not yet. Not the three guys—although if she could catch them together maybe one might let something slip if he thought another of them was being suspected. She had watched two members of the housekeeping staff hide their mouths as they whispered when the DJ took a break and the line for the ladies' room looped into the hallway. Workers knew stuff. Tomorrow she'd try to find one who'd share stories. And Lena—Alice wanted to talk to Lena.

It couldn't be a coincidence that Julian had booked the wedding, and a murder had happened at the resort. What was his real purpose for being there—a purpose that didn't include Lena?

"Julian, what are you involved in?" whispered Alice.

Sylvie and Virgil wanted to help snoop into the murder, so to keep them safe, Alice reasoned she needed to suggest an assignment before Lieutenant Unzicker co-opted them into one of his schemes. He had done it before. Maybe if she could convince them to gossip with the staff who ran amenities or served in the dining room, perhaps then, they'd be out of danger. Cyril was already enchanted by the children's open train carriages that circled the property. That and the all-day apple dessert buffet should keep him occupied.

In the moonlight streaming through the window, Audrey opened her bloodshot eyes and tilted them upward to give Alice the look: *Are you going to sleep or what?*

"Wait until you see the resort tomorrow," whispered Alice as she massaged her dog's toes. "And wait until the children see you. Big day tomorrow, girl. I'm just trying to figure out Julian's reason for planning the wedding at the Madtree Resort. Could it be as simple as wanting to get the wedding over with?"

The bloodhound groaned and shifted her face to align with Alice's hip.

"You had a hard playdate with Cooper. Remind me to give you a bath before we visit the resort. You're a bit doggy."

Before sleep, Alice's last thought went to Unzicker not wanting her near this crime. Did he think she might protect Julian if he were involved with a murder? Alice didn't want to observe the actual crime scene, but as she closed her eyes, she saw Elizabeth's finger draw across her throat.

Every murder is terrible, but this one seems ugly, brutish, and personal. Who wanted to kill the man-beast?

Chapter 9

The staff at the Madtree Resort leaped to help Alice's three house-guests with their six small suitcases and four shoulder bags.

"Careful with that one," called Cyril. "That one holds my pills."

Before she left for her suite, Sylvie drew Alice aside and put her finger to the side of her nose.

"Virgil and I will be out and about after lunch. We planned a scare-crow walk for later. Cyril will hang out in the café and eavesdrop. We need to get to know the players in this murder."

"Please tell him it's not a good idea to tip off anyone." Alice felt her jitters grow as she imagined Cyril pushing his way through the café, asking guests, *You got something to do with this murder?*

"Oh, Cyril will be fine. Eavesdropping is his excuse to take it easy."

"Make sure you all look like you're having a good time," said Alice.

Her face turning curious, Sylvie's head tilted. "You do know that even with that dog, younger strangers see your age first. At best that translates to non-threatening in a young person's mind. At worst—a nuisance. Now imagine what they think when they see me and Virg. Or Cyril? Don't worry about us. If we see anyone being suspicious about what we're doing, Virg and I are experts at talking about cemeteries. Nothing like talking about old dead people to put younger folk right off."

She cackled and patted Alice's arm before rejoining Virgil, who stood next to a young man with a stacked luggage carrier.

Audrey's eyes danced at all the new smells in the lobby. Her nose bounced into many unsuspecting crotches as Alice waited for a room key. She apologized for her dog to many new embarrassed friends.

"Sorry," said the clerk. "Your room doesn't seem to be ready. If you'd like to take a seat in the lobby?" He looked at Audrey. "Or outside? We'll let you know when the room is available."

A text came in from Lena. *Meet me at the Dinner Bell Café on the patio in twenty minutes. I'll buy coffee and pastry. Gotta talk.*

Elizabeth hurried out of her office to personally greet Alice.

"Good, you have your dog." Her forehead wrinkled. "I didn't quite realize how big she is. I thought she's supposed to be low to the ground."

"You're thinking of a bassett hound."

"How much does she weigh?"

"A skosh over one hundred pounds." Alice took a cloth out of her pocket and wiped Audrey's mouth. "She's had her morning walk and a bath. Sylvie even made her pretty by brushing her fur." Seeing some anxiety and doubt in Elizabeth's face, Alice added, "We're about to go outside. To the patio. The room's not quite ready."

"Good. That'll work. It was quite a night with the police here. In two minutes, Lieutenant Unzicker wants to talk to me. Will you be around later? I have something to show you."

"Does he know about an absent employee?" whispered Alice.

"No. And I don't plan to tell him. Nor should you."

"Elizabeth, you need to know I won't lie to Lieutenant Unzicker. If he asks me a question, I'll do my best to answer him. But . . .in the past . . . I have held back details when I don't know if they will be helpful."

"That's all I want. You'll be at the Dinner Bell?"

"With Lena on the patio. Remember, she's a retired baker. She wants to try the resort pastries."

"Yes, good. Remember to watch what you say," said Elizabeth, who looked toward a wall and caught her reflection in a mirror. "The travel reporter is definitely here. Everyone is talking about him or her." She licked her lips and opened her mouth to check her teeth for smeared lipstick. "By the time you finish, I'll be ready to take you on an excursion. I want to show you where Frosty lives. Let's secure your luggage so you don't have to lug pieces around."

Elizabeth raised her hand and a woman came forward. Alice followed as the woman gathered up and dropped off her one bag and Audrey's two into a cloak room with a lock. Alice kept her backpack, reasoning that one never knows what might happen.

"I really don't think it should take very long for this murder to be solved," said Elizabeth.

"Huh?"

"Three bags, Alice? And a backpack?"

"One for me. Two plus a backpack for Audrey—dog food and treat supplies, entertainment, and clean up." Alice didn't want to explain the list of Audrey's toys or favorite blanket or other coverings to protect the resort bed and chairs, not to mention all the cloths to wipe Audrey's slobber. Seeing Elizabeth still scowled, Alice pointed to one bag. "What goes in, Elizabeth." Her finger pointed to a second bag. "And what goes out." Alice peered over her shoulder and pantomimed the twists and turns every dog walker knew.

"Oh," said Elizabeth.

One police officer stood near a historical display of apple cider bottles. Guests passed through the lobby nodding and saying "Good morning" to anyone who made eye contact. Alice guessed the tension of the previous day influenced the heightened politeness.

She corralled Audrey, who wore a lime green vest emblazoned with black lettering: *Working*. Together they found Lena on the patio. A large coffee thermos and a tiered plate of untouched pastries sat on the table. Audrey wiggled with pleasure as Lena finished eating the leftovers of peanut butter French toast with Fluff and chocolate cookie crumbs.

GEORGANN PROCHASKA

"My grandchildren left their breakfast for one more splash in the swimming pool. These pancakes are too good to waste." She licked marshmallow Fluff from her finger.

Lena liked to make sure everyone knew who she was. The day after her wedding, her hair tumbled with blond curls, and she wore a copper-colored, long-sleeved T-shirt with sequins spelling out *Bride*. A long wrap hugged her shoulders. With the sun high in the sky, the day wasn't as chilly as the early morning had been.

"I take it the children are having a good time?" asked Alice.

"A perfect spot for wee ones. But my sons promised to take the older kids to a big amusement park closer to their home, one with several roller coasters. An excellent idea before the whole pack of them become bored and ornery and drive the rest of us crazy." She dusted powdered sugar from her fingers. "After noon, I'll have time to look into this murder. Is Audrey happy to see me or has her nose detected a couple of these sweets filled with cream cheese?"

"She does like cream cheese," said Alice with a grin. "But remember, she sometimes has a touchy belly. Please don't give her that glazed long john with a bacon strip." Alice opened a bag of treats. "Tran's chicken farm has a new line of dog treats called *Keep Me Happy*. Look at the package."

A bloodhound's black and tan face appeared with her long tongue licking her nose. "I didn't want to say anything while you prepared for the wedding, and the packaging just came out four days ago. Audrey's the model."

"We have a celebrity. Oh, look how the photographer captured her loving eyes," said Lena. "Well, here's to Audrey." Lena took a big bite of a pastry that resembled a boat. Powdered sugar fell onto her chest and whipped cream squished onto her chin. "Eat up because it will be only me and you. Julian's somewhere, and my sons and daughters-in-law are at the pool watching the kids and having mimosas made with apple cider. Can you believe the resort thinks this tray of pastries is supposed to feed four?"

MURDER COMES TO MADTREE

Alice watched her dear friend and helped herself to an apple slice. "Is Julian okay?"

Lena's nose wrinkled. "Don't ask. He was up early this morning and didn't even shave before he left our room. At least he remembered to kiss me before he was out the door."

As the two friends ate and Audrey munched a dog treat, Lena spent the next several minutes sharing the compliments she had received for her shimmering flapper dress. Dusting powdered sugar from her chest, Lena took a breath. "Now, tell me everything I didn't catch yesterday. Start with the murder and end with why Julian has gone funny—and I don't mean ha-ha."

"That's my question to you. What's up with Julian?"

Before either woman could comment on the new husband's mood, they heard the loud, screechy voice of a woman.

"Give me that camera. You're not taking my picture."

"No way," yelled the familiar voice of Rikki, the wedding photographer. "I wasn't taking your picture. In fact, you're in my way."

"Then I'll move right after you delete the picture you took."

"Okay, okay," said Rikki. A pause followed. "That better?"

Alice and Lena looked at each other. "Why is she taking pictures today?" mouthed Alice.

Lena shrugged. Within a minute, a woman in her middle forties powerwalked past the patio doors. She wore tight shorts over a thick lower body and an overly clinging stretchy top over her soft upper body. Alice wondered what special occasion had caused the woman to binge in weight loss which caused her upper body to lose weight like a deflated balloon. Her hips and thighs stubbornly maintained plumpness. The fabric of her sleeves cut into the doughy flesh of her arms and bulged the wrinkly rose tattoos surrounding the name *Wayne*. Her penciled eyebrows were a bit too high on her forehead and too dark. Her elaborate eye-makeup was smudged as if she had been crying. Even her thin, spiky hair looked like it needed bolstering. All in all, she resembled a bowling pin.

Rikki joined Alice and Lena at the table. The twenty-year-old wore skinny pants and a flowing white shirt with slits almost to her armpits. Her black hair was tied at the back of her neck, and her once Kelly-green eyes were a bright periwinkle. Alice first met Rikki when the young woman had charmed Alice's grandson in a summer romance.

"You need coffee and a pastry?" asked Lena. "The ones with raspberry jam aren't as good as mine, but the apple hot cinnamon will tingle your sinuses." Lena licked her fork. "Is everything okay?"

Rikki's smile was smart-alecky as she sat down. "All okay." She fiddled with the digital camera. "Delete is never final until you empty the trash." She held up the camera to show the woman's picture.

"Who is she?" asked Alice.

"I don't know her full name. I was here on Thursday to scout locations for photo shots. I caught her in a couple photos with the dead guy. At least that's what Lieutenant Unzicker said when he inspected my pictures last night. He asked me to try for a clearer picture. There are a few other pictures he's interested in. So that's my assignment today. To catch a few more interesting heads before they check out of here."

"You've got a picture of the dead guy?"

"Yeah." Her fingers punched at the camera before she turned it in Alice's direction.

Alice almost said, *the man-beast,* but she knew the phrase would trigger a reaction from Lena.

"He's got to be twenty years older than she is." Alice studied the picture. "He has that scruffy, thug-look down. Do you know his name?"

"Wayne Rasmus." Rikki rose and snatched a small Danish.

"Wait," said Alice, "do you know the name of the woman he was with?"

"Yeah. Pepper. Why?"

"Her reaction to having her picture taken seemed a little extreme. You said you caught pictures of them on Thursday?"

"Yeah." Rikki's eyebrows lifted. "You want me to follow her?"

"No, not at all. Taking pictures for Lieutenant Unzicker is much more useful," said Alice.

"Okay, see you later." With that, Rikki charged toward the pool.

"I do love her work," said Lena. "So creative. But I also see her working for the police department one day. Oooh! Maybe as a private eye. I think she's caught the snooping bug from you."

Alice sighed. "Maybe. But I think butting into other people's lives has a lot to do with running around with my grandson last summer."

"We women do love a sturdy body," teased Lena.

"You, Julian, and Francis arrived on Thursday. Do you remember seeing Pepper and the dead guy, Wayne Rasmus?"

Lena shook her head as one finger poked at the cream protruding from an éclair.

"Now," said Alice, "what's up with Julian?"

"He's behaving like a cake that came out of the oven and fell. His poof is deflated. I don't think it's anything I did. For the last two weeks, he's been jumpy, and when we arrived a couple days ago, he became downcast. Then tense. I saw your face at the wedding. I know you noticed his misery. Alice, he didn't stay with me the night before the wedding. I had that big bed in the honeymoon suite all to myself."

Alice never imagined she'd ever ask Lena the next question. "Why didn't he sleep with you?"

"He said it went against tradition." Lena rolled her eyes.

"I never thought of him as a tradition guy. Where did he sleep?"

"Probably threw himself another bachelor party with his friends. I've no idea where he slept. I asked his daughter, but she hadn't seen him since our ceremony practice on Friday."

"Was he hungover?"

"That's the odd part. No. Only gloomy." Lena's nose wrinkled. "That's not quite correct either. He was serious."

"While he was away from you," asked Alice, "could he have seen something connected to the murder?"

"If he did, he didn't say, but I don't think he did. The murder seemed to surprise him. And it doesn't account for his moodiness in the last few weeks."

"What do you know about his friends?"

"Francis, the *recent* minister, is nice, a kidder in a raw way. Like he wants to make a person embarrassed or angry enough to say something stupid. He told Julian that when he married me, he got many pounds for his dollar. What is it with these guys and fat jokes? Really!"

"Julian loves you. Did he say anything to Francis?"

"Only to me. He said I shouldn't take Francis seriously."

Alice bit down on her back teeth to stifle a reaction. "What about Artie?"

"I met Artie the night before the ceremony. He works for the resort, and he checked in that all was going as we expected. Smiles a lot. Friendly. He's been helpful with entertainment suggestions for my family."

"Julian worked with Artie to make the wedding arrangements?"

Lena nodded.

In the comfort of being with a friend, Alice filled in the very few details she knew of the murder, leaving out Elizabeth's request for Audrey to sniff Frosty's living quarters, but including that the Bottom Ridge crew wanted in on this case. Even Cyril planned to comb the dining room for murder stories.

"You want to meet for dinner and gang up on my new husband?" asked Lena.

"Love to," said Alice as she reached over to squeeze her best friend's hand.

"While I have you here and we have nothing much to do for the next five minutes," said Lena, "I want to know what happened between you and Wells Gabriel. I thought you and he might . . . attend my

MURDER COMES TO MADTREE

wedding together. It's been three years since Baer passed away. Wells seems like a nice guy. Why have I been seeing him around Limekiln with our neighbor Gretchen?"

"You want to know now?" Alice was shocked.

"Yes. I tell you everything about what's going on with me and Julian. Getting a personal story from you is like pulling teeth. I thought you and Wells had something."

"No. Nothing."

Lena leaned toward the table and lowered her voice. "Nothing nothing? Not even once? Why not?"

"Okay, if you want to know."

"I do."

"Wells will be a good friend because he saved Audrey when she was a puppy. It's no wonder Audrey has anxious behaviors. Almost dying of hunger in a dog crate will do that. Like I told you before, Well's wife was seriously ill, and they couldn't keep Audrey. I don't know about her next owner, but I rescued her in her adolescence. But, Lena, Wells and I have nothing else in common. One night we sat in my backyard at the picnic table and talked until dark. I know he still feels guilty about giving up Audrey."

"Having affection for Audrey's gotta be good," interrupted Lena.

"It only makes us friends. After one long talk, it didn't take us long to realize, despite the threat to my grandson last summer, Wells and I had shared everything we had to say. We used up our conversation."

"Alice, I don't believe you. No one can use up conversation."

"He misses his wife."

"And you miss Baer. So what?"

"He wants a wife who's sweet."

"You're sweet . . . sort of." Lena's head bobbed to the side. "I mean you're a nice person."

Alice's chin came down and her left eyebrow rose. "It's not enough to build a relationship."

"Okay, I wouldn't describe you as sweet," said Lena. "But you're . . . organized and smart and . . . thorough. Alice you're *very* thorough."

Alice chuckled at Lena. "Exactly. I get the impression his wife adored Wells, hung on his every word, and dropped everything the moment he entered a room. She loved cooking, and he's come to believe women instinctively are drawn to crafting. He told me how his wife designed cards for all occasions. He proudly tells of her talent making Halloween costumes for his sons when they were little."

"Oh, dear." Lena's mouth widened as she hissed a quick intake of air. "That's not you. Forgive me, you had great ideas for kids, but didn't you accidently put glue in your son's hair?"

"Baer shaved Peter's head that year," said Alice with an embarrassed laugh. "I think that was the year we used Baer's Aunt Marlene's mink hat and sent Peter off to trick-or-treat as Attila the Hun."

"I'm sorry Wells rejected you, truly." Lena looked disappointed.

"He didn't reject me," said Alice with a slight squirm. "We have a mutual understanding and a friendship. Since he moved in next door, I've covered for Gretchen when repairmen come to her house. Wells is skilled, but he doesn't like finishing a project. He's like a precise surgeon—but not inclined to stitch up an incision. So, Gretchen and Wells go out for the day, and I greet the professional plumber. I'm sure Wells has noticed the repair work, but I think he's grateful not to have a nagging reminder."

"Got it. I know how you have to see a problem through to the end."

"So, we are all friends. Audrey looks forward each day to playing with their dog Cooper. Wells and I trade dog stories, otherwise, I happy to be like Aunt Marlene—useful." Alice's head tilted and her eyes sparkled.

"Alice, *useful* is not a glamorous descriptor," sighed Lena. "It makes you sound like a broom."

"Changing the subject, if you have your laptop, how about looking up the names of Julian's two friends."

Lena sat back. "Are you saying you think Julian's friends are involved in this murder?"

"Probably not, but we need to start somewhere. And Julian's mood is off. Can't hurt to find out what's bothering him."

"Okay. Arthur Levitsky and Francis Brandau."

Alice wanted to add Frosty's given name to the list, but so far Elizabeth hadn't volunteered it.

"Has Julian talked about Francis?"

"All I know is that after Vietnam, he moved away from Bottom Ridge and now handles fishing excursions in Wisconsin, maybe near Lake Superior. Red Rock or Red Shores sounds right."

Alice smiled. It was a start at building profiles. "Elizabeth wants to see me in a while. I'm going to push her for more information."

"Alice, do you know what I have never, ever done? Never did a deep-dive research into Julian Mueller. Maybe a snorkel research, but not a full-bottom-of-the-ocean dive." She raised her palm. "I know—odd for me. I took the Octopus Man at his word. I think I know how I'm spending my afternoon when all our guests leave. Let's see what my Google apps tell me about Levitsky, Brandau, *and* Mueller."

Audrey stood and Alice took one last sip of cooled coffee.

"By the way, I cracked who's the reporter on the property," said Lena. "It's that woman who yelled about the murder."

"The tangerine woman?"

"Oh yeah. She's got some act going. I plan to track her down and tell her details about my wedding. You know, talk about human interest stuff? A murder as the backdrop for a wedding? I should at least get a good paragraph." Lena pointed to her shirt. "Bride. Can you see me as the lead photo of the story?"

Chapter 10

With Audrey riding in shotgun position and Alice directly behind her dog, holding onto the harness, Elizabeth drove the thirteen-row tandem tram across the Apple-Butter Train tracks to the outskirts of the resort property southeast of the inn. Each car of seats snaked follow-the-leader fashion until Elizabeth slowed in front of a weathered plywood trailer anchored in an apple orchard of barren apple trees. Outside the trailer was a bicycle next to an old-fashioned farmhouse windmill that squeaked.

"This is where Frosty lives." Elizabeth pulled a set of keys from her jacket pocket and slid out of the driver's seat. Alice watched the agility of the younger woman. Dressed in black dress pants, a long reddish-orange top, and spiky heels, Elizabeth glided as she walked over packed dirt and gravel. Alice studied her own attire: hiking boots, jeans, a beige long-sleeved top, and a puffy beige vest. She followed Audrey from the tram to Frosty's door. Alice looked at the sky and listened to a couple of birds. Away from the center of the resort, gone was the rhythm of apple picking, apple packing, cider making, and guest enjoyment.

All three entered the trailer. The smell of bleach and stale smoke made the air stuffy. Elizabeth's hand came to her nose. Audrey sneezed, and Alice cleared her throat.

"This is it," said Elizabeth. "What do you think?"

Given the circumstances, the bleach smelled like guilt, and Alice had nothing to say—yet. She expected Frosty's living quarters to be stereotypical of a working guy living alone: strewn with worn clothing and odd bits of litter. Instead, the inside was spartan. Bed—made as if he were in a military boarding school. Table with chairs carefully tucked forward. Burners clean, pots shiny. Alice opened the small refrigerator to six items logistically placed according to use, two bottles of beer prominent. The few pieces of clothing that remained were stacked according to color, from dark to light. Even bath towels were obviously newly laundered and carefully folded.

His home told a story: rough-hewn on the outside, inside a highly unexpected care bordering on persnickety. Pillowcase without a wrinkle. No pair of shoes waited in a closet or under the bed. No comb. No toothbrush. No hamper of clothing to launder. No pajamas.

"Does housekeeping change linens and towels for him?" asked Alice.

"No. Housekeeping doesn't enter the trailer. They only drop off fresh linens once a week." Elizabeth looked around. "I've had the trailer checked before now. Everything seems okay other than he's packed up."

"Is his trailer always this clean? Does he normally use bleach?" asked Alice. She glanced at several wire extensions draped across the ceiling and carefully taped down the walls to lamps.

"Orderly? Yes," said Elizabeth. She too looked at the wiring. "Those wires give me the creeps. He likes to live off the grid as the kids say. The limited electricity comes from something he jerry-rigged. As to bleach? Can't say. I'm not here that often, but housekeeping mentioned yesterday that as they stood at the door, they noticed an odor of cigarettes and bleach . . . when they came to deliver fresh towels . . . and to check if he were back in the trailer. But he was gone."

"Has no one seen him lately? Does the staff have any guesses?"

"No one in the cider barn or in packaging would know of his

comings and goings. I asked a very few at the inn. No one seems to want the responsibility of getting him fired—so no. No one has shared anything."

"And is Frosty on Lieutenant Unzicker's radar yet?"

"He hasn't asked a single question about him." Elizabeth glanced at the room. Her fingers rose to her lips.

"Does Frosty ride or walk about the grounds?" asked Alice.

"Depends what we need him to do. He owns a bicycle. It's outside." Elizabeth bit her lip.

Thinking a search of the trailer with Audrey might prove useless, Alice still looked for any personal item that might help Audrey track the missing man. Open drawers and surfaces wafted bleach.

"Audrey, take a good sniff," said Alice as she pointed to a chair with a worn tapestry seat. The bloodhound's nose swept across the chair and lunged back. "Audrey, find."

The dog's nose went to the floor in the trailer. Her ears swept like little brooms. After trotting up and back, she barked at the door, and Alice followed her dog outside. A rapid, cross hatch sniff of the grounds around the trailer ended with Audrey sitting down, her eyes expressing confusion.

"The trail is cold," said Alice. "The scent is probably too old for Audrey to follow or he rode away in a car. Who might be the last person to see Frosty? Maybe Audrey can get a hit from a different location."

"I don't know who to ask," said Elizabeth, "It's been at least three days since he disappeared. Do you think he is in danger?"

"I don't know. It's curious that he's disappeared. You have no idea who he has a beer with?"

"Anyone who works here, I guess."

Alice wondered why Elizabeth dodged complete answers. Didn't she want to find Frosty?

All three rode back to the inn in the tram. This time the hound sat next to Alice in the seat behind Elizabeth. Audrey's tongue hung out, her eyes closed, ears flapped as she balanced on the tram's hard-plastic seats and nudged Alice as she swayed with the rocking motion. Alice told Elizabeth of her upcoming meeting with Unzicker, and Elizabeth promised to have her staff keep a protective eye on Sylvie, Virgil, and Cyril.

"Thank you for their suite. I'll pay for whatever they need," said Alice.

"You will not. To have this murder settled, you all are my guests for as long as it takes. There's a chance that the reporter who is interested in safe vacations for the disabled will notice and talk to Cyril. An elderly man with a walker at a resort during a murder investigation? It has to be a good image for us, right? And it's an image I'm willing to pay for. I think you should talk to Artie."

The name startled Alice. "Artie? Polo shirt, sport coat guy?"

"Yes, my older brother. Have you never met him? He's in charge of reservations and group events."

"I've met him, but I never made the connection," said Alice. "I thought he just worked here. Your maiden name is Levitsky?"

"Elizabeth Levitsky Madtree. Try writing that on an application line."

"Oh," said Alice, "when Julian wanted to settle on a place for the wedding, he worked with Artie, your brother."

"Artie and Julian have been friends since a few years after Vietnam. He was so happy Julian moved out of that dreadful town of Bottom Ridge and to Limekiln. It gives them a chance to meet up. You know, guys bolstering each other's spirit. We were all happy to accommodate Julian for this wedding."

"It was beautiful and the reception lovely. Our older guests from Bottom Ridge were impressed."

Elizabeth stopped the tram in a round-about circular drive near the inn.

"That's Artie. He has an eye for detail and a regular historian for every event he has planned. After my divorce, Artie hired himself onto the staff and has stayed four years. He knew I was in a bad way, and he has this ability to zero in on a problem and find a path out of it. I hired Frosty on Artie's recommendation. We needed someone in the kitchen who understood meat." Elizabeth's hand waved as if considering more detail.

"Frosty's a chef?"

"No, he's a butcher's son, and his mother was a chef. I told you, the kitchen buys sides of meat, and Frosty prepares the cuts for our chef. It's almost funny, but two of our kitchen staff have their own favorite knives for the work they do. And don't ask them to share." Elizabeth made a face and checked her watch.

"Are Frosty's knives in the kitchen?"

"No, he's very protective of them, like I said." Her eyes lowered. "He never leaves them where someone else could touch them. Apparently, knives are very personal. He must have taken them with him because they aren't in the trailer or the kitchen."

Silence followed with Alice feeling the enormity of a clean, staged trailer.

"Then, I'll ask your brother about Frosty."

"Do that. Artie has been known to protect me from what is really going on," said Elizabeth as she looked again at her watch. "I have to go." Elizabeth left the tram in the circular drive in front of the inn and walked inside.

Seeing a bench under a tree, Alice took Audrey to sit, and they both watched a staff member drive the tram toward the scarecrow maze. She knew her questions for Artie would have to wait. Her head buzzed with the brother-sister Elizabeth and Artie. In her mind, she created a scattergram of relationships. Besides the brother and sister, Alice mentally circled Julian and Artie—old friends, plus Julian and Francis—even older friends from Bottom Ridge. Frosty and Artie were friendly enough for a job recommendation.

"Maybe the friendships make up one big circle," said Alice to Audrey. Her biggest worry was Julian. "Julian, what are you involved in?" whispered Alice to no one.

Before he left the trailer a few days before, even with his cleanliness nature, would Frosty have thought to wipe surfaces in his own home with bleach? Because that was a tactic more in keeping with Julian's knowledge of Audrey—bleach to dilute the human scent. This was the third day Julian had been on the grounds of Madtree.

Alice's foot scuffed at loose gravel.

If this goes badly for Lena, who's going to pick up the pieces, thought Alice.

"Because, Audrey, not even your sloppy kisses will save her from hurt if Julian is involved in a murder."

Chapter 11

To give Audrey exercise, Alice walked her dog toward the edge of a stand of apple trees and scanned the rows for anything she thought to be unusual. Many of the trees with ripened fruit removed sounded dry and crackly in the gusty wind. Audrey's ears perked up with each strain or snap, yet she wobbled forward, happy with soft dirt underfoot, not gravel.

The tram with parents and singing, young children in Halloween costumes meandered toward a large gazebo with an ornate painted sign: Mrs. Penrose's Story Time. Virgil and Cyril sat in the last seat of the tram. A stocky woman dressed like a Raggedy Ann doll stood outside the gazebo clapping her hands and waving. She wore a red yarn wig and red gingham dress with a white apron. Her stockings were red and white striped, and her cheeks had bright red circles. Red gloss of lipstick made her mouth look like a bow. Both Alice and Audrey stopped to watch as she directed the parents and children to a long table filled with apple juice and cookies.

"We have apple butter snickerdoodles, apple butter thumb prints, and apple butter oatmeal cookies."

Alice couldn't help but smile at Mrs. Penrose's enthusiasm and animation as she gestured toward the cookies and rubbed her stomach with delight at each mention of eating apple butter. Children stacked cookies onto plates and took seats at colorful child-friendly tables and chairs near the orchard. After snapping pictures with their phones, the parents and the two elderly men found grown-up chairs in the dappled sunlight.

"Before we have story time, say hello to Mrs. Tricklebank and Audrey," said Mrs. Penrose.

"Hello, Mrs. Tricklebaaannnk, hello, Audreeee."

Kids shouting their names and making the syllables linger in the air made Alice clap her own hands as she encouraged Audrey to answer them with a long, singing howl. Audrey pulled forward. None of the children, however, looked to race to Audrey's side. Alice waved again and said, "Thank you, Laura Leigh."

"Ple-ease," said Laura Leigh with the drama of pretended shock. "I'm in Story Time character. The children know I'm Mrs. Penrose, if you please."

"Of course. My apologies," said Alice. "Thank you, Mrs. Penrose. Children, also say hello to Mrs. Penrose."

A loud, elongated song of children's voices held the vowels of Penrooozzz, and Audrey once again joined in with her dog song.

Alice had known Laura Leigh Penrose for at least twenty years. As a face painter, she entertained young children at birthday parties. As a storyteller, she performed at libraries and schools. Laura Leigh's world was filled with joy, amazement, gratitude, and wonder. To Alice, all children needed moments with Mrs. Penrose's world.

"We're about to hear a story!" said Mrs. Penrose. "Right after face-painting time. We have a lovely story about a grasshopper to tell. Maybe if we are all good, Mrs. Tricklebank will come back to see me in an hour? Right here at Story Time?" Laura Leigh's eyes widened, and Alice nodded back. "Now, who wants a big, green bug painted on his face?"

Most of the children raised their hands. So did Virgil and Cyril.

Chapter 12

Alice sent a text to Lieutenant Unzicker: *Free whenever you are, but I have more questions than answers.*

She checked on her room, but housekeeping still hadn't completed the cleaning and staging for occupancy.

"Can't have you tracking in orchard dust," she said to her dog.

Taking the leash with a firm hand and grabbing her backpack, Alice again walked outside toward a quiet bench to clean Audrey's toesies. Families visiting the orchard for the day lined up for the scarecrow maze. Adults and children jammed the miniature golf course. The air filled with the sounds of joy. Alice opened her backpack. The hound, however, had other plans than sitting quietly for a brush down. Audrey's neck snapped to her right, and her tug almost pulled Alice to her knees.

"Hey!" said Alice rising from a deep knee-bend and catching her balance. She was no match for Audrey's determination. At times in the past as they walked to the slough, Audrey's interest followed a skunk. Here at the inn, Alice suspected her dog might be hungry and the scent she followed perhaps a juicy hamburger or bacon being delivered to a room. Still, she allowed Audrey to hotfoot forward. One never knew what intrigued her dog. Often these wild goose chases created wonderful stories to share later with friends.

Audrey tried to bound her way toward the back of the building.

Quite parallel to the ground, Alice's arm strained with each step. At a back doorway into the inn annex, Audrey barked for entrance. Luckily, a sign read the door was locked after seven p.m. Opening the door, Alice followed her hound to one of the guest rooms. Audrey barked again with insistence. Her tail wagged.

Loud voices of anger came from the room. "Dammit."

"Julian?" With one knuckle, Alice rapped on the door. "It's Alice and Audrey."

More yelling followed, some shushing, a scuffle, then quiet. Audrey's nose twitched. Even Alice detected cigarette smoke although the inn claimed to be smoke free.

"Just a minute." More muffled talking followed before the door opened a crack.

"May we come in?" Alice knew the look on Julian's face. He had been caught. At what, she didn't know—surely not because of the smoke—but his face reminded her of the many times of seeing smoke melt away in a breeze from the boys' washroom. Boys never expected a six-foot-tall lady teacher to haul her armload of books and papers into the washroom and catch them smoking. Kids never ran because Alice knew everyone at Limekiln High. All the smokers looked guilty and hung their heads. Only one boy ever tried to shed responsibility. "I was holding the cigarette for a friend."

Julian checked over his shoulder before he opened the door wider for Alice and Audrey to enter. Someone in the room had been smoking, but it wasn't the three men she saw. Julian remained at the door. Francis, still wearing his clerical collar, sat on a chair at a small desk. Artie lounged on the bottom of one of the queen-sized beds. Alice purposely dropped Audrey's leash—exactly what the bloodhound seemed to want—and the dog beelined for the bathroom door. Audrey barked for entrance.

"Dammit, Alice," said Julian. "You've got to go."

"Is someone else here?" Alice thought her innocent tone precisely caught the moment.

"Better find out what she knows, or rather what my sister may find out," called Artie. His eyes tilted up to look at Alice not with curiosity but with scorn smudged with guilt.

"Okay," said Julian, anger and frustration in his voice. "Have a seat, Snoopypuss." He walked to the bathroom door. "Frosty, we're busted. I told all of you none of this would work."

Chapter 13

As air rushed into the bathroom, it disbursed a cloud of smoke. Frosty slow walked out, balancing a cigarette like an additional appendage. He wasn't what Alice expected. Wearing jeans, a dark work shirt, and sandals, he had the bearing of a warrior and the confidence of a jockey. He was a man in his sixties, muscular and rugged, head shaved, and stood no taller than five feet two inches. His mouth was tight, eyes mere slits. Deep hollows in his cheeks signaled tension when he stared down at Audrey. His apparent callousness unnerved Alice. She felt this man capable of killing. Certainly, capable of harming Audrey if he felt annoyed.

The bloodhound, however, was oblivious to any danger, and her tail banged against the edge of the bed with delight. Alice dove to contain Audrey before her hound lunged at Frosty's crotch. Once trapped in Alice's arms, Audrey had no chance to explore the new guy.

"Crotches," she called to Julian. "Sorry, Frosty, she likes the personal touch when she meets someone. I apologize." Alice wrestled with her hound to keep her polite and safe. She didn't trust Frosty.

Julian pushed himself in front of his friend and acted as a protective barrier. Jumping to his feet, Artie urged everyone to sit down. "There's nobody dangerous here. Right? Julian said your dog's not a biter." Then looking like he controlled the moment, Artie waved his hand through the smoke around Frosty. "I asked you to stop smoking. Housekeeping will smell it and tell Elizabeth."

"I thought *you* were in charge," said Francis. He pulled a pack of cigarettes from his pocket and lit up.

"Are you begging for us to get caught?" The heavier, shorter Artie stood toe to toe with Francis, who flicked the cigarette into a waste basket.

"Very nice," said Artie. "Cause a fire." He picked up the basket and carried it to the bathroom.

Alice nestled her backside onto the floor and pulled Audrey to her lap. The dog's stretchy tongue swiped at her own nose as she twisted to take in the essence of four men. Alice too inhaled deeply and hoped her knees wouldn't twitch with the hostility in the room.

Francis folded his arms and glared at the others. Alice wondered if something were about to break. In a disgusted tone, Francis said, "Now what?"

"Introductions," said Julian. His voice was almost calm as he addressed his companions. "You know Alice. I've told you about Audrey." Julian slowly lowered his body onto the edge of a hard chair near a window. "Alice, you know my friends. As you've probably guessed, this guy is Frosty." His thumb pointed in the direction of the shortest man.

Artie and Francis looked self-conscious as they softened their shoulders and rigidity left their spines. Frosty didn't look in Alice's direction but clutched the drape and pulled it back less than an inch to peer out the window.

"If anyone can help, she can," said Julian. "I get that you don't trust the police. But Frosty, you need somebody out there poking around for details on who killed Rasmus."

"Someone's trying to set him up," said Artie by way of explanation.

"I want to hear from her," said Frosty. He moved to lean against the opposite wall. "Why should I tell you anything?"

"Well," began Alice, "Elizabeth is concerned and asked me to find you. She took me to your trailer. It was so strange, Julian. I couldn't find anything Frosty wore. It was like all the personal items of scent were removed. Odd, don't you think? Frosty, you're very tidy. And your bleach bill must be enormous."

The men avoided her eyes. Julian's chin dropped to his chest.

"Lieutenant Unzicker is a good investigator," continued Alice. "He's a friend to Julian, Lena, and me. It won't be long before he senses you're a person of interest simply because you're missing."

"I went *missing* before the murder happened. I have an alibi."

The men in the room nodded like bobble dolls on a dashboard.

"Maybe so," said Alice. "Also, there are three elderly people out there asking questions because they have nothing better to do. Julian, I don't want them hurt. Elizabeth promised me that the staff will watch them and make sure they're safe. Does anyone believe I can convince them to stop pestering other guests and staff?" Julian and the other men looked peeved and fidgeted. "They can be persistent. So, you see, Frosty, you'll be found. Julian already knows investigations are a process of elimination. Better to be ruled out early as a suspect."

"Lady, when I leave this room, no one will find me," said Frosty as he slid to the window and crumpled the drape enough to glance out again.

"He does have a set of skills," said Artie.

"So does Audrey," said Alice brightly, but her heart hammered. The dog's head rose with her classic ha-ha-ha face. "Yes, you do, my pretty girl with your big beautiful nose."

Julian turned to face the small man. "You don't want to run for the rest of your life for something you didn't do. Your skills saved you in 'Nam, but they're not necessarily good in Midwest farm country. Aren't you tired?" For a moment everyone was silent. Julian leaned back in the chair, turning his head to face Alice. "Let me guess. Virgil told Cyril about the Christmas we took down a killer."

Alice nodded. "Don't forget Sylvie," said Alice. She caught Artie's eyes. "Her nickname is Leatherneck. She was a little timid with our first murder case because she didn't trust Lena and me, but she's since hit her stride with the second. She's a gardener. For her, catching a killer is like eradicating weeds. And speaking of nicknames, why are you called Frosty?"

"It's personal," said Frosty.

"Pardon me," said Francis. "I've got a soft spot for those three, but are we really going to trust Frosty's life to three elderly people and a woman with a pet dog?"

"I know her. I seen her work." Julian pointed again to Frosty with his thumb. "We took Frosty out of the picture before Rasmus got here. Who knew the guy would get killed?"

Julian looked at Alice. In her peripheral vision she saw Frosty grimace.

"Frosty's the only guy here who knew Rasmus other than the murderer," said Julian. "He's got history with the victim. Alice, I don't care how much respect you have for the cops. You think Lieutenant Unzicker won't target him? He's been missing. We know he looks guilty." Only the air conditioner made sound. "She's the only hope he has," uttered Julian to his friends. "Alice, you in?"

"It wasn't me. I didn't kill Rasmus." Frosty looked nervous, as if he might bolt the room.

"May I ask how you four met?" asked Alice, hoping to soften the tension.

"We just did. Over bacon, wasn't it?" Francis grinned, the same grin as at the wedding, the grin that wasn't a grin.

Alice wasn't about to accept more cloaked explanations. She decided to throw some weight around. "In Vietnam?"

"Why 'Nam?" asked Francis.

Alice explained what she knew about Julian—Army medic in Vietnam in the late Sixties as the Tet Offensive ended, sometimes on foot with a unit, sometimes on a helicopter. Francis, the Marine on the Laos border about the same time. Both men grew up in Bottom Ridge and enlisted.

"Gentlemen, you're of an age. Is Vietnam the link or not?"

Audrey's nose twitched taking in a scent Alice couldn't detect.

Artie said, "Early Seventies for me. Frosty too. Hated the red mud and the syrup humidity. So what? But none of us knew each other in 'Nam."

"Of course, I knew Francis in Bottom Ridge, but I didn't meet Artie until years after we all got home," said Julian.

Francis rubbed his upper lip with his index finger. "Aw, hell. You have any idea what went on there?"

"Some," answered Alice.

"Good, because that's all I'm saying."

"I was a forward observer," said Artie before he added, "Communications. If there's such a thing as front-line stuff, that's where I was. See Cong—call it in. Track incoming. Need an extraction, call for help. Bullets regularly whizzed past our heads. You've no idea what a bullet sounds like." His tone was patronizing.

"Actually," said Julian, "she does, Artie. Alice isn't a bake-cookies grandma."

"But I was only shot at once, and I wasn't the target," added Alice. "You're right, Artie, I've no idea what you experienced. I've been lucky to have good people watching out for bad guys with guns. So, if not Vietnam, how'd you all meet?"

They looked to each other. The question on their lips seemed to be: How much do we tell?

Artie spoke first about guys coming home to blend into family life but feeling guilty about leaving year-long, tight friendships behind.

"Friendships? That what you call it?" said Francis. He made a sound and turned his shoulder to Artie.

"Lots of guys packed those memories away," said Artie. "Some . . .

even years later had issues—not sleeping, revisiting experiences at un-usual moments. Many of us were reluctant to share that with the VA. Veterans just got together on their own, shared recovery stories, or hos-pital humor."

"Some pretty dark sh——," Frosty paused. "Pretty dark jokes."

At the reference to jokes, all four men snickered but didn't choose to share examples.

"We drank beer," said Julian.

"And we talked," said Artie.

With a groan, Audrey flipped onto her back, and Alice's fingers drew designs in her dog's belly fur.

"Did Rasmus join the group?" asked Alice.

"No," said Francis. "He wasn't part of any patrol."

Alice concluded, *But he was in Vietnam, and you all know it.*

"Any idea what he did during the war?"

"He was a jerk," said Francis. "A big, arrogant, jelly-belly jerk."

"But he was a jerk long before he ever got to 'Nam," said Frosty with anger.

Alice knew looking up military records for soldiers in Vietnam was nearly impossible for Lena. Afterall, individual records from the 1950s Korean War weren't scheduled for release until the 2020s. The release for Vietnam records probably after 2045. But if Rasmus had a reputation for trouble before he arrived in Vietnam, maybe Lena could scour her newspaper app for stories before and after the war.

Who might want the jerk dead?

One look at Frosty told Alice, he wasn't ready to share his experi-ence with Rasmus. She needed to prove something to him first.

"Any idea who killed Rasmus?" asked Alice.

"Probably someone who knew he wasn't such a nice guy," said Francis with that smile that challenged.

"How did he spend his time at the resort?"

Artie answered. "He was here with a woman. Pepper Finwall. She checked in with him on Thursday but left after dinner. Far as I can tell, Rasmus was alone until housekeeping found him Saturday morning. Well, except for the killer, of course."

Alice asked if the rooms were coded to record how many times a guest went in and out.

"Sorry. No. We use old-fashioned keys to open doors, not magnetic cards. Elizabeth likes to keep things quaint. Pepper received a key when Rasmus checked in, but like I said, she left until Saturday—arrived back here a little before the wedding. The police stopped her from entering the room."

"She's still here," said Alice.

As if he didn't expect Alice to know, Julian's face registered surprise, and he said, "The police have talked to her twice."

"Do you think she killed him?" offered Alice.

"Unlikely," said Francis. "Have you seen her?"

Alice wondered what caused his scorn. She didn't answer but asked instead, "Any of you have details on how Rasmus was killed?" asked Alice.

The four men glanced at each other with gestures of innocence similar to those boys used to hide a truth.

"Oh, for pity's sake. You want my help, then tell me. Was Rasmus stabbed? Throat cut? Dismembered?"

Julian looked away, but like Elizabeth, drew his index finger over his throat.

"And you all knew this before the police got here because Artie runs the reception desk and receives information from housekeeping. Right?"

No one spoke. Laces on a pair of shoes became interesting to Julian, as Francis lit another cigarette, and Artie ripped it from his hand, and Frosty tapped his toes on the floor.

Julian cleared his throat which drew everyone's attention. Still, no one had anything to say.

Alice didn't reveal her other conclusions. *Because Artie runs registra-tions, he knew of Rasmus' intention to visit the Inn where Frosty worked. And you all started covering for Frosty when Julian arrived on Thursday and warned him to bathe his trailer in bleach before he went into hiding. Francis strapped a knife to his ankle—such a foolish move. But was the knife meant to protect Frosty from Rasmus, or did he strap it on after learning of the weapon used in the murder?*

For now, Alice trusted that Frosty wasn't the murderer. Despite Artie throwing out the name of Pepper Finwall, she guessed Rasmus's lady friend wasn't guilty of murder either. Probably both Frosty and Pepper were too short. Julian was tall enough and had the upper body strength. Francis had the leverage of height. But Alice doubted Francis had the inclination to be an active-duty Marine again. His snarly be-havior struck Alice as a man disgusted, not a man on a mission.

Alice checked her watch and scrambled to her feet. In a bound, Audrey was at her side.

"I have an appointment. Sorry, gentlemen, gotta leave."

Julian blocked her way. "You never answered me. Are you in?"

"If you mean am I going to reveal Frosty's location to the police? Not yet. Will I choose to trail him if he leaves the property? Well, Audrey enjoys a good challenge. I guess my answer depends on how desperate his behavior is."

"You'd never find me if I did," fired Frosty.

"Whatever you say," said Alice as she pushed past Julian and walked toward the door.

"Really, Alice," said Francis with that annoying grin, "Frosty knows ways to stop a dog. None of them are pretty."

Alice's back straightened, her height became apparent.

"I wouldn't try it." Alice's stare was deadly. "Julian can fill you in. Vietnam had its own rules, but so does rural farm country. I'd have thought, Frosty, you'd have figured that out by now. Francis, you must remember what Bottom Ridge was like when people developed an undesirable attitude toward someone who was not a townie. Frosty, right now people, like Elizabeth, are trying to help you because they believe in your innocence. Wonder how that could change if you killed my dog?"

Julian's voice turned to a squeal. "No one's talking about killing Audrey."

"How did he get his nickname?" demanded Alice.

"He was a tunnel rat," said Francis with outrage. His anger took control of his face as he struggled. "The . . . the . . . *enemy* burrowed tunnels for storage, for cover. Tunnel rats went down—alone—to blow up their world—he survived. Get the picture? No fear."

Julian said, "Don't mean nothin'." Artie looked wounded. Francis nodded and repeated as a conclusion, "Don't mean nothin'." Frosty went back to peering out the window.

Alice knew she had hit a nerve. Jaws turned hard. No one glanced at each other. Alice patted her dog and moved to the door. No one else moved to say a polite goodbye. As the door closed behind her, Alice heard the men swear and grumble accusations.

Half-way down the hallway, Alice stopped and took several deep breaths to calm the beating of her heart. If someone went after Audrey, how far was she willing to go to stop him?

Finding a bench near the elevator, Alice pulled Audrey close and took out her phone to call James Kennedy, dog trainer and veteran of Vietnam.

Jim had come to her rescue when Audrey arrived at her back door, starved and lost. Jim taught Alice games to play with her dog, activities that focused Audrey's nose on a scent. But mostly, Alice learned to read her bloodhound's body language and make them a team.

As briefly as she could, Alice explained the death of Wayne Rasmus and Julian's strange behavior. However, she slowed the explanation down when it came to the tunnel rat and shared the phrase Julian and Francis repeated. She wanted to know if the phrase carried weight.

"Hmmm, *nothin'*. You bet," began Jim. "Haven't heard that for a long time. Yeah, it carries weight. You can be sure whatever they referenced is serious. Guys I knew saved the phrase for the horrific scenes or behavior they saw. Too crazy to be real. You think Julian has something to do with the murder?"

"Don't know," answered Alice.

"You remember how you told me your eyes well up with tears whenever you hear a child's cry of despair, that for you that sound triggers a memory of another little girl?"

"Long time ago. Nothing I could do. I was too young." The memory of *No, Mommy, no* crushed Alice's heart. Even now she could picture the child's trembling hands and bubbling tears before the first strike came.

"Remember that moment when you talk to veterans. Lots of things can be triggers for us. Cracking bubble gum can even call up unwanted memories. My advice? Tread lightly."

The call ended with Alice feeling apprehensive, but she had an appointment with Laura Leigh, and at this particular moment, she could use Mrs. Penrose's stories of grasshoppers.

"We'll get there, Audrey, in our own time. Secrets always come out."

Audrey gave a *darn-tootin* sneeze that made Alice chuckle even as she dug a towel out of her backpack to wipe away her dog's slobber.

Chapter 14

Lieutenant Robert Unzicker trotted up from behind Alice as she walked Audrey toward the colorful ribbons flying from the gazebo stage of Story Time.

"I don't want you helping on this investigation," said Unzicker.

"So you said yesterday."

"Time to go home, Alice, and please take your houseguests with you." His voice cast concern.

"And good afternoon to you too," said Alice. "Why do you want us gone?" She wanted to ask him what had happened, but not when he was in Lieutenant-mode.

He looked annoyed. "Sorry. We've been doing repeat interviews all morning. Look, I don't like the way this guy was murdered. The case could turn dangerous once we get close to the killer." His tone changed from police officer gruff to that of a friend. "Alice, I don't want you hurt. I'm asking you to be reasonable and leave."

Alice had never been thrown off a case before. Well, not really. Other warnings to her about standing down were mere suggestions. But this time, her friend Bobby was serious.

Once she had left the room occupied by Julian and his friends, Alice's intention was to acquaint Unzicker with small details from her conversation with the four men. But if she wasn't supposed to be involved at all . . . well, she was just annoyed enough to clam up and wait for the right moment to share. Besides, who knew how information on Frosty might spin Unzicker in the wrong direction? The lieutenant was sure to have questions, and she didn't have answers. Questions that might get her a patrol car escort home.

"I can't exactly leave today," said Alice. "Elizabeth has asked for us to be here as a kind of support system. She feels having Audrey on the property will help calm guests so they don't flee. And she recognizes the benefits of having three elderly people engaging with guests. Can't be too much wrong with the resort's safety if Sylvie and the Deke brothers enjoy themselves. You've heard there's an undercover reporter on the property, evaluating the accessibility of the resort? Do you know which guest is a reporter?"

"No. I heard that rumor too." His attention drifted to the apple orchard and diverted to the picker cabins in the distance. "It's all Elizabeth and Artie have talked about. I don't like this case. What's your answer? Can you convince Sylvie, Virgil and Cyril to leave?" asked the lieutenant.

"What was their response when you told them to go home?"

"That they have reservations to play miniature golf."

"Did they mention the breakfast buffet and afternoon snack table before dinner?"

Unzicker's head dropped. "Yep. Along with face painting and the scarecrow walk. They're pretty impressed with cucumbers in the chilled water jugs."

"Did you talk to Lena and Julian?" asked Alice.

"He's another one! All their wedding guests are gone. Where is he? I can't find him. He's apparently not with Lena very much. She's indicated he doesn't seem preoccupied with a honeymoon if you know what I mean." Then, sounding more frustrated Unzicker added, "I don't want any of you hurt."

"I'm not fond of getting hurt either," said Alice. "Maybe if I knew more, I could convince the others to leave."

The lieutenant's mouth wrinkled. "I'm not convincing any of you to pull up stakes and go home, am I?"

"Probably not."

"What have you learned about Wayne Rasmus?" asked Unzicker.

"He was a jerk," repeated Alice remembering Francis's description.

"You can say that. Alice, he has a long sheet. Juvenile record. Dishonorable discharge from the military. Prison for selling drugs. Prison for plowing his car into the front of a bar and killing one man, severely injuring another. He's been out of prison for nineteen days. Now what do you know?"

"He was in Vietnam, but you know that. According to hearsay, he wasn't lean like we picture combat soldiers, but he was tall— you know that too. His lady-friend checked in with him but left the property. Then the morning of the murder, she was back. No one has mentioned details of his past, just that they don't like him. Artie probably took his reservation, but I don't think he actually met Rasmus until he showed up. So far, I haven't been able to see Julian one-on-one to get him to cough up details." Alice wanted to ask what Unzicker knew about the delay in reporting the murder, but she asked instead, "Who's your suspect?"

"Angelo Killian—a person of interest."

"Who's Angelo Killian?" Alice's eyes widened with surprise as her shoulders relaxed. Even Audrey sat down and looked up at the lieutenant.

"You haven't run across the name? Elizabeth never mentioned him to you?"

"No."

"He's a staff member who's missing."

"Oh. Elizabeth mentioned she wanted to keep his given name private. She called him Frosty. I understand he missed work yesterday and today."

"He's been missing longer than that."

"Elizabeth took me to his trailer, but Audrey couldn't hit on a scent," said Alice feeling a little guilty at not mentioning their trek. "Elizabeth fears something might have happened to him."

"We've also checked the trailer. Covered his identity pretty good. No photographs, no documents, nothing personal. When did you plan to tell me about this guy?"

"Nothing to tell. Like I said, Elizabeth was worried. She doesn't want him to be another victim."

"The bleach smell didn't tell you anything?" asked Unzicker. "Because not every killer thinks to wipe his home with a strong-smelling cleaner."

Alice couldn't make eye contact with him. "Audrey and I arrived this morning. I haven't been assigned a room yet. I'm not up to speed."

Audrey rose and gave a tug toward Laura Leigh, still in her Raggedy Ann costume. The face painter waved at Alice with big swooping gestures.

"Sorry, Laura Leigh is expecting us for tea. Before we go, have you been able to obtain a physical description of Frosty, I mean Angelo?" asked Alice. "Because I heard he is five-feet two and bald. Makes me wonder how such a little guy manages to kill a much bigger, taller man-beast."

Unzicker's eyes narrowed. "Wayne Rasmus was a big guy."

Alice caught his unease. "Rikki showed me the picture she took."

"We learned when Angelo was in Vietnam," said Unzicker. "He was one of those guys who—let's just say they trained to go beneath the ground and clean out an enemy nest. For him to be alive today, he had to be good and resourceful He might be a nasty piece of work, Alice."

"Can you tell me more about the wound Rasmus received?" Knowing how investigators rarely gave details about the crime scene, Alice added, "I'm only asking because scuttlebutt says he was cut with a sharp blade."

"I think I mentioned before it was a precise strike," said Unzicker.

"No call for help?"

"Not that anyone has shared."

"No thrashing about?"

"No, this guy had practice. He knew what he was doing."

Unzicker held back additional details. By the sour look on his face, she knew the cut wasn't a slash in fear, but it was precise like hate.

Alice waved to Laura Leigh and called, "I'll be right there."

"I need to find Julian." Unzicker reached down to pet Audrey's shoulder. "Be careful. We're seeing something that smacks of a professional or at least professionally trained, like a combat soldier."

"But probably not a *short* combat soldier," clarified Alice.

"At this time in the investigation, we're not seeing the evidence other than this was well thought out and planned."

"We'll all be careful. I promise." Alice turned to go when she remembered one last thing to tell Unzicker. "Lena is occupied with why Julian chose the apple orchard resort for their wedding site. She's researching everyone, even Julian. I'll let you know what she finds. Now I must have apple tea with Mrs. Penrose."

"Tell me she's not a suspect on Lena's list," said Unzicker as his hand swept over the top of his head.

Alice grinned. "She's not. But don't you wonder what dark, lovely, moody stories she might be able to tell on Halloween night?"

"*Oh, the Places You'll Go,*" teased Unzicker, referencing Dr. Seuss.

Alice's imagination caught the magic of titles. "Maybe: *The Cat from Madtree Orchard* could be one or *The Wonderful Wizard of Madtree.*"

Both raised their hands in small waves to Laura Leigh, and Alice left to join her. After a greeting, Alice explained the game she and Unzicker had played.

"I like it," said Laura Leigh. "*The Owl with Piercing Gray Eyes* or *The Girl Who Spied a Bad Man.* Because in an orchard, Alice, can be many beings who see surprising things."

Chapter 15

"As long as I'm still in costume, let's have tea here in the gazebo on this beautiful Sunday. Have you had lunch?" asked Laura Leigh as she poured tea into flowery teacups.

Alice blinked as her stomach growled a response. Audrey's head tilted with curiosity. "I had pastry with Lena on the patio this morning, but now I'm hungry. I lost track of time."

"I've been told that the children from the inn have canceled out for the last session of my day. I guess they've gone home early. Probably the murder scared off their parents."

"You're not packing up to go home?" asked Alice.

"Certainly not. The children from the cabins texted they plan to attend the last show. They always do. Every Sunday. They'll show up soon, but we have time to talk."

Laura Leigh reached under the table and pulled out a small cooler. "The kitchen always provides me with tea sandwiches. Do you mind chicken salad on apple bread?"

"Sounds good."

Laura Leigh handed over a thick, wrapped sandwich. "Do you believe the size of this *tea* sandwich?"

As she unwrapped it, Alice saw the bread wasn't made with apple sauce, but with chunks of apples. The aroma was heavenly. It even captured Audrey's interest. Her face came close to Laura Leigh's elbow.

Feeling guilty about her limited supplies for her dog, Alice put her hand to her vest pocket. The hound slipped closer; her nose waited an inch away. Front paws tapped and her tongue licked at her nose in an earnest expression of pleasure. The treats from Alice's pocket disappeared in seconds. With an exaggerated magical hand trick of reaching behind her to the backpack, Alice produced a dog bone in front of her hound's nose. Audrey's body wiggled like a child as she settled back down for a good bone-gnaw.

"This last group of children were timid eaters and left some cookies for us," said Laura Leigh. A breeze caught a piece of red yarn of her wig and flapped it above her head. "The snickerdoodles were popular, but the thumb prints are left for our dessert. I've forgotten. Can Audrey have a cookie?"

"I try to watch her sugar intake because she sometimes has a touchy stomach."

"Understood."

"It's always good to talk to you," said Alice, "but it seems to me you have something special to share?"

Laura Leigh filled the pouch of her cheek with chicken salad on apple bread. First, she hummed as she chewed, then explained her irregular storytelling jobs at nearby libraries as well as those at the resort—one on Friday afternoon, three on Saturday, and two on Sunday afternoon.

"I'm not here all the time," said Laura Leigh once she had swallowed. "Isn't that something about the murder?" Laura Leigh focused on the mayonnaise oozing over the edge of the soft apple bread and caught it with her tongue.

"Unexpected," said Alice even as she thought murder can happen anywhere.

"I saw you talking to Elizabeth after the wedding yesterday, and today you're here with Audrey. May I ask you if you are looking for Frosty?" Laura Leigh's voice was light, as if her question had no consequence.

"Why do you ask about Frosty?"

Laura Leigh's voice dropped from her expressive Story Time persona into a normal range for an adult. The entertainer act was gone.

"Because he's been missing for a few days. Usually he drives the tram to Story Time. It's not beneath him to allow me to paint his face first as an example to the children. Sometimes he joins in and becomes a story character. He particularly likes *The Little Engine That Could*. He's a small man and can make such faces and sounds of an engine climbing a hill." Laura Leigh sipped some tea and looked toward the orchard. "Last week some twin boys called him *poop-face*. I have no idea what prompted that, but he didn't mind. We all had a giggle." A slight breeze carried the smell of apples being pressed into cider. "No one seems to know where Frosty is."

"Laura Leigh, Lieutenant Unzicker is interviewing guests and staff. I think they're still gathering information about the murder itself."

"Yes, yes. Probably so. Lieutenant Unzicker is another one I can count on when I'm painting faces or telling stories. He always engages with the children." Her face turned serious. "Here's my question: do you think . . . Frosty is a victim or a person of interest?" She sat back like a doll on the shelf. Her painted face not in keeping with her concerned eyes. "I'm worried for him. What's going on?"

"I don't know," said Alice. "Elizabeth's also concerned. By now the police know he's missing. I'm sure he's not another victim. If he were, staff would have found him by now." Alice felt guilty not sharing more. "But since you worked with him, what are your guesses?"

"I've known Frosty for almost four years. He's a generous . . . conflicted man, but lovely with children. Hard worker."

"Conflicted?" asked Alice.

"As a retired teacher, you probably have experienced when a child is trying too hard to please." Alice nodded. "Frosty has that trait, as if to fill a hole in his heart or make amends. Do you know what I'm saying?"

"I do."

"Up until a few months ago, he was settled into his life here at the apple orchard. Like I said, he helps. I know he's a loner, but he's willing to please everyone by doing a task without complaining. You don't find many men like that. He reminds me of my father."

"What changed?"

Laura Leigh hummed, paused, and allowed her eyes to catch a view of the faraway cabins. "He started to be agitated and distant in August. By September, he was okay around children, but I couldn't get a word out of him once the kids were gone. During Story Time, he participated, but a few times he faded into the background. Not a word out of him. No toothy smile. I thought . . . I have no evidence of this . . . but I thought someone, maybe in his family, died. Grief hits people differently."

"You have no idea what happened?"

"Not at first." She unbuttoned a pocket on her apron and removed a piece of paper and held it tight in her hand. Her words came fast. "Alice, I don't mean to violate anyone's trust, but someone other than me needs to know this. Before the children come from the cabins for storytelling, I need to tell you what one girl, a daughter of one of our pickers, told me. I wrote her experience down so I wouldn't forget."

Laura Leigh unfolded the paper and told of an eleven-year-old girl, Maia, who overheard an argument between Frosty and another man. A tall, heavy man. A loud, angry man. The argument happened the Monday before the wedding. The two men weren't yelling, but the taller man shook his finger in Frosty's face. Maia particularly heard the bigger man say, "*See you soon, Kill-again.*"

"Except for school, Maia isn't supposed to be away from the cabins when her parents are picking, but one of the women who works in the cider house snuck her dog onto the property, and like all kids who love animals, Maia wanted to see it. That's when she caught the argument—as she hid to keep her family from seeing her.

"Then on Friday, the same big man walked to the outskirts of the cabins. He spotted the kids and asked Maia and the younger children if they knew Angelo Killian. They all said *no* because the little ones only know him as Frosty, and Maia was afraid of the bigger man. He offered them money if they could find him. The next day, of course, Rasmus's death blew up the resort, and I haven't seen her today. I don't know what Maia understands about any of this, but she knows the big man was bad.

"The argument and the man's questions made her afraid. Who was safe for her to tell?" Laura Leigh's fingers went to her chest. "Mrs. Penrose, of course."

"There's no way to tell if the man she talked to was Wayne Rasmus?" asked Alice.

"She said the same man who offered them money also argued with Frosty."

"Does she know Frosty's actual name? Could she have confused Killian with Kill-again?"

"No confusion. The younger children don't know his name, but Maia does, and she's old enough and smart enough to distinguish between *kill again* and *Killian*. But she is timid and cautious. No wonder she didn't cooperate with an aggressive stranger. Children are sensitive to a pointed finger."

"She's a smart, observant girl," said Alice.

"She's very certain he said *kill again*, and not in a teasing way," said Laura Leigh. "I wasn't sure who I could talk to. I made her go over the details while I wrote them down." Laura Leigh smoothed the note paper in her hand and turned it for Alice to see.

"Would Maia be willing to talk to the police?"

"Absolutely not. That'd be way too scary."

"And you think the man who approached Frosty was Wayne Rasmus?"

"I have no factual evidence, but that's my guess."

"Maia said the first meeting happened on Monday?" asked Alice.

"Yes. I talked to her on Thursday afternoon when I came for details about the children registered for Friday's Story Time and then again on Saturday afternoon. Maia was paled with fear and found me here. I trust her. The children from the cabins sometimes have a heightened sense of danger. Parents warn them not to get into trouble. They are to be invisible. So, they have a fear of authority. For them conflict means a parent could lose a job or be deported."

Alice's mind threaded timeline details together. Lena and Julian arrived Thursday along with their family members. Their wedding happened Saturday morning. According to Artie, Rasmus and Pepper arrived on Thursday for him to check in, probably around three, but Pepper didn't arrive to stay until Saturday morning when Rasmus's body was discovered.

Maia's description of the big man seemed to match the one Lieutenant Unzicker gave, but that meant Rasmus was at the orchard on Monday. Could there be a second big man trying to help Frosty or hurt him?

Alice read Laura Leigh's short, choppy sentences.

"What do you think it means?" asked Laura Leigh. "With this murder I don't know what to do. I can't go to the police because I don't want Maia to be frightened or for her to get into any trouble." Laura Leigh bit her lip.

"It's disconcerting in light of the murder," said Alice. "Maybe *Kill-again* is a joke from an old school chum who knocked books out of Frosty's arms. Or someone on a soccer team. Players always talk about killing an opponent. Or because this is an apple orchard, maybe it's a reference to beating Frosty at a drinking challenge 'to kill it drinking cider.'"

"My only contact with him comes when he participated in stories with children," said Laura Leigh carefully. "I know he smokes because I can smell it on him, but, Alice, I've never known him to have a drink."

"Not even a beer?"

"Absolutely not," said Laura Leigh. "He once told me it took him too long to get sober."

"A play on his name?" muttered Alice. "Could that be it?" Her thoughts stumbled over *Again*. Until she discovered more, there was no reason to pass Laura Leigh's scribblings to Unzicker. She would, however, tell the lieutenant about Rasmus maybe being on the property as early as Monday. Well, eventually. She needed to lock down a few details and avoid pulling Maia into the investigation.

"I hope that's all it is. Boy talk," said Laura Leigh with doubt in her voice. "But the murder—because my other thought . . . oh this is so dark and so not in keeping with the Frosty I know. I do read adult books full of suspense. I know . . . could it be . . . that Frosty's a hitman hiding out at the apple orchard, and the murdered man is his handler? Do real life hitmen have handlers or agents?"

Julian's friend, the athletic old veteran Alice watched walk out of the bathroom, could certainly kill. If he was a tunnel rat as Francis said, Frosty had probably killed men many times with little emotion. But that had been his job. And while Alice had little to no experience with hitmen, she doubted hiding out in an apple orchard for more than three years was how a hired gun worked. Or that the tall man had met him near the cider house to hire him to kill someone. Nah. Not likely.

"I think you can put your mind at rest. I doubt that Frosty killed the man at the inn."

"Good. But why can't anyone find him? Are you positive he's not a victim?"

As Laura Leigh spoke, Frosty-the-warrior danced through Alice's mind. Nothing about that man hinted at a compliant model for face painting or an actor in Mrs. Penrose's story telling. Something had changed him from the man Laura Leigh knew and the friend Julian willingly protected. But why did Frosty threaten to run?

"I don't see him as a hitman. And I believe he's too strong to be a victim, even of someone much bigger. I don't know what is going on, but do you mind if I keep your notes?" asked Alice.

"Please do. I want to help, and you're the only person I trust. Please destroy it if it's only some stupid, embarrassing school-boy taunt."

Alice looked at the paper again and dreaded Julian's role in whatever was going on. Unzicker might see Julian's protection as obstruction. If Julian and the others kept hiding Frosty, all might be accused as accessories after the fact or accomplices.

Audrey's head came to Alice's lap with her nose against the treat pocket. Alice took a cloth from her backpack. "Babes, your mouth is covered with slobber from grinding down that bone." Seeing that bits of bone attached to fur and nose, Alice wiped her dog's mouth, upper chest, and soft black nose. "She really throws herself into eating."

"Are you supposed to reward your dog when she hasn't done anything?" asked Laura Leigh.

"But, she has," said Alice, knowing she indulged Audrey way too often. "She sat here politely while we had tea. You've no idea how much energy she has or how many miles we log. I'm always happy when she's not up to mischief like hiding my car keys or tucking my bra into couch cushions."

"Oh look. The children are coming," said Laura Leigh. "It's time for me to resume my role of Mrs. Penrose, storyteller, and prepare for the last performance of the day. Like I said, the children from the inn have canceled out. All my attention will be on the children from the cabins."

Mrs. Penrose placed a call to the kitchen to remind them of more cookies and cider, tidied up her face-painting table, and touched up her own makeup. Five children approached Story Time from the picker's cabins south of the scarecrow maze and next to a grove of Winesap Apples. The taller girl with dark hair, glasses, and a ponytail walked behind two rambunctious younger boys who swatted and tried to trip each other. In front were two little girls holding hands and skipping until they noticed Alice and Audrey. They all stopped dead, but the older girl nudged the two little girls. Coming up slowly behind them was an older woman, a grandmother by the looks of her, but one younger than Alice by at least ten years.

Back was Mrs. Penrose's expressive voice full of joy. "Come on. It's time for stories." To Alice she whispered, "The tall girl is Maia. Might be best to talk to her without Grandma."

Alice waved at the children. "Hi, are you excited about Story Time with Mrs. Penrose?"

One boy nodded, his eyes drifting to the table that once held trays of cookies. He touched his cheek with one finger and asked, "Penguin?" The other boy pointed to his arm and boldly said, "I want a snake. Like the one the priest at the inn has."

Alice confirmed for Mrs. Penrose that a man at the inn indeed wore a clerical collar and had a whopper of a snake tattoo on his arm.

So, strangers, indeed, put the children on high alert. Francis had impressed this boy. For Alice, the request of a snake helped to prove she could trust Maia's observations.

"How about I give you a bright green snake with yellow spots? Cookies are almost here."

"Audrey and I have to leave," said Alice as she moved a step closer to Maia. "Mrs. Penrose, is it okay for Maia to help me tomorrow after school? Audrey's a good girl, but sometimes she gets bored with just me to walk her. I could use some help."

Maia's eyes sparkled.

"An excellent idea," said Mrs. Penrose. "I'll clear it with her grandmother."

All eyes went to the children's grandmother, who arrived with the youngest grandchild.

Audrey took a step forward in the direction of the children. The little ones backed away, but the girl with glasses gave a shy nod and reached for Audrey's ear.

"Oh! That can't be good," said Laura Leigh softly, tugging at Alice's sleeve and pointing to the maze. All discussion of Maia and Audrey stopped.

Beyond the trees, they saw a police officer sprint past the swimming pool and into the scarecrow maze. A small cluster of men ran with the second officer but stood back from the entrance.

"Wonder what's up," said Alice. Both Alice and Laura Leigh eyed the action. The small children skirted to the gazebo table and grabbed the remaining cookies, but they watched the maze.

"Whatever, it's not going to ruin my time with these children," said Laura Leigh. "You go along."

Seeing she couldn't help with the children and Audrey being crowd-curious, Alice walked her hound past the waiter delivering a tray of cookies and toward the maze that now had an audience. Her plan to catch Julian alone fell apart. Before she could ask, the crowd told of a boy and his dad finding a knife plunged into the straw of a scarecrow. They presumed the smear of red was blood.

Standing with the gathering, Alice noticed new fear replaced their initial excitement at hearing of a murder the day before. If this knife were the murder weapon, the killer was still around, and he didn't care if a child found the bloody weapon. Was the killer taunting the police? The resort? Frosty? Or was it someone in cahoots with Rasmus?

Chapter 16

The rest of Sunday afternoon, families with young children drifted into clusters, whispered of the danger of staying at the inn, and walked with heads down to pack up and leave. The police asked questions, otherwise, remained silent. Unzicker waved off Alice as she approached, but Lena came to her side.

"We're staying!" stated Lena, and Alice nodded. "I'm not leaving until I know what's going on. Dinner in an hour? At five-ish?"

"Sounds good. I'll ask the Bottom Ridge guests to join us unless they've filled up on happy hour appetizers," said Alice.

"I'll corral Julian. I'm not taking any excuses this time. And no Francis. I want to catch Julian without a firewall of friends."

Alice planned to spend the next hour walking Audrey, feeding Audrey, playing ball with Audrey, and grooming Audrey to be presentable at dinner. But her mind was on *See you soon, Kill-Again!*

What did it mean? Frosty had worked for Elizabeth Madtree for almost four years. According to Unzicker, the prison system released Rasmus in September. Alice didn't have the impression that Frosty and Rasmus were old friends.

And now this knife, perhaps the murder weapon or a joke. Maybe we are all looking at this the wrong way. If the killer is still around—probably so—the death of Rasmus did not fulfill his purpose. Okay, a former cell mate of Rasmus?

But then with Rasmus dead, the killer certainly wouldn't still be here. Did the kid who found the knife play a joke for the attention of his father? Kids can be like that, but this kid was young and with his father. Probably not yet a fine-tuned schemer.

Alice and her hound walked away from the entrance of the maze to the far side where the stacks of hay were shorter and allowed her to spot scarecrow creations designed by children. A baseball player, another a boy scout, a ghost, a ballerina. Every summer, the Madtree staff hosted a competition for the most creative scarecrows. Scouts, Bible schools, baseball teams, as well as local library book clubs for children, came up with ideas and clothing for their scarecrows. Now, bails of straw and canvas curtains formed the maze. Alice imagined children giggling at finding their Halloween drawings attached to sheets of canvas with scarecrows looming nearby. Adults easily meandered behind their children with phone cameras ready.

Why did the culprit wish to introduce fear into this idyllic setting by leaving a knife behind?

"Mrs. Tricklebank!" yelled a woman. Alice looked up from her concentration on the maze. It was the tangerine woman she'd seen outside the inn after the discovery of the body, the woman who'd stayed in the room just below the murder site. "I'm so glad to find you. And you have a bloodhound. It's about time someone took my situation seriously."

She took Alice's arm with a firm hand and escorted her back toward the inn.

"I'm sure the police are taking this very seriously," answered Alice. The woman was older than Alice first thought. Perhaps in her early sixties, she wore lime green shorts and a matching quilted jacket. To Alice the woman didn't have the demeanor of Lena's conclusion that the golfer was a reporter. "What's your name?"

"Bernadette. They haven't found the murderer yet, have they?"

"I've been walking my dog," said Alice. "The only new development I know is the activity in the maze."

Bernadette ignored the maze and rattled on about her breakfast with her husband Lester, the movie they watched the night before the murder, and her detailed description to the police the morning after. The same man who stood in Bernadette's shadow the previous day, now waited in the doorway of the inn, checking his watch. He turned briefly, caught Alice's eye, and weakly smiled at her as his chest puffed with a deep breath. Bernadette remained oblivious to him as he patiently waited to catch her attention. Instead, as she walked with Alice, Bernadette began a deep analysis of the television murder mystery that had kept them up late. With one look over his shoulder at the two women, the weary man slipped back into the inn and walked toward the bar.

"Am I keeping you from your dinner?" asked Alice.

"Dinner? No. Lester doesn't mind waiting because we heard someone back upstairs in the murdered man's room. I think the killer might be using the room as a hiding place. The police have cleared it, so what better place is there to hide? Or he left something behind and has gone back to retrieve it."

"It wouldn't be unusual for the police to look at the murder site one more time." said Alice.

"It wasn't the police." Bernadette's eyes enlarged.

"Maybe forensics," said Alice.

"Nope. Why would they be dropping marbles on the floor? Somebody was upstairs being awkward and rolling marbles on the floor. What could they be looking for? I told the police, but I think they brushed me off when I suggested the murderer went back to the room."

"Maybe housekeeping?" asked Alice.

"No. Marbles! Why would Housekeeping drop marbles? Anyway, Lester and I never heard the squeaking wheels of that cart the housekeeping women push. So, I went upstairs to check what was going on. Lester said I was being a baby with worry. I tried the door to the room, but it was locked, and everything was silent. Lester said my imagination is overactive. Lester said if the police do investigate, now they'll find my fingerprints on the door. Am I safe?"

Alice doubted anyone could hear squeaky wheels from the floor above. All the hallways were carpeted.

"I know sounds can be worrisome," said Alice, "but despite having keys to open doors, all the doors lock automatically when they close."

"Can I ask you to go upstairs and tell the police what you see?"

"I'm only a guest at the inn. I don't have access to someone else's room, definitely not the site of the murder."

A small knot of guests stopped by the elevator as they noticed Bernadette's sharing. Alice felt uneasy.

"You've reported the suspected intruder already. Right?" asked Alice.

"I did. The officer said he'd pass it on, but I think he believes I'm a nutcase. He behaved like I was annoying."

"I don't know what to suggest," said Alice.

"People are saying one of the workers is missing. Could he be hiding in the room above ours? It would be a perfect hide-out because the police have already searched it."

Alice's mouth twisted. "Highly unlikely. Police go back to crime scenes all the time."

"But don't they have to let you and your dog go into the room. Let the dog sniff around. Find something or someone."

Alice did have an itch to visit the murder site. Forensics focused on useful bits of residue like hair, broken fingernails, and blood. Police generally charted the layout and movement in the room, but sometimes a little nonsense detail like a shirt being freshly laundered and hung up with all the buttons buttoned told a story. Alice wondered if she were to visit the room what would be the lingering odor? An odor to excite a dog's nose?"

"I'll see what I can do," said Alice.

As she spoke, Artie came out of the elevator flanked by three employees of the resort.

"We are sorry for this scare, Mrs. Livingston. The police have searched the room in question but have not found any new evidence—only an overturned planter. But just in case, forensics will be back for a second look." In a louder voice for all to hear, Artie announced, "We have warm apple cider and pastry on the patio. Staff members will keep you informed through a text to your phones, and the police have promised to make a statement."

Artie's smile was tolerant as he whispered, "Your room is ready, Alice." The way he cast a look at Alice, caused her to feel a chill. Alice's guess: the police had found something.

The other guests near the elevator dispersed for their special late-afternoon treat.

"Wait until I tell Lester, someone is finally taking me seriously." She looked over her shoulder. Her voice was breathy. "Where's Lester?"

"Bernadette, it's good to be with people. Why don't you join the others on the patio? As we came in, I saw the staff turning on the outdoor heaters. Maybe ask your husband to join you. I believe I saw him go into the bar."

"In the bar? He better not be. The number of medications that man takes is terrible. He knows better than to add alcohol. Unless he's more upset than I thought. He's sensitive. Probably worried about my safety."

Bernadette spun around and headed for the bar.

Alice checked her phone for text messages. Nothing from Unzicker. Apparently, the police chose not to share. Nothing from Julian, but that was expected.

"Ready for old-fashioned gossip-mongering at dinner?" wrote Lena. *"Room service in our honeymoon suite. The whole gang is coming except for Francis. Time to pose theories."*

Chapter 17

Alice felt weary with the events of the day. The white, crisp sheets on the bed looked inviting. Knowing she would be exhausted after dinner, she opened Audrey's bag and removed furniture coverings for chairs and particularly the bed. Those lovely sheets deserved protection from a hound who loved to snuggle her face onto Alice's foot. With the coziness of every piece of furniture protected, Alice and Audrey left for dinner.

Although she had Elizabeth's permission to take Audrey anywhere on resort property, including the dining room, Alice knew dog slobber sometimes put people off. Room service was the perfect plan.

A little after five o'clock, the temperature dropped as gray clouds moved in. Alice and Audrey walked behind the Bottom Ridge guests and listened politely to Sylvie's tirade against the chill outside as she, Virgil, and Cyril entered Julian and Lena's honeymoon suite.

No one really expected older snoopers to brave the autumn air, but all three announced they would have rejected dinner if Lena and Alice wanted the romance of dinner under the stars. The tall heaters flamed around young diners to keep the cold away. Young drinkers also huddled in puffy jackets near the fire pit. All around the inn, pathways glowed with strings of orange fairy lights.

"What are they thinking?" asked Sylvie. "Cool, damp October

drafts are freezing our bones, and that manager thinks to turn on something that has an open flame? Anyone might rush about and knock into one of those things. Then whoosh. We're crispy."

"I saw you with Unzicker and Laura Leigh," said Julian while lifting the lid off a tray of bruschetta. "Anything special to report?"

"I'll wait until later," whispered Alice into his ear. "No reason to be in the middle of details when dinner arrives."

Cyril stood up and pushed his walker past the bedroom door. Rather than continue to the bathroom, his attention diverted to the bedroom ceiling.

"Hey, why do you have mirrors on the ceiling? Our suite doesn't have these."

"Think about it," said Sylvie with criticism in her voice. "Honeymoon suite? You're not that old." She went into the bedroom and took his arm. "Now, look way up." Cyril twisted his neck and looked up at himself. "See. All your wrinkles fall right out of your face by looking up."

"I never noticed that before. Say, that grasshopper painted on my face looks pretty good." He turned his face back and forth, admiring the bug Laura Leigh had painted.

"Imagine if you were in bed," said Virgil. He still had a small white moth on his forehead.

Cyril's eyes widened and his eyebrows drew together, not with understanding but with confusion, as he looked at Lena and Julian. "You two are in your sixties," he accused.

"Thank you for that assessment," said Julian, clearing his throat. "Now can we all take seats. Lena ordered the bruschetta for us to nibble, but we have to call in our dinner choices to room service."

After a half hour of defining caramelized versus glazed and fricassee versus meunière, the friends placed their orders of roasted chicken and vegetables. While they waited, Sylvie asked, "Did you all hear about what happened this afternoon?"

"A boy and his father found a knife stuck into a scarecrow," said Alice.

"Virg and I were behind them," said Sylvie. "The boy kept running ahead and running back to his dad. I think he wanted to scout out the twists and turns of the maze without disappearing too far ahead. He was the one who found the murder weapon."

"*The* murder weapon?" asked Alice. She had caught Lena's rolling eyes.

"The police were very interested," continued Sylvie. "They closed off the maze until everything was inspected."

"Where was it exactly?" asked Lena.

"A long-handled knife pinned a sleeve to the straw body of the scarecrow. The twelfth one into the maze," said Virgil. "No one could miss it."

"You didn't touch it, did you?" asked Lena. "Did the kid touch it?"

"Please. This isn't our first murder investigation," said Sylvie. "We're not amateurs and that child was too scared to touch it. He just ran to his dad."

Lena sat forward in her chair. "Did Lieutenant Unzicker say it was *the* murder weapon?"

"Not in so many words," answered Sylvie. "But who else would leave a big stainless-steel chopping knife in a scarecrow dressed like a road construction worker? I think the killer chose that display because it had a traffic cone." She eyed the others. "It's a reminder. A warning."

From what Unzicker told her, Alice could have argued that the chopping knife wasn't the murder weapon. It crossed Alice's mind that any one of the teenage guests might have imagined a good joke on adults. Even though the resort was lovely with many creative activities for little children and adults, teenagers were at a tricky age to entertain.

"Couldn't have been there that long," said Julian. "The maze has regular guests. Usually a backup of people in line."

"You're saying someone went into the maze with seconds to spare and jabbed the knife into the scarecrow," said Lena.

"Had too," said Julian.

"Any child could have found it," said Virgil. "Of course, it could be a diversion. Make the police think that it's the knife used in the murder."

"The dad called the police as soon as he saw it," said Sylvie.

"Unzicker never mentioned anything?" asked Julian as he turned to Alice.

Alice shook her head. She hadn't spoken to him. He was busy assessing the threat. If she were correct, Alice counted the knives in question: First the blade used on Rasmus. Second the knife strapped to Francis, and now the third in a scarecrow.

When the food arrived, the older friends plus Julian sat at the table for four. Lena chose the hassock as her table. Alice's plate balanced on a wooden luggage rack next to a wall—so much easier to police the bloodhound's quick tongue. Audrey ate her regular dinner, but once she had finished, Alice pulled strips of chicken from bones and fed several to the seemingly famished hound.

As they finished with apple crisp and vanilla ice cream, Lena said, "Now, Alice, what have you got?"

"Lieutenant Unzicker wants all of us off the case," said Alice.

"Not happening," said Sylvie. "What else?"

Unsure of Julian's role as protector of Frosty, Alice carefully edited out details from her private conversation with Mrs. Penrose. Instead, she described the isolation of the gazebo and the limited time Mrs. Penrose spent on the property. She also told of Bernadette, who'd heard noises from the room above her.

"She said she heard sounds of marbles dropping on the floor. The police promised to check it out."

Cyril wiped his mouth with a napkin. "That poor woman. I spent a little time with her husband and spoke some to Bernadette. She's scared to death to leave the resort in case Lieutenant Unzicker needs her."

"Why does she think the police need her?" asked Julian.

"She's in the room below. She did hear marbles rolling across the floor," explained Cyril, "and that's after the murder. Poor woman's terrified. Feels like a sitting duck."

"Cyril, I don't get it. Why does she feel like she's in danger?" asked Julian.

"For one, her husband's in that wheelchair. Poor guy's probably at least twenty years older than Bernadette. She worries about having a room on the second floor. If there's a fire, how's she going to get him into a wheelchair and down a flight of stairs?"

"Why are they on the second floor?" asked Lena.

Cyril shook his head. "That woman. She's afraid of a peeping Tom. I heard staff say she was very picky about what room she wanted on the second floor."

"But why if her husband's in a wheelchair?"

"I don't know. Maybe she's afraid he'll wander off. Lester has dementia. When I talked to him, he only recalled his first wife. He doesn't know Bernadette's the woman he's married to now. She had to keep reminding him. At my age, I've seen it before. Poor guy's mind has backed up in time."

Alice perked up. "In a wheelchair? I thought I saw him in the bar. He was standing up and not that old. You saw him in a chair?"

"Yep. The guy you saw musta been Gavin."

"Who's Gavin?" asked Lena.

"His attendant. Gavin doesn't like to be called home attendant or care giver. Gavin helps Bernadette's husband with dressing, bathing, getting around, you know."

"My mistake. I thought I saw her husband holding her putter," said Alice feeling unconvinced. Her eyebrows drew together.

"Yes, that'd be Gavin," said Cyril. "Bernadette has a bad back. She can't golf on the big courses. This trip was for her to try miniature golf. When they travel, Gavin comes along to help. I told her it's a good thing she's staying because a barber shop quartet is scheduled for tomorrow. She and her husband can't miss that. What?"

Lena had stood, her palms tipped upward. "What, indeed? Think about it. A woman with a disabled husband? Her with a bad back? She likes to golf? Don't you see? When I'm right, I'm right."

"Lena, I know you think she's the reporter for a magazine, and she may very well be," said Alice. Her mind was dancing around the wheelchair and the man attendant who stood in the doorway of the inn with a putter. Something in his behavior had an unsettling intimacy—something more than employer and employee.

"Yes, Alice, the reporter. One of those three is the reporter everyone's expecting. One a photographer. Cyril, when you were with them, did they take photos of the resort?"

"Not that I saw, but we were waiting for that waitress to refresh the cucumber water."

"I'm guessing they're a team," said Lena. "The man in the wheelchair tests accessibility to activities. Bernadette's the writer. Gavin's the photographer. Or maybe the old guy is the writer and Bernadette their cover, so no one suspects—I don't know I haven't figured out the logistics." With a spark in her eyes, Lena said, "All I know is that they're evaluating the inn for a story."

"Lester wasn't faking dementia. I'd know," said Cyril. A scowl registered his disapproval.

"Sure," said Lena with a wink to the others.

"Let's get back to the knife," ordered Julian. He looked scared. "Did you say it was a butcher's knife? Did it look like a hatchet?"

"Not so bulky. It wasn't a cleaver" answered Sylvie. "It was sturdy and probably used for chopping vegetables. In a fight, maybe good for slashing?" Her arm moved as if it held a machete.

"Kinda clumsy weapon to use in a murder," said Julian.

"I heard Lieutenant Unzicker ask one of the officers to question staff in the kitchen to see if any guest has been in there with a request," said Virgil.

Julian's eyes went to Alice. When she didn't pick up the discussion of the knife, Julian looked relieved.

"Hey, why is no one talking about the murdered guy's girlfriend?" Lena paused until she had everyone's attention. "Alice and I saw her get ratty with Rikki when her picture was taken. So why is that? I think she killed him in the middle of the night when he was asleep. There's another couple that's got a twenty-year age difference between them. She was probably after his dough. Now she has to stay on the property to avoid suspicion." Lena dusted her hands. "What's her name?"

Julian answered, "Pepper Finwall."

Lena missed so many details about the murder scene that Alice didn't have the heart to correct her. Unzicker was convinced the killer was a man. Sure, the murderer most likely surprised Rasmus because there was no evidence of a struggle. The man appeared to fall straight down without a fight. Lena's guess of a female assailant was good if Rasmus had been found in a chair or a bed, but he wasn't. And size of the killer did matter. Pepper was too short.

To push Lena into another direction of thinking, Alice said, "Rasmus just got out of jail. How much money could he have?"

"Oodles," said Lena. "What if he were a thief and hid the money before he went into jail? Maybe he's a bank robber, and after all these years, his gang wants their share."

The discussion continued for another forty minutes with the friends repeating details about the murder, questions about Bernadette's husband really being in a wheelchair, and catty criticism about chubby-thighed Pepper Finwall, fiancé to the deceased. The evening broke up when Sylvie announced she had a big day planned tomorrow and wanted sleep. Virgil rose slowly.

"Bed's a good idea," said Alice while giving a patient Audrey a pat on her side.

"What a day," said Cyril and off he went, walking slowly behind his brother and Sylvie.

Once the door closed on the guests, Lena said to Alice, "Now what do we know about the missing guy called Frosty? Do we like him for the murder?"

Chapter 18

"Cupcake, how . . . um . . ." sputtered Julian.

"This is supposed to be our honeymoon. What do you think I've been doing all day when you haven't been around? Research. That's what. People talk—maybe not to the police, but the staff is anxious."

Julian said a couple more *ums*, several *sorrys*, before asking, "What did you learn?"

"Sounds like you two need a private talk," said Alice.

"We do," replied Lena. "But that doesn't mean we can't share part of this with you."

Lena put together a list as only she could. "Rasmus is a bad guy who probably learned the trade from his dad. From newspaper stories and several local police blotter entries, his dad was a conman and a drug dealer. Always in trouble. Rasmus himself has a history of not obeying the law. I wrote down all the sites. I bet Unzicker was able to find many more." Lena turned to face Julian. "I understand wanting to help a person in Rasmus's path. What I don't get is why you excluded me. Me!" Her hands went to her hips.

"Julian, take us through how you know Frosty and Artie," suggested Alice.

Lena's fists unclenched and took Julian's hand. "Remember I know some of this already. I did research on you, too."

Julian took a deep breath and described a bunch of guys getting together over raucous breakfasts, telling jokes no lady wants to hear, sharing stories only other veterans could appreciate.

"Guys need to be with guys sometimes. Frosty, Francis, and Artie had their own experiences to deal with. It's not like we were nuts, but sometimes vets get flashes from the war. Maybe a soldier's face or that of an enemy. One time I was at a picnic with my daughter when she was ten or so, and all the kids were running through a sprinkler and laughing. It was their screaming with delight that triggered . . . for three seconds, I saw Vietnamese kids running and screaming. I felt dizzy and my heart hammered. I called up the guys to have breakfast. Talking helped."

Lena squeezed Julian's hand. "I know about the nightmares."

"I don't remember them," said Julian as if cloaking the truth.

"Still, not often, but they do visit you," said Lena.

"When Frosty called you or Artie," said Alice, "and told about Rasmus knowing about his location at the apple orchard, you all felt he needed support."

"Like he and Artie have helped me. We don't judge what other soldiers did over there."

Alice tried to smile with understanding. "Something like a bunch of muddy-pawed dogs throwing themselves into a pile for a nap. None of them care if another has a little dirt on its muzzle."

"Yeah, like that."

With an air of relief, Julian repeated the story of Rasmus contacting Frosty. In Vietnam, Rasmus worked in moving supplies—some assigned, others improvised and illegal. When he was about to be released from prison, Rasmus reminded Frosty that they shared serious secrets. If he didn't help him now, the inn might learn of Frosty's wartime past both the using of drugs and the looting of enemy dead.

"That can't matter now," said Alice. "There has to be more."

"Really," said Lena. "Your friend is afraid that someone will learn he took drugs during the Seventies? Julian? Really?"

"If there is more, he never told me."

It was the kind of answer that made Alice cringe. Technically he was being correct, but his phrasing built in hide-and-seek nuances. Maybe it was true that Frosty never told Julian, but Frosty may have told Francis. And Francis may have relayed truth to Artie and Julian. Alice also felt Julian knew because of the way he raised his chin with a sort of defiance. *Loyal to the end*, she thought. *A fierce defender*. No doubt about it. Julian knew of a secret. So did Artie.

Staring back at the two women, Julian said, "Let's see how long he can keep his job when they realize he once had a habit and lifted someone else's property."

Alice kept quiet.

"Okay," said Lena. "I still don't think that matters. It was years and years ago. It was war. No one gives a flying fig about that stuff now."

Julian cleared his throat. "Look, Magpie, I saw an opportunity to support Frosty and finally get married. There's nothing wrong with that. If Rasmus was coming to the orchard, then Artie, Francis and I could keep him safe. You and I could invite the whole family for a lovely outdoor wedding." Julian shrugged. "Artie thought it sounded efficient."

"Except, this wasn't like helping a pal change a tire," said Lena. "Frosty's anxiety had to spike. I know yours did."

Seeing her friends' faces redden, Alice asked, "Why didn't Frosty take off right after he heard Rasmus intended to contact him?"

Julian took a moment to compose his answer. "If Frosty took off, the problem wouldn't be over, would it? Artie told him we'd have his back. He could hide at the inn. The four of us would confront Rasmus together." He turned to Lena, "Magpie, I'm never worried or anxious."

Lena rolled her eyes and her voice rose as she spoke. "I'm not calling your plan stupid, but if the police find out you all were plotting against a guy who turns up dead? Julian, I can't even . . . what must the police think?" She stood and walked around. "Why did it take four of you?"

"It just did."

"We'll talk later," said Lena. "Just the two of us. Alice, how does the timeline square with what you know?"

Alice was careful about divulging the pieces of the story she knew. No need to reveal witnesses. But she repeated that Rasmus got out of jail sometime in late September after spending years in prison for manslaughter.

"They must have had regular correspondence, right?" asked Lena. "How did Rasmus know where Frosty lived? Do you see him looking it up online?"

"No. Frosty's careful about exposure. He said they never wrote back and forth," said Julian, "except for two letters recently. He was surprised Rasmus found him."

"Julian," said Alice, "are you aware Rasmus was on the property and spoke to Frosty as early as Monday?"

Julian's body reaction was physical. The information hit him with a jolt. "No. He never said. I didn't know. How'd you find out?"

"It doesn't matter. Rasmus was seen shaking his finger in Frosty's face. He never mentioned the meeting?"

"No."

Julian spilled the events he knew. Wednesday night Frosty went into hiding. Julian and Lena had arrived on Thursday to prepare for the wedding. Julian and Francis took turns keeping an eye on their old friend. For whatever reason, Frosty thought his life was endangered and wanted to leave the resort. They took him at his word and didn't ask for a thorough explanation. Artie assumed it was better to take on the devil on the turf they knew rather than allow Frosty to flee to an unfamiliar location. At the resort, they could help protect him.

Alice added to the story: On Thursday a big man who may have been Rasmus asked for Frosty. When he couldn't be found, the man—probably Rasmus—offered money to a person on the property for information.

"Sorry, Love Bug," said Lena to Julian, "this makes no sense. Rasmus writes to Frosty to tell him he's going to be released, contacts him on Monday. Frosty still believes his own life is threatened and goes into hiding. Then Rasmus is murdered?"

"It only makes sense if there is another menace out there," said Alice. "Julian, do you know who the real threat is?"

Julian tightened his lips and kept silent.

"Okay, let's try this. You mentioned Rasmus wanted Frosty's help," said Alice. "If Rasmus knew his own life was in danger and part of his plan was to force Frosty to help him, do you know of any leverage Rasmus had over Frosty?"

Silence.

"Julian, you talked about the bond that forms between soldiers. Maybe Rasmus thought he had that kind of bond with Frosty."

"No, they didn't have that sort of trust. You don't threaten a friend into helping you."

"Now that Rasmus is dead, why doesn't Frosty come out of hiding?" asked Lena. "You said he didn't do it and has an alibi for the time of the killing."

"It's . . . hard to explain."

Alice thought, *Hard to explain because there is something more.* "Does he have any idea who went after Rasmus?"

"He says no."

"It could be someone Rasmus knew in prison," said Lena helpfully. "A big brutish guy who thought Rasmus's bunk was better than his. Or Rasmus didn't show respect to the . . . what do they call them in the movies . . . a boss?"

Julian smiled and lowered his eyes. "I doubt it. Magpie, you do have flair."

Lena's eyelashes fluttered.

Alice picked up the conversation. "We need the truth from Frosty. I can't believe a guy in prison would turn to an old buddy he hasn't seen in over forty years. Lena's right. How does he even know where to contact him if Frosty's been living off the grid, as the kids say? Somehow Rasmus knew his whereabouts."

"And the chopping knife? Why did the murderer stick the knife into a scarecrow?" said Lena.

"If it was the murderer," said Julian.

"It does sound like Rasmus wasn't his only target," said Alice. "Or did someone try to complicate the investigation by throwing yet another knife into the mix? Maybe someone like Francis who wants to protect a friend?"

Both Lena and Julian began talking loudly at the same time. Julian defended his friend, and Lena charged ahead with Francis's nickname *Gut*. It took several minutes before they both settled down. The verbal scuffle ended with Julian admitting, "I don't know."

"It's been a long day," said Alice. "How about breakfast tomorrow? Maybe we can talk to Francis."

"Good idea," said Julian. "Alice, in my soul, I know Rasmus wasn't killed by Artie, Francis, Frosty, or me. But I agree, Frosty needs to open up, tell the story he keeps to himself. I'll also talk to Francis. You know his nickname has nothing to do with the war. Even as a kid, Francis was called *Gut* because he loved fishing. None of the rest of us were thrilled to clean a fish. Francis loved it. It wasn't any surprise to me that he retreated into fishing when he came home from war. While on duty, he was assigned to a bad spot near the Laos border. It's true that he and Frosty swapped stories, and Francis might be a little closer to Frosty than the rest of us, but if Francis wanted to kill someone, he would have shot him."

"Are you sure? Because he kinda scares me," said Lena. "Remember you told me about him wearing a knife before our wedding."

"It was Frosty's knife. He wore it . . .as a last-ditch effort . . . in case something bad happened. Believe me, he was relieved to surrender it to the police."

"Frosty has experience in Vietnam with both a gun and a knife," said Alice.

"Look, he was in demolitions. Yes, he went into tunnels. And yes, he shot the enemy and sometimes used a knife. He also used grenades. He's lucky to be alive. You ever see pictures of those tunnels. Guys like Frosty were recruited because of their small frame. Most of them never came back. I wouldn't have his memories for . . ."

Alice and Lena kept silent with their own memories of the Seventies.

"He couldn't exactly brag about his drug habit or the men he killed. If he made mistakes? Ah, does anyone care about a guy like Frosty? How long is he supposed to pay a price?"

Lena put her arms around Julian. "It will be okay, Julian. Frosty has the best orchestra of snoopers looking out for him even if he doesn't know it. So do you. We'll all get through this."

"I'll . . . talk to . . . the guys first thing tomorrow morning," said Julian. "Maybe they'll have details."

As Julian escorted Alice to the door, he managed to look grateful. "Thanks. I didn't want to share too much from these last few days."

"One last question?" asked Alice. "When you arrived on Thursday, did you happen to notice Rasmus?"

"There was too much going on. I'm not sure I'd recognize him now even with the picture Unzicker's officers have circulated. Why?"

"Rumors. Maybe verify with Artie exactly when Rasmus and Pepper checked in. I'm wondering if Pepper received her key on Thursday when they checked in or on Saturday when the staff moved her to a smaller room? If on Thursday, she had access to Rasmus the night of the murder."

"Okay, I'll ask Artie."

"Also, how did he spend Thursday while Pepper was on the property. Did they have lunch together? Dinner? Did they play miniature golf? Was Rasmus seen at the bar talking to another woman? To me it appears Rasmus allowed his murderer into the room or at least never had suspicions about the mystery killer. Tomorrow we talk."

"Yes, ma'am. And thanks."

Chapter 19

Alice awoke to Audrey's wet nose sniffing her ear. Her hand wiped the wetness away as she squirmed to a new position. Perhaps Audrey needed more room. But three soft *eh . . . eh . . . eh* from the dog's throat convinced her to turn on the light, crawl out of bed, and layer on sweats.

"You want to go out now?" A quick peek out the window proved morning was a long way off.

Audrey stood at the door and glanced over her shoulder at Alice.

"Okay." Alice rolled her shoulders to shrug off sleep and attached Audrey's harness.

The night carried a chill of dampness and the beauty of silence. Audrey found the right spot, and Alice yawned as she waited for her dog. Old-fashioned street lanterns dotted the property and strings of orange fairy lights marked edges of sidewalks. Alice guessed all were still lit to help allay fears of the darkness after the murder.

Audrey gave a tug forward. "What's this?" said Alice. "We never take middle-of-the-night walks. Well, almost never."

When her hound's tail wagged with interest, Alice knew they weren't alone. She stopped Audrey to scan what lay ahead. A cigarette burned in the darkest of shadows, shrouded by greenery near the miniature golf area. Trusting her dog's tail of excitement, Alice moved ahead slowly. Within ten feet a chill crossed the back of Alice's neck.

A man sat on the ground, his knees drawn close to his chest, forearms resting on his knees. Alice smelled the smoke as the cigarette glowed.

"I'm walking my dog," said Alice. "May I ask what you're doing out here so late?"

"Smoking," said Francis. "The owners are touchy about smoke being offensive to other guests."

"Aren't you supposed to be guarding Frosty?"

"He snores. Can't sleep with the noise. Artie said he'd take a shift and give me a break. There's a bench. Join me if you want."

In the murky shadow as she moved forward, Alice spotted the bench. She was curious about Francis and a little frightened. All notions of going back to sleep were gone.

"I like the night," said Francis. "Less complicated. In the daylight I close my eyes and hear noise. Out here, I can throw on a light jacket and listen to the music of night breezes. No thinking required."

"Mind if I ask you questions?" asked Alice.

"Mind if I don't answer?" He gave a grunt of a laugh and took a long draw on the cigarette. "Shoot."

"What happened the morning of the wedding? You and Julian were late for the service and seemed nervous. I can't imagine it was his wedding jitters."

Francis puffed on the cigarette, and Alice felt his answer was silence. But as he tapped the cigarette into the ground, he said, "We knew pretty early something had happened. Artie stopped us from going to breakfast. He brought us a cart of food and told us to hold tight. Told Frosty to be prepared."

"Artie brought you breakfast?"

"Yeah. Why is that strange?"

"This was what time?"

"I don't know . . . after eight?" Francis's shoulders shrugged at the importance of the time, until he said, "No. Now I remember. It was a quarter to nine."

Sure, shot through Alice's mind.

"I assume Artie had been alerted about the murder," said Alice.

"Yeah."

"Here's the thing," said Alice. "I'm thinking that before breakfast is rather early for housekeeping to enter a room for clean up."

"Never thought about that. Guess you're right." Francis lit another cigarette and sucked in the smoke, holding it, before expelling a long, slow cloud from his mouth.

"Artie told Frosty to be prepared. For what?" asked Alice.

"To run? To hide? I'm not sure. Artie took his time to report the murder, I'll give you that. We didn't get murder details until he came back."

"What did you do while you waited?"

"Ate fast. Dressed fast. Frosty packed what was essential to him in case he had to run."

Alice craned her neck to catch a glimpse of his face, but he wore the leafed bushes behind him like a cape. Only his long white hair caught bits of silver light.

"His knives were important to him?" asked Alice.

It wasn't until Francis lit yet another cigarette that she saw he was amused and nervous. "You want to join me?" He offered her the second lit cigarette.

"No, thank you."

"Yeah. Frosty's carving knives. Lots of luck ever touching those. We all get attached to treasures." Francis cupped a cigarette in the palm of each hand, darkening the shadow where he hid. "Artie came back and told us housekeeping found Rasmus dead. After that, Artie called the police. That was maybe after ten."

"Why didn't Artie call the police right away?"

"Jeez, the guy was clearly dead. Didn't matter when the police got there." Francis blew a smoke cloud up into the air. "Artie wanted to figure out a plan. He didn't want the resort—what's the word—*be-smirched*. That's it. He had his sister to consider."

"And how do you do that when you've discovered a body?" asked Alice. "Did he tamper with the crime scene?"

"No. He knows better," said Francis. "You touch something, you leave a piece of you behind. No. Artie's plan was to calm down house-keeping for one thing. Make sure no one started hysterical sharing of resort details. And to notify his hyper-sensitive sister."

"What the police saw was the way housekeeping left the room?" asked Alice.

"Yep. Artie might have decided to let a buddy know that the guy stalking him just had his lights turned off, and let that buddy take stock of the danger he was in."

"Why would Frosty be in danger? From whom?"

"Beats me," said Francis. "That's when I asked him for one of his two ankle bracelets."

"I'm confused." No way was Alice going to leave this discussion even though Audrey went belly down. Her breathing became deep with sleep.

"The ankle knife," said Francis. "It's military grade. Frosty's not too keen on guns. Too noisy. A knife doesn't tell other enemy that you're coming."

"By my count that's four types of knives the police know about: the murder weapon—very sharp, Frosty's kitchen blades for his meat-cutting work, the military knife with a chip in the blade, strapped into your ankle holster, and the scarecrow knife."

"Guess so," said Francis. "I strapped on one, but the police don't know Frosty has another. We weren't certain how things were going to go, but Julian said we should play normal and go ahead with the wedding . . . if the cops allowed it. Best thing I did? Put on my clerical collar."

Francis's hand adjusted his white collar.

"What is so special about the collar?"

"I have no idea. It seems the collar demands respect and trust. Who

MURDER COMES TO MADTREE

knew? People see the collar, and it doesn't matter that I got a tattoo of a snake, or that I wear heavy metal T-shirts, or that I was ordained on the Internet. I'm not taking this off until I'm back in northern Wisconsin. Maybe not even then. Can't hurt to bless the fish to bite."

"The plan was for Julian to get married and for Frosty to hide?" asked Alice.

"Frosty wanted to run right then, but Artie talked him down. Too many people were already outside because of the wedding, and the usual day-tripper families waited in lines for miniature golf and the swimming pool."

"When the first officer arrived, did he see you had a knife?"

"I'm not stupid. I surrendered it first thing. I didn't want to get shot. Anyway, we knew Frosty's knives weren't used in the murder. No harm letting forensics knock themselves out proving the knife was clean. Clearly not the murder weapon. Nothing about it made it suspicious, and the cop we talked to seemed to know that. Of course, we didn't tell them that Frosty kept his for protection. Julian begged that the wedding be allowed to continue. That's why we were late. The police here are pretty agreeable, but they still might tangle Frosty into the murder."

"If you surrendered the knife when you met the police before the wedding, what was the point of strapping it on in the first place?"

As a cigarette came to his lips, Alice saw he was grinning.

"In the time before Artie called 911, we hunkered down. We weren't sure where the enemy was or who he was. I was ready for a surprise. When the cop showed up, I wanted to show them I'm mellow and agreeable too. Show him none of us had the murder weapon. Hush!"

They both heard footsteps on the sidewalk coming toward them. A Limekiln police officer first appeared as a silhouette. He carried a large flashlight in one hand. The other hand rested on his holstered gun.

"What are you doing out here?" he asked. "Oh, Mrs. T., I didn't recognize you or Audrey. She looks like she's stuck under the bench."

Audrey's head came up and her tail thumped the sidewalk, but she stayed under the bench.

"She was asleep, but Officer, did you notice how she angled her way to get ear scratches from Francis Brandau? None of us seem to be able to sleep tonight. Francis, our officer friend is Officer Briar with the Limekiln Police Department. We worked together one Christmas when a man was murdered."

Briar nodded his head in Francis's direction. "Understood. I think it might be better if you all went into the inn, or at least, go sit on the front porch. All the lights are on, and no one will mistake you for someone you're not."

"Excuse me, Officer," said Francis. He stood up, moved two strides closer to the orange fairy lights along the path, and adjusted his clerical collar. "Is there a real danger tonight?"

Briar's shoulders relaxed. "The resort's never had a death, never mind a murder. Makes everyone jumpy. Better if you announce where you are by being in the light of the front porch."

"Got it," said Francis. "Thank you, Officer."

Alice, Audrey, and Francis followed the paved walk to the porch of the inn where rocking chairs lined up for comfort. The air was cool as Alice and Francis rocked. They kept silent until Officer Briar followed the path toward the outbuildings.

"Told ya about this collar. Didja see him loosen up when he saw it?"

"I never would have thought," said Alice.

"You know, you scare Julian," said Francis.

"How's that?"

"He's used to women like Lena."

"And that would be . . . what?" Alice felt her temper rise like it always did when someone criticized Lena.

"A girl. She's soft and scattered. Lena gives Julian a purpose. She's musical from what I hear and wild. She wants a man in her life, and Julian's willing to protect."

"She's my best friend," said Alice. "Lena has the biggest, kindest heart. I think they'll be happy. If nothing else, she'll pull him into adventures and new experiences. Last week they went to the Button Museum."

"How does the man contain the thrill?" His chuckle sent him into a coughing spasm.

"She's a whizz at research, absolutely amazing at finding dark corners."

Francis stretched his long legs forward. "She won't find anything on me. Like Frosty, I'm off the grid."

"Not likely," said Alice. Holding up her hand, she began to count. "One: your Internet ordination. Two: your fishing business. Three: you have an address and a cell phone. Four: I'm guessing you're good at your job, and that means somebody has probably written a review. Five: public records have birth, marriage, and any run-in with law enforcement. Six: if you appear in any picture with a client catching a big fish, and it's online, you're not as anonymous as you think. Lena taught me all of that."

Francis stopped rocking and pulled his legs back toward the chair. He appeared deep in thought. "Some guys had a harder time during the war than others."

Alice kept quiet and waited.

"Laughing helped. Young guys out of high school thought up gotcha jokes, like every day was April first, but soon the war reshaped what they thought was funny. One guy imagined bowling where C-4 was wrapped in concertina wire. I don't have to tell you what kind of strike he wanted."

Alice leaned toward Francis and touched his jacket sleeve.

"It wasn't me. It was some young guy. Funny how memories come back." His middle finger kicked away a cigarette into the bushes.

Alice thought their discussion of Frosty was over. She hated to leave him, but his eyes had gone to a place far away.

"Are you going in soon?"

Francis turned to her with a snarky grin. "You're more like me than Lena," said Francis as if revealing a truth.

"What?" Alice was stunned. "How's that again?"

"Julian tells me you butt into other people's lives. You're a control freak . . . like me."

"Too many things in this life move way beyond our control," said Alice. "No way do I think I can control them." Alice felt irritation seep into her cheeks and remembered Lena's statement that Francis liked to irritate people as a joke.

"Doesn't mean you and I can't smooth out the rough edges in other people when we see them," said Francis with a grin. "So, I strap on a knife to help protect a friend. You take in the most badass dog, known for being intrusive into personal space. We both understand baby steps for control. We're fixers."

"Fixers, huh? Tell me about your fishing excursions," said Alice, hoping to redirect the subject. His mentioning that he was a fixer sent a cold rush down her spine. Despite his explanations of helping Frosty, what else did he do?

"Artie likes to talk things out, but the best way to repair a guy is to give him the silence of fishing. And a beer or two."

Alice gathered Audrey's leash and scooted to the edge of the rocking chair. "Morning will be here soon, and my girl is bent on catching a nap where she can."

She stood to leave. His voice deep, Francis said, "I know you, Alice Tricklebank. You never flinch. When I threatened Audrey, you fired up. You threatened back, and you meant it. Julian told me about the risks you take." His tone put her on defense.

"Ah, well, very few risks," said Alice, hoping her tone was flip. "I'm a grandmother with a slobbery dog. That's all."

"Still, you don't rattle easily. You're quick and perceptive. You have ego, but you don't put it on the line unless something you love is threatened. I saw all that in the room when you first met Frosty."

"Okay. Have a good night." Alice rose and opened the front door of the inn for her and Audrey to enter. Warmth brushed her face and chased away the chill in her clothing.

Francis said, "Alice." She turned to face him as he lit a match and held it like a candle. "You don't need to be hanging on some guy's arm like Lena does. You fix other people's problems. The difficulty with that . . . I've seen too many men die as they carry out a mission. Careful, Alice, you're playing a dangerous game." For a moment Alice didn't move. "Bless you, my daughter," Francis chuckled his way into another coughing spasm.

"Have a good night," said Alice as she walked down the hallway a little shaken. *What was that about?*

She was tired. Tomorrow she'd sort out how their conversation should have gone. Now she wanted to escape into sleep. The only impediment? Why was housekeeping at Rasmus's room before breakfast?

Chapter 20

Julian knocked at Alice's door a little after dawn as she dressed for Audrey's morning walk.

"Frosty's run off. Francis was supposed to watch him to keep him safe, but last night when he came back to the room, Artie saw him pour three fingers of whiskey into a glass. He must have drunk too much and fell into a deep sleep. When I got there for my shift this morning, Francis said he overslept. Frosty hasn't been gone long. The coffee in his mug was still warm. Francis is checking the grounds of the resort to see if he just stepped outside. What are you doing?"

"Audrey and I are going after him." Alice laced up her hiking boots. "Artie watched him last night while Francis stepped outside to smoke. My guess is Francis found it hard to sleep without whiskey."

"How do you know that last night he didn't sleep through until morning?" asked Julian. His eyes narrowed.

"Just do."

"The other guys are right, Alice. You'll never find Frosty," said Julian.

"We'll see."

Alice wondered how long Francis had stayed on the porch and how long it took for coffee to cool. She reasoned that before dawn Frosty awakened, made coffee, and saw his chance to escape. Was Frosty's head start fifteen minutes?

Maybe, he left just at the half-light of dawn. If on foot he'd move slowly in dim light. That will give us a chance.

She checked her backpack for supplies. She knew Frosty would make this search as difficult as possible, not endangering Audrey, but her. He'd set a difficult course to target Alice's determination, to challenge her commitment as a pursuer. In her sixties, Alice still felt the drive of youth, but her ankles and knees sometimes proved tricky and after long, long walks with Audrey, her spine always burned. By contrast, Audrey eagerly accepted each new game of peekaboo as her personal mission.

Medical supplies? Check. Water and treats? Check. Protective clothing and eyewear for both of them? Check.

"Julian, he won't put something on the trail that might harm Audrey's lungs?"

Julian paled. "No. He's not a monster."

"Francis said Frosty had ways to stop a dog." Alice didn't make eye contact. She almost didn't want to hear.

"Francis doesn't know what he's talking about."

"Okay," said Alice. "You'd tell me if I needed to take precautions."

"I'm not saying he won't make this difficult. But no, not harmful and not life-threatening. He doesn't have time to construct a bear trap. This is farm country."

Alice's mind began listing sacks of poison and repellents found on many farms to control insects, vermin, and weeds. "Not every farm is organic," said Alice.

Julian's mouth opened and closed. "What will you do for a scent?" asked Julian. "I'm sure Frosty wiped every surface in the room with Francis."

"That's easy," said Alice. Grabbing her gear, she walked the hound to the room Francis and Frosty shared and steered Audrey to the draped window. Tapping her fingers near the spot where Frosty had held back drapes the day before to watch for his enemy—whoever that enemy was. Alice waited for her dog to do that clever thing of picking up a scent in a room filled with stale cigarette smoke.

Audrey took a nonchalant sniff and turned toward the door.

"Always amazes me," said Julian. "So simple. You wonder what she smells."

Alice had no time to respond. They were out the door and headed toward the back exit of the annex. Alice had expected Frosty to move through the apple trees in the orchard. This time of year, guests were drawn to the scarecrow maze, not the busy apple orchard with workers already in the trees. But maybe his memories of cabin children waiting for an early morning school bus set his path toward the cider building, through the apple storage area, and down a gravel utility road.

Like a mother who might worry about a child's bare feet, Alice felt uneasy about Audrey's paws on gravel, but the bloodhound loped ahead with her usual stride. Audrey's nose made her oblivious to the surroundings. Trailing that scent was all that mattered.

The first field of dry, weedy stalks whipped Alice's thighs. Despite the temperature lingering in the fifties, heat from the ground rose to Alice's face. She wished she hadn't layered on an additional sweatshirt.

It took a moment for Alice to recognize the smell and vocalizing of moving water. Frosty made the mistake of all those who tried to escape a bloodhound—thinking water washed away the human scent. Up ahead was a shallow stream of water with a pretty, three-foot waterfall.

"He doesn't know skin cells are oily and float. Or that you have webbed toes," whispered Alice, "and love water."

When they reached the stream that poets might describe as a burbling brook, Alice was ready to march across the water with Audrey, imagining that Frosty hoped the water would carry his scent downstream and take them south while he traveled east. Audrey, however, splashed in, and for the next several minutes both dog and handler slopped against the slow current and navigated the slippery stones beneath their feet.

"Okay, maybe putting leather boots on you would have been stupid in this water," said Alice.

Underneath forty-foot tall, overhanging willow trees, Audrey cut through the leaves and left the stream. Alice did battle with dangling, drooping branches that hooked her curly gray hair, stole her cap, and challenged her balance. Another field of weedy, spent flowers followed, but at least Frosty's scent emanated from a rocky, well-used prairie path. Alice adjusted the cap on her head to shade more of her face.

It crossed Alice's mind that Frosty's escape didn't take him to the highway. He wasn't planning to hitchhike. He didn't have an accomplice ready to drive him to a hideout. She wasn't sure he had a plan, other than wearing Alice down and eluding Audrey's nose.

Several minutes later, Audrey made a sharp right and left the path behind. Her loose skin and ears flapped, and she picked up the pace and followed the scent to an old, abandoned farmhouse with a wide porch. Most of the windows were broken or missing. Most of the roof shingles worn or gone, the unpainted boards dry and cracked. But among the stands of five-foot tall thistles, extra tall white phlox competed for space. Alice pictured a thin mother, probably like her own aunt, tending a kitchen garden. Maybe she wore a home-sewn flowery apron to gather beans or chicken eggs. Maybe she wiped away a child's tears with the same apron. Like so many farm women, she probably shared peaches from her cellar storage of canned fruits and vegetables with neighbors.

The hound pivoted around the house and walked past it to a broken wooden fence. No reason for Alice to search. The previous owners of the home and Frosty abandoned the idea of taking refuge here. Ahead was an out-of-control patch of silver maples.

Pretty trees alone, or at least groomed, but untended—what a nightmare, thought Alice.

Thousands of silver maple saplings of various heights jammed together in a thicket longer than a football field and as dense as a wall. Several dozen old, towering silver maples, still holding their leaves, stood like the bulwark of a fortress, shoulder to shoulder, sardined, entangled, daunting. Surely, nothing as big as a man—or woman—could get through it. But a squirmy little guy or a determined bloodhound, maybe. If she tried to play it safe and cut around the trees, Audrey might not be able to pick up the trail again for a long time, and she'd lose Frosty.

Audrey beelined for the trees.

"Oh sure," whispered Alice. "You'll have a tough time, but you'll do it. Frosty probably can wiggle though. But me, the big, awkward girl? Okay, I'm ready for scratches and gashes."

Alice stopped and pulled out protective eyewear for her dog and herself.

"You're not going to like this. Call me a grandma. I don't want your eyes scratched. And I promise not to embarrass you by telling Jim or your friends that I made you do this."

Audrey thrashed away from Alice's concerned fingers, but Alice's intentions were stronger. The dog eyewear slipped into place, and Audrey pushed through the trees, following Frosty's scent to a spot big enough for an adult male raccoon to crawl through.

"We're not going through there, are we? How do you expect me to fit?"

The bloodhound ignored Alice and went belly down and crawled among the thin weeds, saplings, and mature trees. Alice questioned how badly she wanted Frosty, but her pride said yes. Her knees complained as she first crouched and then slithered on her stomach, grateful for her boots digging into the earth to propel her forward as if she climbed a horizontal ladder. A new, bright bother gave her a nudge. Her sock felt twisted and burned the arch of her foot.

"Sore muscles tomorrow for sure, and now a blister."

Audrey remained committed and ignored the smell of dirt and putrid dead animals. Alice was the one who flinched. Finally, Alice noted the dim light give way to ribbons of sunlight. With a groan, the hound stood, and Alice gave a sigh of relief. They weren't out of the trees, but at least they could stand up.

She pushed young branches forward out of her way; they managed to slap back. She tucked in her chin and felt dust collect on her lips. Twigs pulled her hair. She could barely see what was beyond, other than they moved toward sunlight.

When they finally emerged from the thicket, there was another field. This time Audrey managed to pick up more burrs on her legs and belly. Her right shoulder was already coated with drying mud.

Alice was thirsty and hot despite the cool breeze. Audrey was panting. Alice wondered if she should stop for water or take on the challenge of the corn field up ahead. Alice touched the dog's tail, a signal that usually made Audrey stop, but Audrey remained committed. She wouldn't stop.

Years ago, farmers planted their corn arrow straight with walking space between the rows. This more modern field, however, didn't allow for anyone walking leisurely through rows. Alice suspected the density of the thickly packed rows prevented people from stealing a more desirable crop of sweet corn several yards away. Farmers were careful like that. Hide a crop of flavorful corn destined for the farmer's market behind the less desirable field corn, used for bio-fuel or cattle feed. At ten feet tall, the drying crop of field corn looked mighty, but if she guessed correctly, up ahead would be an opening where the sweet corn had already been harvested. Both she and Audrey would stop to drink water in the open space.

The dried cornstalks closed in around Alice. She tilted her shoulders and shimmied sideways to follow her dog through the tightly packed rows. Her first gash—quite like a papercut—drew a droplet of blood on the back of her hand and came from the edge of a dried corn leaf. Another ripped at her cheek. Unscathed, Audrey *doggedly* shoved forward.

When Alice heard voices, her stomach cramped. Maybe she was wrong about Frosty not meeting up with rescue. Two voices cut through the rattling of dried cornstalks. One man sounded angry.

Too late now, thought Alice. *They'll have heard us rustling through the corn.*

But as Alice and her hound reached the opening in the field corn, it was to a distinctive crop of marijuana, at least eight feet tall. Two men with rifles stood over Frosty who sat on the ground. He'd also had a rough time with the path he followed: dirty, muddy, scratched, disheveled. In addition, a fresh bright red bruise sat on his cheekbone. One that looked suspiciously like the result of a hard punch to the face. A holstered knife lay ten feet behind the two men as did a leather wrap with other knives and a small backpack. Alice guessed the two men knew to search an uncooperative Frosty.

One man turned and pointed his rifle at Alice. "You helping this guy? We know somebody's been creeping around. That a sniffer dog?"

He looked angry, and Alice felt her mind begin to stack up defenses. What could two people in their sixties do to defend themselves from much younger growers of marijuana who were built like gladiators and held rifles?

Audrey was clueless to the danger. Her tail wagged with great joy, and she wanted to greet Frosty with her find. Alice patted her hound's side, proclaimed her a good dog, and produced a small treat from her pocket.

With his rifle still raised, the second man guarding Frosty turned to look in Alice's direction. "Oh, man. Mrs. T.? I haven't seen you since high school. Is this your new doggo?"

Chapter 21

Alice hadn't seen Josh since he was a skinny kid in high school, so she hadn't recognized his increased height or broadened shoulders, but the glimmer in his eyes was familiar, and his peculiarity of adding *oh* to the end of some words, a distinct identifier.

"Josh?" said the other man. He pronounced the name with caution.

"It's me," said Josh looking directly at Alice. He gestured with his gun by touching his chest with the long barrel of his rifle. "Is this crazy-o what? What are you doing here?"

"We're playing a variation of ding dong ditch." Alice wrinkled her nose and pointed to her opponent on the ground. Josh's face tightened as he also looked at Frosty.

"Cops around here are sensitive to a guy ringing a doorbell and running away," said Josh. "Don't make it tough for the rest of us trying to stay under their radar."

"No, no," said Alice. "Frosty said he could put down a trail that Audrey couldn't follow. I said nothing stopped Audrey once she caught a scent. I know we look a dirty mess. He gave Audrey a real run. And me too. All three of us need water. Isn't that right?" She shot a look at Frosty, daring him to contradict her.

"Yeah. Yeah. The silver maples were a battle to get through. I thought they'd stop you for sure. You got Bengay in that bag of yours?"

Alice grinned. "Sorry. A little too strong for Audrey's nose."

"How'd the dog follow me through water?" asked Frosty with a glare.

"I don't know the doggo," said a smiling Josh. "But I coulda told ya nothing stops Mrs. T."

"I see you have a nice healthy business," said Alice. Her arm swept in the direction of the marijuana.

"We do. This is the last for this season. We'll begin cutting the field corn soon . . . so we'll lose our camouflage. Man, this land is made for marijuana. Tuck it behind a wall of field corn, anyone who flies overhead can't tell the difference between crops. They only see green. From the air, one green crop looks pretty much like another unless you're in a chopper and specifically looking for our crop. Harvest naturally comes before the field corn is cut. You know someday all of this is going to be legal. Washington and Colorado are raking in cash."

"Josh? What are you thinking?" said the other man, shaking his head. "He was armed." All three looked at the ankle holster on the ground and the leather pouch of kitchen knives.

"Relax, John-o. Mrs. T. isn't one to talk. They aren't here to steal either. Are you?"

"Nah. We stumbled on you, and we're sorry," said Frosty. He gave a side-eye to Alice.

"Josh?" repeated the other man with more force. "They know!"

"Whatdaya think? We aren't going to kill them, and believe me, we're not scaring her. Hey, Mrs. T., will ya promise not to tell about our crop? In a couple years, it's all legal anyway. I'll take you to dinner after my first million." Josh looked super pleased with himself.

"What about him?" asked John. "What says he doesn't report us to the police?"

"He has his own troubles," offered Alice in a hushed voice. "He won't tell. For him, this was a kind of practice, if you know what I mean. Besides if he says anything, I'll have to tell the police what I know about him."

"Way to go Mrs. T. See I told ya. She's okay." He held the rifle with one hand and pointed the barrel at the ground.

"Hey kid, I'm not exactly cozy with the cops, right now. And I'd like to keep it that way." Frosty rolled to his side, protecting his knee, and he stood with difficulty and dusted his hands. "Look. She and I had a bet. She won. Okay? She wanted to prove to me a dog could beat an old grunt like me." Frosty nodded with respect in Alice's direction. "I got it."

"You're running?" asked John.

"I might need to, yes."

"Why?"

"Drank too much hard cider at the apple orchard," lied Frosty. "Overstepped. Slugged Artie Levitsky. You know him?"

"Sure do."

"Artie's not gonna squeal to the cops," said Josh. "He has his own secrets. You got problems with Artie? Come back and talk to me." Josh's eyes twinkled. "Can we give you a lift? You both look ragged. But Doggo's bright-eyed."

Audrey wagged her tail.

"Josh? This is insane. Tell me you're not thinking of giving his knives back," said his partner.

Josh's eyes measured Frosty and then looked at Alice. "I think John-o's right. We'll keep the knives."

Fury entered Frosty's expression. "You're not keeping my knives."

"Yeah, we are. Until Mrs. T. comes to my house to pick them up. You okay with that?" He nodded at Alice.

"Sounds good," said Alice. "As long as you don't touch the knives and leave fingerprints. The police might want to check those if they get their hands on them."

"No prints, huh? You got it."

She raised an eyebrow that sent a message to Frosty, *Don't even!*

John's chin fell with defeat as he shook his head. "I got a bad feeling."

"Cool it, man." Josh's voice took on more threat. "Mrs. T. and me are friends. She keeps her word."Then in a softer voice and looking at Alice, he said, "She coulda busted me at prom when Samantha and I split a jar of olives and a bottle of gin.Talk about sick. She got us home, no one the wiser, and I still got to graduate." Josh raised his rifle in a kind of respectful salute.

"Your grandmother would have killed me if I hadn't," said Alice, smiling back at Josh. "Can you drop us off about a mile from Madtree's orchard at the rest area along the interstate? I don't want Frosty taking a ribbing from his friends about losing to Audrey."

"Will do," said Josh. He turned to Frosty with a face drained of empathy. "You called yourself a grunt? Well us, too. Remember 2004—Fallujah? John-o and I enlisted after high school. You old guys like to tell how tough things used to be. Fallujah left us with memories too. John-o and I have no problem killing an enemy. Understand, you have a problem with her, we can make you disappear. Are we clear?"

Frosty nodded.

"I will gratefully pick up the knives in a few days," said Alice. "How about I bring cinnamon apple donuts?"

Josh's face recalled his classic grin filled with merriment. "See, I told you she's reasonable." Josh patted Audrey's side. "Good job doggo."

Chapter 22

"You can take off if you want," said Alice to Frosty as she encouraged Audrey to climb up on top of the picnic table set back from the comfort stop and the busy interstate. "But if you do, my first call will go to Lieutenant Unzicker. Rather than a confrontation, why don't you sit and talk to me? I've got water, and the vending machines in the shelter have sodas and treats."

Audrey's head came up with expectation. *Treats?*

"I feel naked without my knives. Gimme a water," said Frosty as he grabbed a bottle and joined Audrey on the tabletop. He placed his feet on the seat of the picnic bench. Alice opened a water and poured it into Audrey's travel bowl. Once the hound had lapped the bowl dry and stretched out on top of the wooden table, her head squirmed under Alice's arm, and her wet mouth rested on Alice's lap. Alice opened her own bottle of water, and Audrey's tail drummed Frosty's back.

"You carried all this stuff on our trek through those fields?"

Alice sighed. "I do feel like a mule at times, but yes, I travel ready for picnics or emergencies like you do with your pack." She took a gulp and some of the water spilled down her chin. She quickly wiped it away with the back of her hand. "I think we should talk because frankly, I'm tired."

"I got nothing to say."

"Okay, I'll talk instead. I imagine you're thinking of running which is a very bad idea." She looked at Frosty who leaned forward with one forearm on his knee, his hand cradling the water bottle. "So, after my call to the lieutenant," continued Alice, "my next call goes to James Kennedy. Do you know him?"

"Nope."

"He has two hounds ready to search at the drop of a hat. He's been searching with dogs ever since Vietnam. He knows his stuff. Audrey and I train with him. And because of his background, Jim knows seven dog-handlers—some in their thirties—who live in the county and work with tracking hounds. Young, physically fit people who love a good hunt. Know what I mean? Not tired and old like me . . . or you."

Frosty's cheeks puffed before he blew air through his lips, derision obvious.

"It really doesn't matter to me if you want to run through more fields. There are other hounds and fresh handlers ready to follow." She stopped to take another drink of water. "And you do have other possibilities of hiding. Caves, for example. Maps at the library have all the nooks and crannies marked. Kids have been exploring them for years. Six months ago, Jimmy's hounds went in and found a runaway kid. Do you like caves?"

"Not particularly."

"You probably wouldn't like our old coal mine shaft. Jim and I aren't familiar with the coal veins, but an old miner still lives in Limekiln. Says he knows the mine like the back of his hand. You see, he went down the pit at sixteen. Experienced miners put him through his paces. Taught him not to be afraid of the dark when the lights go off. He's eighty-five now, but super fit. Up until ten years ago he gave tours until the shaft elevator became dangerous. Probably he will love to show off his talent. I hear space in a coal mine gets pretty tight."

"I know about underground. I'm not particularly interested in going back down a hole in the ground."

"That's right. Julian said you were a tunnel rat."

"Demolitions. If a patrol spotted a suspicious hole in the ground, they called us to explore. We cleaned up what we had to and defused explosives."

"You went down not knowing how many enemy soldiers hid beneath the ground and did hand-to-hand fighting in the dim light. A lot of you didn't get home."

"Sure didn't."

"You are brave."

"If brave means stupid, then yeah."

Alice couldn't read his facial expression. He didn't appear annoyed, defeated, or shamed, but Alice felt his sadness. Something lay deep. She waited a few minutes before she said, "I think your initial choice is to run through fields. Of course, overland means the police can also call in an air corps of drones. Did you see the wedding photographer?"

"No."

"Nice girl. She practices with a hoard of young people who also have drones. Again, a group of young people who love a good hunt. In the short term, you could put all these threats to rest. All you have to do is kill me. That might get you at least two hours of freedom."

Frosty scowled at Alice. "I didn't kill Rasmus. No reason to kill you."

"Whew! Good to know, because this rest stop gets lots of traffic. If a traveler notices a body of a woman and her dog, he's sure to call it in. Audrey and I are too big to hide easily. And my former student back there will keep his mouth shut to protect his crop, but he might speak up if we go missing. He was a fiercely loyal kid. Used to be skinny. Did you notice how muscular Josh became? I guess training for Fallujah probably did that. He looks like he's continued weight training or at least martial arts. I don't know John."

"The guy who slugged me?"

"He didn't go to Limekiln High when I taught there. Don't know him at all."

"Can I trust your boy—Josh—to give back my pack?"

"You can. I promise to pick it up in a week."

"Okay, I get it. But I'm not going to hand myself over to the police to be arrested."

"Why do you think you'll be arrested?" Frosty frowned and remained silent. "Want to hear my plan?" Alice lowered her voice as if they were conspiring.

"What?"

"Drive back to the resort with a lawyer. Turn yourself over to Lieutenant Unzicker for questioning. He's also one of my former students. You need to tell the police what you know about Rasmus."

"Of course, that cop's a former student. Julian told me you're a pain-in-the-ass."

"I know," said Alice with a wide grin. "Proud to be one."

Frosty closed his eyes.

"Explain to the lieutenant where you've been," continued Alice. "Tell him you knew Rasmus was coming. He wasn't a guy you wanted to meet, so you went away to think. Staff told you he got himself killed. You've no idea by whom."

"I don't know who knifed him."

"There. See. You got the idea. But fibbing to police—iffy results. Lying—downright dangerous."

"I don't know a lawyer."

"I do." Alice's voice sounded chipper.

"Let me guess—another former student?"

"As a matter of fact, yes. But she will cost you the whole story. Who is Rasmus to you?"

"A guy." Frosty's upper lip curled.

"No kidding? A guy? Then you may as well start running because I need to call Lieutenant Unzicker."

"Okay, okay. I knew Rasmus in 'Nam. He moved . . . supplies . . . plus drugs."

"Which you bought?"

Frosty nodded with a head wobble of uncertainty. Alice focused on her word *bought* as the precise word of contention.

"Rasmus wasn't in demolitions? You just knew him from being at the same base camp?"

"Yeah. More or less."

"Maybe you *traded* items you *found* for drugs?"

He twisted to glare at her, and his rigid jaw stopped a denial.

"I know soldiers sometimes removed items from enemy dead," said Alice. "Trophies. I'm of your generation. I had uncles in WWII. Classmates in Vietnam. Julian was a medic—not sure if he collected anything, but some soldiers do. I'm guessing because of your assignment during the war, you had access to personal items that some soldiers might see as souvenirs. Items that were easy for you to pick up. Maybe from a tunnel." Seeing Frosty's jaw still tight, Alice added, "One of my uncles happened upon a German handgun while cleaning up after a World War II battle. He said one guy in his unit liked to collect family pictures the enemy carried, but my uncle wasn't the sentimental type. He went for a gun."

"What if I did *find* a thing or two?"

"And traded for drugs."

His silence confirmed her thoughts. *So what, indeed. How does swapping loot for drugs contribute to a murder nearly forty years later?* She was fishing for a clue to his agony.

"And when Rasmus came back to the States? What happened then?" asked Alice.

"He continued selling drugs. I heard he did jail time. When he got out, he got in trouble again and went back to prison." Frosty paused before he added, "I was still over there when he first wrote to me about his troubles. Another note came later when I returned to the States. But that was it until the two notes this year."

"He hasn't been in contact with you all these years?"

"No. I moved around a lot. Lost direct contact."

Frosty explained how the letters stopped after the first two. Rasmus entered his first prison sentence, but other knowledge came through rumors he heard from former soldiers. Rasmus didn't resume his contact with Frosty until his latest release drew near.

"I got a letter with curly handwriting. A woman's hand, you know. It was kinda like the way my sister writes. So, I opened it. It was signed *Rasmus* but I swear it was written by a woman. It said he had to be careful with what he wrote while in prison. The first note arrived over a month ago. Surprised the hell outta me because I didn't know he knew where I was. He said he wanted to talk. Somebody was stalking him, threatening his life . . . and mine. The second note arrived over a week ago, written by him. I already knew he was out because Artie told me about Rasmus's online reservation. He was coming in with a lady friend. Can you believe that?"

"How do you think Rasmus found you here if you haven't been in touch?"

"I don't know."

"Did you tell anyone about the last two notes?"

"Artie. Like I said, I asked him to watch reservations. I called Julian because in group I shared what a cold-blooded snake Rasmus was. Julian called Francis." He took a long drink of water, draining the bottle. "What I can't figure is how he can afford this place when he's just out of the joint. What scam raised enough cash?"

"Maybe scamming money got him killed?" Even as she said it, Alice knew it couldn't be true. Why then was Frosty implicated by a kitchen butcher knife stuck in a scarecrow?

Alice let the questions circle in her mind while she reached for antiseptic from her backpack. She applied the spray to her scratches. Audrey raised her head with a groan and jumped off the tabletop.

Her nose wrinkled as she watched Alice. No way did the hound like the smell of antiseptic.

"You want some?" offered Alice to Frosty.

"Nah." He glowered as he looked at her. "You got a pretty good scratch on your face. Next to that scar."

Alice touched her cheek and remembered the burn of a bullet that slid over the top of her skin last Christmas.

"It's a reminder to be careful." She applied more wet antiseptic to the cut, then put the spray away.

"You got crazy eyes. Too round and gray. Anyone ever tell you they're scary, like a hawk's eyes?"

Alice had heard it many times, but she said, "No. No one ever did. How about we get back to the story: You knew when to disappear because Artie told you the date Rasmus would arrive."

"Yeah."

"And Artie, Francis, and Julian also knew Rasmus was your drug source back in Vietnam?" Alice waited for a response, but Frosty stared forward toward the highway. "Okay, you called Julian after the first note from Rasmus." The muscles in his face hardened. "Because that's about the time Julian took charge and scheduled the wedding at the resort. He wanted to be here to help. Let's see, you knew over a month ago that Rasmus booked a room at the resort, but other than your three friends, you never let anyone else in on the secret. Not family, not co-workers."

"I guess. But you're wrong on him booking a room. He was in prison. That lady friend had to make the reservation for him."

"Her name is Pepper. Does that ring a bell?" Frosty shook his head. "You think she wrote the notes? You said the handwriting was curvy like your sister's."

"Maybe."

"But you didn't take off and leave the area—which I find strange." Frosty shook his head again, and Alice took an exaggerated breath. "Something's not right in your story."

"I didn't kill Rasmus." His voice revealed frustration.

"See, to my way of thinking, who cares about a guy who used to sell you drugs forty-some years ago? You don't want to meet him, you don't. But you did meet with Rasmus on Monday. He shook his finger in your face and called you Kill-again. You tell anyone about that?"

His face had paled. "How'd you hear that?"

Alice shrugged. "I hear things. Maybe Rasmus meant it as a joke, a play on your last name, but the term makes it sound like you and he once killed someone, and his visit meant the two of you were going to kill again."

"I never killed nobody I wasn't supposed to."

"Did Rasmus?"

"Look, some guys used drugs to take the edge off or to stay alert." His eyes shifted to an unfocused place. "The heat over there cooked a guy's thinking. And then there were the officers. They sent us out, not always knowing what-the-hell they were doing. They got out of West Point and spent two minutes in 'Nam ready to tell us how things were gonna go." He shook his head as his forehead wrinkled.

Alice felt the tickle of truth.

"Funny you should mention officers. My brother went to school with a guy who served in Vietnam. He told us this story of playing a joke on the officers in their quarters. Regular soldiers used to wait for night and shoot randomly at the officers' buildings. He said it kept them on their toes. Can you believe that?"

"It's called *fragging*," said Frosty without making eye contact. "The slang comes from fragmentation weapons. It was more serious than a joke. Shooting at a building was a first warning. If they didn't take the hint, the next patrol might be dangerous. Maybe a stray bullet. Maybe a fragmentation grenade at their feet."

"I thought it sounded serious," said Alice. She lowered her volume. "Did Rasmus kill someone he shouldn't have?"

Frosty's whole body slumped. His one hand gripped his knee, and a long pause followed. Audrey climbed back onto the tabletop and curled into Frosty, whose hands found her soft ears. He took a deep breath. "A lieutenant, just out of West Point. Hardly had any charm school training."

"Charm school?"

Frosty took a deep breath as if he found Alice's lack of vocabulary aggravating. "It's slang for having no practical knowledge of survival. The jerk wanted to bring order to the war zone. Thought we needed clean-cut fun." Frosty shook his head.

"Rasmus couldn't allow that—could he? He had to defend the chaos of war. He wanted to keep soldiers on edge to keep his black market going." Frosty looked away, toward the highway. "You saw Rasmus kill a lieutenant?"

"Yeah."

"Did you report him?"

"No."

"Why?"

"I was too young at the time. Didn't know any better. Maybe I was bored or homesick. Head in a fog. Maybe I was always in a hole and tired of killing—tired of men I knew getting blown apart. What possible difference could it make if one more lieutenant died? They seemed to die every day. With my mission—demolition—it wasn't a good idea to get too invested, too close to anybody."

"It hurt less when they go," said Alice. "Do you think Rasmus looked for you because you were a witness?"

"Maybe. I don't know." Frosty looked miserable.

Alice related her conversation with Laura Leigh. The storyteller liked Frosty because he reminded her of her father. His playful nature with children pointed to his respect for kids as he joined in with storytelling and face-painting.

"She said you encouraged them to call you Frosty."

"Sounds different when they say it. More friendly."

"I imagine they're thinking of the snowman."

"Again, maybe a different snowman than what I was," said Frosty.

"It doesn't matter to you if the children are guests or children of the pickers, does it?"

"Nah. The best thing about kids? Their innocence and honesty," said Frosty.

"I heard one of the kids called you poop-face."

Frosty attempted a laugh at the memory. "Poop-face. I guess to him I look pretty old."

"Kids are why I stuck with teaching for a lot of years," said Alice. "How'd you meet Julian and Francis?"

"We told you in our room. In group. None of us wanted to make the trip to the V.A. You know attitudes were different then. Besides, we didn't feel broken, just angry. We looked at the V.A. as a place for physical injuries. We thought anyone there was a clueless . . . a book-reader, a know-nothing who never experienced madness or what it's like to come back in the real world? A few years after the war, once I was sober, the ghosts came back. It helped to be with other guys. That's when I told them about Rasmus."

"But not the whole story."

"What do you mean . . . not the whole story?"

Alice knew from her teaching days that adults, like children with a mean truth, rarely reveal complete details on the first go-round. There was the matter of the knife left in the scarecrow maze. If the killer murdered Rasmus, why was he still around? And why did Frosty run? To Alice the link was obvious.

"I don't understand why Rasmus came to see you," said Alice.

"I didn't kill Rasmus! I don't know how to make that clearer." He pushed away from the dog and stood up.

"Angelo," said Alice using his given name for the first time. Even to Alice, her voice sounded motherly. "You're way too jumpy to explain yourself to the police, lawyer by your side or not. Unzicker will know you're holding something back, and that alone will cause him to focus on you as the murderer. I know you didn't kill Rasmus. First, you're too short. Unzicker said the blade was sharp and the cut just enough to create a concentrated blood pool. There was one desk chair and that had only speckles of blood. No furniture turned over, therefore, no fight. Whoever killed him was of similar height. If it were you, my guess is that you'd have had to make him sit. There'd be lots more blood. Of course, you could have asked him to get on his knees, but I can't wrap my head around a heavy-set, old guy kneeling to allow *you* to kill him, particularly since he spent most of his life in prison. Unzicker said he wasn't the iron-pumping sort. You see what I'm saying? You're way too short—Rasmus too much girth, probably with bad knees. Still, the police will look for details to rule you out. Any of your lies will delay the process. The real killer could slip away. Now let's go over your story again after I call my lawyer."

"I don't need a lawyer."

"Yes, you do. Gilly'll introduce you to Lieutenant Unzicker." Alice placed a call to her friend and lawyer Gilly Chapel. "I have a sticky situation," she said and briefed her on the problem. Gilly, who loved a juicy, complicated case, said she'd clear her schedule.

"While we wait," said Alice, "tell me about Artie the morning the body was discovered. I know he brought breakfast into the room. Awful early for housekeeping to go in to clean a room."

"The housekeeper didn't go to clean the room. Artie said a guy called for clean towels. She went in to deliver a stack, found the body, and reported it to Artie."

"We know Rasmus didn't make that call because he had been dead for a few hours. It wasn't you because Francis and Julian spent the night guarding you."

"They did."

Alice believed him. "Why would the killer make a phone call for someone to enter the room and discover the body?"

"No idea," said Frosty.

"My guess," said Alice, "to flush you out. One down. Very dramatic, to be sure. And one to go."

Frosty hung his head. "Was the knife in the scarecrow also a message to me?"

"Someone's ratcheting up the heat—wants you to do something stupid like running."

Frosty stared at the interstate as if it were too far away.

"While we wait for Gilly to pick you up, explain Rasmus and Vietnam. If it's your only link to him, tell me the name of the lieutenant that Rasmus murdered."

Chapter 23

Shortly after Gilly took her new client into safe hands, Julian picked up Alice and Audrey at the rest area. He and Alice settled in the front seat of his car with a squirmy Audrey in the back seat, but her big head draped between them. A cord of slobber accented Julian's upper sleeve. His face tilted to the left, apparently trying to avoid Audrey's decoration.

"She likes the front seat," said Alice.

"In my car, not happening. Too much drool on the windows," said Julian. "You couldn't find Frosty?"

"Audrey found him."

"Did he get away? Where is he?"

"I'll tell if you tell about your group of Vietnam veterans who went to breakfast. But I want us to talk in front of Lena" said Alice. "I have research for her to do."

"Deal."

As Alice turned in her seat to check on Audrey, she felt a twinge in one knee and a swelling thickness in the other.

"I'm in trouble," said Alice.

"How so?" asked Julian.

"Crawling on the ground with Audrey played havoc with my body. I'm really going to feel it tomorrow."

"But you're always in shape from walking Audrey."

"Well . . ." Alice straightened forward and felt a sharp pain run through muscles next to her spine. "Maybe being a certain age is catching up to me."

Julian grunted but chose not to speak. They drove in silence until Alice asked, "Tell me again how Angelo Killian got the nickname *Frosty*."

"Lots of guys had nicknames for everything. They might sound innocent but weren't," said Julian. "A grenade launcher became *Thumper*. 'Get Thumper,' they'd say. Innocent sounding, right? Bunny rabbit testing the ice to see if it's safe. Nah. Firing off launchers isn't a sound a guy can forget." Julian repeatedly hit the dashboard hard and fast with his hand. *Bam, bam, bam!* "Maybe the men around him should have called Angelo *Thumper*. I understand he was fast and lethal. The guy was cool about death. Some said *frosty*."

"So the name *Frosty* had nothing to do with drugs?"

"I don't know. Maybe. When we first met, he was detached. Men I knew over there dabbled with pot, but no one I knew got hooked. When they left for home, all the nonsense was put behind them. A few guys tried harder stuff. Frosty mentioned he had to get straight when he came home. We met him after that." Julian's voice softened. "He . . . told us he witnessed a murder while there. Not war-dead stuff, but a murder. With all he saw and did, that murder is the thing that eats at him."

"Maybe he should tell about it now?"

"Alice, what good would it do?"

"Ever think maybe Rasmus came face to face with revenge? Or that the killer's second target is Frosty?"

"Damn," said Julian. "I hope not."

Chapter 24

"What!" said Lena.

"Magpie, it's me. Let me in," said Julian.

"Where were you?" Lena sounded peeved as she threw back the security latch.

"I went to give Alice a ride back to the inn."

The door opened. "Unzicker was here looking for you. He thinks I'm in on the obstruction. He said we both could face jail time."

Alice heard Lena's anger as she stomped away from the door. "If I miss my honeymoon because you . . . you . . ."

"Let me talk to Lena alone," said Julian to Alice before going into the honeymoon suite. "I might have some explaining to do." He threw the security latch across the door frame to prevent the door from fully closing.

"Make it fast," whispered Alice. "I've got a feeling Unzicker may show up annoyed."

Alice's ear lined up with the opening, and she pushed the door enough to peep through the crack. Julian faced Lena, holding both of her shoulders. He turned to Alice before finishing his serious conversation. Lena stayed silent. Finally, he wrapped Lena in his arms. When she broke free, Lena rolled up a thin resort newspaper of daily events and whacked Julian on the upper arm. *Whack. Whackwhack*!

"I knew you had an ulterior motive," said Lena, "but I never actually believed you'd do something so stupid as work against the police. You've been *hiding* a friend from the police when a guy has been murdered? Unzicker comes in here and thinks because I'm your wife, I must know what you're doing. How stupid does that make me look?"

Alice entered the room with a waggy-tailed Audrey.

"It wasn't like that." Julian shook his head. "I guess the topic never came up."

Whack.Whack. "Oh, like we've all been oblivious to a murder at the resort."

"Let's close the door and talk this through," said Alice. "I have questions. Julian might have answers, and Lena needs to know what's going on so she can do research."

Mentioning research seemed to calm the newly married couple. Both sat—not together on the couch, but in opposite slouchy, upholstered chairs.

For the next ten minutes, Julian apologized, and Lena stopped threatening him with the rolled newspaper. She explained how cute it was that Julian took charge of the wedding arrangements, but as the wedding day drew near, Lena saw something was off. A man like Julian ignoring her wasn't like anything she had experienced.

"You made me feel alone." Lena's eyes became weepy. "And old."

Alice shoved the conversation toward her talk with Frosty: his drug arrangement with Rasmus and witnessing a murder. She reminded her friends of Unzicker's access to documents of Rasmus's past: juvenile record, black market in the military, dishonorable discharge, jail, more drugs, manslaughter, more jail time.

"Julian, do you know the name of the man Rasmus killed in Vietnam? Because when I asked, Frosty went silent."

"Honestly, he never told us the guy's name," said Julian. "He just admitted he saw the shooting in camp. It wasn't an accident. Rasmus unloaded his rifle into the guy. People who weren't in the war don't know what combat was like. Hell, some guys there didn't know the full experience. You come back to the real world, and neighbors think you're either a killer or a hero. Either way most of them think you're nuts. Yes, bad things happened. But most guys learned to deal. Not everyone turned to drugs. We came home, got jobs, did the best we could with family. I don't talk about the war because people don't get it. What was Frosty supposed to do? Say, 'Oh, I saw someone get shot, but I was hopped up on drugs'?"

"But why refuse to identify the victim now?" asked Lena.

"Is it possible, Frosty did more than witness a murder?" asked Alice.

Julian's face flushed as if he were ready to defend the honor of a fellow soldier. "I don't know. You think he was part of it?"

"It could explain why the killer is still around. Why he stabs a knife into a scarecrow—another warning to Frosty, perhaps?"

Alice gave Audrey a little push in Julian's direction. The bloodhound hopped up to share Julian's chair and pirouetted trying to find a place for her paws before plopping into place on Julian's lap. Luckily for her, Julian slid over to one side although he didn't look pleased. The hound's butt wedged between the comfy arm of the chair and Julian's thigh. His arm instinctively wrapped around the dog's back and scratched her opposite shoulder. Slowly, Audrey's body grew saggy until her upper half draped across Julian's thighs, her bones seemingly disappearing in contentment. His fingers continued to scratch.

"Look, I don't know everything about Frosty," said Julian, "We met in group, maybe five years after the war."

Lena's face softened. "And I don't know anything about your war experiences."

"The war took down my best friend, Riley," said Julian softly. "Over there I did my job. Chose not to get too close to any of the men in the field. Came home after my time. That's all anyone needs to know."

Lena moved forward to the edge of her chair. "I know you still react to the sound of helicopters and look to the sky as if someone called for medevac."

Julian rubbed his calloused hands together and then rubbed them up and down his tattooed arms. Audrey twisted her neck to question the break in Julian's back scratching. Alice saw after all these years, Julian still found sharing hard.

"After he came home, Francis headed north to Wisconsin to fish," said Alice.

"Yes, he did."

"Artie came home to an apple orchard," said Alice.

"Not at first. Artie had a background in psychology. He got vets together. Called it repair work. After her divorce a few years ago, Elizabeth needed help with the expansion of the resort. Artie stepped in."

"And Frosty?" asked Lena.

Julian sighed. "We met in Artie's repair work breakfasts."

Audrey rolled her body like a pretzel to allow Julian's fingers to find her belly fur. She jigsawed her body, her head slipped into the space near the arm of the chair, back legs flopped akimbo, and front legs snuggled close to her chest. But Julian's fingers found burrs trapped in Audrey's fur. Carefully, he skirted the stickers by running his fingertips lightly over the animal.

Julian's voice changed as he began to recount veterans at breakfast. They always began conversation with dark, ugly jokes and huge belly laughs before giving way to descriptions of what they saw and did. Frosty and Francis saw the most action and the most death. They were always in danger. Frosty was underground in a tunnel, sometimes with a partner, but a hole in the ground had a one-at-a-time entrance. Frosty faced the enemy, alone.

"Francis's platoon got shot up pretty good," said Julian.

"Do you have a lot of contact with Francis?" asked Alice.

"Hardly any. But when any of us are in trouble, all of us pledged to move into action."

"Francis got ordained for your wedding," said Alice.

"Yeah."

"He promised to stand guard over Frosty."

"Yeah. I know neither of you like Francis," said Julian over the protests of Alice and Lena, "but he's special. In the field, on a tough mission, remember this was Laos." Julian's face became serious. "I met a guy from his unit. Only men close to Francis knew he gave last rites to men who passed. That wasn't his job, you understand. He didn't care if they were Baptist or Catholic. It was something he felt he had to do because he respected the man. Someone needed to notice the tragedy of loss."

It wasn't what Alice expected to hear. She remembered her talk with him and how he said he was a fixer. She said, "Even though he isn't a man of faith, he gave a little bit of comfort to dying men."

"Yeah. He volunteered to officiate at our wedding. He said the universe would like the joke."

Both women sat in silence until Lena sat taller, her face animated as if a light bulb went on. Her pitch raised to almost a screech. "Alice, you're wondering if Francis would kill someone who threatened Frosty."

"Wait a minute," said Julian, his posture firing up to defend. "Francis isn't the killer. Not Francis!"

"I don't think he did it either," said Alice, "but we better consider the possibility before Unzicker asks. Remember, Francis did strap on a knife and then surrender it to the police. Julian, they have to be curious. I'm following a thread, that's all. Do you plan to tell Unzicker that Frosty was a witness to murder in Vietnam?"

"Don't mean nothin'," said Julian. "Francis isn't the killer. He was with me and Frosty that night."

"Sorry, but it might mean something to the police," said Alice. "Unzicker might ask if all three of you were asleep at the same time."

"Probably."

"And Francis slept the whole night through? He never went out for a smoke?"

Lena sat back as Julian's head turned toward a window.

"How'd you know Francis goes for a walk at night?" asked Julian.

"He told me," said Alice, holding back her full encounter with Francis. "But his walk has nothing to do with being the killer because we know the killer called housekeeping and asked for towels. Julian, Francis didn't call for towels that morning, did he?"

"No." Julian's face lit up with hope.

"The murderer wanted the victim found. It follows that the killer knows Frosty works in the kitchen and planted a knife in the scarecrow to frighten Frosty to make a move."

"Which he did," said Julian.

"At least he's safe for now," said Alice.

"I can't imagine seeing a murder during war counts for anything," said Julian. "Not after all this time. Frosty says he was pretty-well wasted. Can anyone trust his memory? When I heard Rasmus was out of prison, and he wanted to contact Frosty, I knew this wasn't good. Frosty kicked booze and drugs when he got out, but it was hard. To have his supply guy come back into his life, not good. Hell, we're all in our late sixties. We're now the blood pressure-Lipitor generation. Why can't people let this go?"

"Because Rasmus is dead," said Lena. "Killed on our wedding day. Julian, excuse me if I don't let this go." Lena finally reached over and took her husband's hand. "Alice?"

Alice summarized the timeline. Before Rasmus got out of jail, he wrote a short note to Frosty about wanting to make contact. Then Frosty alerted Artie and Julian about Rasmus's intention of dropping by the inn for a visit. Rasmus asked his lady-friend to make reservations for them at the apple resort. Julian proceeded to use the wedding as a cover for why he and Francis would be on the property. Artie watched for the name Rasmus to appear in the reservations and alerted Frosty of the confirmed date. The date of the wedding was set. However, before all the players were in place, Rasmus cornered Frosty, perhaps ordered or scolded his old pal on the Monday before the Saturday wedding. When Francis arrived, Artie assigned him an out-of-the-way room, and Frosty disappeared from public view. Rasmus officially checked in on Thursday and looked again but didn't find Frosty. The murder had happened well before dawn on the day of the wedding.

"All of this because Frosty saw Rasmus kill a young lieutenant in Vietnam?" asked Lena. "No one investigated. I know they probably couldn't have regular police during a war, but why didn't military police investigate?"

"Magpie," said Julian, "it's not easy. It was the Seventies. Crazy."

"But surely there was forensic evidence. Just match up the bullets to the gun. Then the gun to the owner."

Julian made sounds of frustration.

"I think what Julian is trying to say is that soldiers might collect souvenirs from the war like guns belonging to the enemy. Rasmus was known for souvenir distribution. Isn't that right Julian?" Julian nodded. "Rasmus may have used an enemy gun to shoot the lieutenant. If that's true, the military would only know the soldier was killed by an enemy. At the time, Frosty didn't open his mouth. Maybe because he supplied the souvenir. Maybe because he was on drugs."

"He said he was a mess when he came back to the States," said Julian. "All I know is the lieutenant was out of West Point and planned to go to the Olympics as a racewalker. It seemed to bother Frosty that the guy practiced that wiggly strut almost every day. He thought it was too cheerful, too disrespectful to the guys getting killed—like the lieutenant didn't care about the insanity of the war."

Alice felt the sting of revelation. That was why Frosty carried guilt. What had he done?

"Julian, he never gave you a name?" asked Alice.

"No."

"To me, either." Alice's chin raised as she looked to her best friend. "Lena, is that enough? West Point graduate with Olympic, racewalking ambitions? Killed in Vietnam? Can you find a name with that?"

"If he was any good, yes, but it may take time. Newspaper stories were sensitive to war death during the Sixties, but in the Seventies, they cut back on personal stories. Too grim. Riled up voters back home. But a West Point grad who is killed before he makes it to the Olympics could make a powerful human-interest story. If I can get a name, I can find family."

"Family?" asked Julian.

"You two can talk about the murder all you want, but—Alice knows this—as a mother, if I had lost a son, I'd want to know the real reason he didn't come home and pick up his life. His mother could still be alive." Turning to Alice, Lena continued, "If I find his name in a news story, I'll look up online memorials. Those usually give a short bio and a list of family members. Even if it turns out Rasmus was killed by a prison buddy, that lieutenant's family has a right to know what happened."

"The death of the racewalker happened in the Seventies," said Alice, "when we didn't have a computer system. You think someone put up a memorial online?"

"Anyone who works on genealogy can post a memorial for any family member, even generations long ago. I've found family memorials for soldiers who fought in the Civil War. If a mother felt the deep loss of her son, she may have requested or submitted a tribute to him, and that might appear with the memorials. But first, I need the lieutenant's name."

"I don't get it, Magpie, why the focus on family?" asked Julian.

Lena gave a big sigh. "You know me. If one of my sons were killed and if there were anything suspicious about the death, do you think for one minute I'd let that go without cornering everyone with a shred of evidence?" Lena's face flushed as her hands gripped the rolled-up newspaper. As she spoke, she continued to roll the weapon ever tighter. "I'd spend years searching for the truth and thinking of revenge."

"Yes, you would," said Julian with a sly grin.

"I know I come up with wild ideas, but Julian, a mother wants answers, no matter how long it takes."

"Rasmus was protected by being in jail," stated Julian. "If someone had found him, there's not much the guy could do until Rasmus got out."

"Frosty never gave any clues?" asked Alice.

"He only said some guy had been stalking Rasmus. Frosty wanted no part of it. How was he supposed to know it wasn't someone from prison? Julian pulled off his bandana and ran his hand over his helter-skelter, thin hair.

"If I find a name, do I tell Unzicker?" whispered Lena as she put the newspaper down and folded her arms.

"Yes," said Alice. "He has more resources than we do. Better to rule out that soldier's murder had anything to do with this current one. Who knows what's in Rasmus's prison record?" Her eyes narrowed.

Usually, Lena's imaginings bordered on the comical, but this time, the revenge scenario passed the smell test. Not a mother or a father, of course, because they would be too old to turn to murder. But a brother might have taken the death seriously. Or another West Point soldier who became a close friend? Or maybe a sweetheart who saw her dreams shattered with the soldier's death? But realistically, she would be in her sixties and probably not able to take on a beefy, guy like Rasmus. Alice thought she heard the spirit of her husband say, *But a son could*.

"Believe me," said Julian, "I hate to be the cold water here, but Magpie, how could anyone prove Rasmus killed a soldier unless Frosty talked? If he didn't tell the lieutenant's name to us guys, he didn't talk to anyone else. After all this time, how would family or friends learn about the murder in 'Nam, find Rasmus at an apple orchard after he's released from jail, and kill him without anyone knowing?"

"Aren't you also asking why a murderer is still here?" Lena's nose rose into the air.

"All I'm saying is, can't we explore that this has nothing to do with 'Nam. Maybe it's someone from Rasmus's jail past," insisted Julian.

"Oh, like you believe that," Lena rolled her eyes. "If he were Rasmus's State-side past, would Frosty be so touchy? Tell me that."

Julian made a sound of frustration. "I have to hit the can." He pushed Audrey from his lap and rose to leave.

"Speaking of telling," said Alice, "maybe we're looking at this all wrong. What if the leaked information about the murder in Vietnam didn't come from Frosty. I mean there could be another witness or participant in the killing of the lieutenant. Maybe a witness is choosing to set things right."

"Or Rasmus could have bragged about it in prison," said Lena, her eyes widening with delight. "You see it in the movies all the time. A guy doing time has to brag about how tough he is. Only this time his story falls on the wrong ears. Next time I see Unzicker, I'm asking about who Rasmus talked to in prison."

Alice felt exhausted and stiff. The pain near her spine sharpened as she attempted to stand up. She pictured soaking in a tub of hot, soapy water. If she did, however, there was always a chance Audrey, the water-lover, might try to join her.

"Come on girl, we need to clean up from our morning excursion and Lena needs to do some searching. No more dilly-dallying." Alice rose from her seat with a groan and moved toward the door. "Ask Julian to gather Artie and Francis for a sit-down to get Frosty to talk—if he gets back to the resort. He needs to finish telling his story. His behavior shows us he thinks he's the next victim."

Chapter 25

Outside the inn, Alice took time for Audrey to chow down a late lunch. A cloudy canopy moved in over the orchard, but off in the distance, Alice could see the apple pickers stripping ripe apples from trees. Their ladders balanced against tree trunks, collection bags drooped around their waists. The process was a ballet of sorts but also mechanical like the pistons of an engine. Up the ladder, picking almost in unison, down the ladder to unload the apple harvest. Back up the ladder the collectors went. The back of Alice's knees strained just watching the apple-pickers lean into their work, and her back throbbed.

Alice hoisted her backpack over one shoulder and said to her hound, "Okay, a quick tinkle before we clean up." The wind carried the scent of a crushed apples and a gust caught Alice's gray hair, causing her natural tangle of curls to tremble. "I'm going to love a hot bath."

Maia rounded a corner of an outbuilding and approached. Alice had forgotten their promised afternoon walk, but she did have questions for the child who had spotted Rasmus with Frosty on Monday. Taking a deep breath, she waved with big gestures.

"I'm sorry I'm late." Maia's voice was timid. "I had to talk to my teacher. Am I too late to help walk your dog?" asked the girl with big glasses that slipped down her nose. She looked both afraid and excited.

"You're just in time," said Alice brightly. "But do you mind if we don't walk? Audrey played a game this morning and now she has burrs in her fur. Can you help me brush her?"

Maia's head bobbed as she took the leash from Alice's hand and led Audrey to a quiet spot under an old oak tree. She settled down and gave the leash a tug. Audrey needed little encouragement to drop next to a child who was willing to pet her.

"She's kinda stinky," said Maia. "Do you have a brush?"

Alice removed a brush from her backpack, and Maia got to work making Audrey's back glisten. It wasn't until Audrey rolled onto her back that Maia caught the burrs on the dog's belly and upper legs.

"You can't brush burrs out because it pulls your hair and hurts," said Maia.

Rather than tear entangled burrs away with a firm brushing, Maia carefully broke each flat burr and removed them one by one.

"I hate it when my mom's in a hurry to comb my hair. Sometimes she pulls it."

They talked about her brothers and sisters, her favorite fruits and vegetables, and living life from cabin to cabin as they moved to each picking site.

"We can pick up all the apples we want from the ground," Maia said. "I like apples because they don't get as bruised as other fruit. When my dad picks strawberries, sometimes we get the mushy ones."

"Your mom and dad pick apples then move south for other crops?"

"Uh-huh. We spend the winter in Florida." Her eyes widened. "Dad said someday we'll live in a real house. Not in Florida. It's too hot." Her hands cracked a couple more burrs and rubbed the dog skin beneath them. "When your hair gets pulled, it helps if someone rubs your skin," said Maia.

"Thank you, I'll keep that in mind for when I have to brush her. Do you like . . .?"

Maia seemed to know intuitively Alice's question and said,

"Frosty? He gave me books when we were here last year. Mrs. Penrose said it's okay for me to talk to you about him."

"When the man shook his finger in Frosty's face, you had to be a little bit scared."

Maia nodded with authority. "I see it a lot. We go to a lot of farms. Sometimes a boss shakes his finger, and somebody gets fired. I didn't want Frosty to get fired."

"But the big man was new to the orchard, right? You hadn't seen him before?"

She shook her head. "No, never before. He was new."

"What was the scariest part of what you saw?"

"Before he left, he said, 'See you soon, Kill again.'"

"Mrs. Penrose said you saw him a second time when he came to the cabins."

"I did on Thursday. He was scary. My brothers and I played outside, and he asked me if I'd seen Frosty, and I said no, and he said he'd give me a dollar if I'd come get him when I did see him, and I said okay because I was scared, but I wouldn't have done it, not for a dollar, because I like Frosty, and the man went away." She kept her eyes on Audrey and played with the dog's wrinkly face.

"You did the right thing," said Alice. "After that, you didn't see Frosty, right?"

Maia shook her head. "I think he's hiding. Away from the bad man." She pulled back from cleaning Audrey's fur and looked at Alice. "Can I ask you something?"

"Anything."

"Is the man I saw the same man who was killed in the inn?"

"He is."

"Will Frosty come back now?"

"Soon. He's helping the police find a different bad man who killed the man you saw."

Her face turned back to Audrey, "Is my dad okay?"

"I believe so. Why?"

"Because."

"If you think there is something that could help Frosty, I prom-ise not to tell anyone. I promise." Alice's heart hammered. What if she couldn't keep this promise to Maia. What damage could a broken promise do to this child?

"Not everyone gets to live in cabins. The men without families live off the property, sometimes in campers." Maia turned shy. "I heard people talk about a knife. What if Mr. Levitsky remembers that my dad And the other apple pickers have harvesting knives? They're about this long."

Maia held up her hand and pointed at her palm.

"About three inches," said Alice.

"I don't want my dad blamed. We'd have nowhere to go."

"Oh, Maia, this has something to do with a long time ago, Frosty and two bad men. Your dad is safe. You and me, your dad, even Audrey— we just need to wait until the mystery gets settled by the police. But if you see anything strange, tell the police. Or if Mrs. Penrose is around, tell her. Or tell me. Okay?"

Maia nodded but not with confidence.

"Do you know that I used to teach school, and that nice policeman who has been walking around, he was my student. He used to stay after school and ask me questions just like you did today with your teacher. You can tell him anything. Now, what books do you like?"

For the next several minutes, Maia filled time with stories she loved. Audrey responded to the child's attention by squirming into new brushing positions.

Alice's heart slowly returned to normal, wishing someone would crack open the case. *Come on, Lena. Work your Internet magic.*

Chapter 26

After leaving Maia, Alice had planned to go back to her own room, take a long, hot shower, and stay in for the rest of the night. But Pepper Finwall waylaid her and Audrey from the resort lobby to a deserted hallway, away from the curious eyes lingering at the entrance of the hard cider bar. Pepper sipped at a golden-brown drink and huddled close to the wall. Audrey sat between the two standing women, her head tilting in one direction and then the other.

"I've been over this and over this with the police," said Pepper. "Me and Wayne Rasmus were pen pals. I got his name through our church, and I wrote to him every week for four years. We fell in love. Is that a crime?" Her movements were huffy, her lips pouty. "We planned to get married when he got out, but he had something to do first. Everybody here seems to think I should talk to you because I'm done talking to the police."

The first time Alice noticed Pepper, she appeared to be a woman used to lively makeup of overly darkened eyelashes and brows. But now her eyes puffed as if she had recently been crying. Without her usual theatrical style, she looked fragile. Her thin hair had flattened. Alice guessed she was no more than forty-five. Her skin was blotchy and wrinkled with spidery paths. Her legs were thick and her arms thin. She wore baggy shorts and a bulky raspberry-colored sweater. Her feet flattened into flip-flops. Alice thought Rasmus might have seen her as a pliable mark.

"Is that why the two of you came to the orchard?" ask Alice. "One last stop before leaving the state and getting married?" A staff member walked by with a room service cart. A waft of roasted meat caught Alice's nose and her stomach growled. When had she eaten last?

"Yeah. He had to see a buddy and square things. He said a guy owed him. Then we were going to get married and go to Montana. He said after being in prison, he needed wide-open spaces and a job. You know, it's hard to get a job after you've been to prison."

"What kind of job was he interested in?" asked Alice.

"He was once a blackjack dealer. Casinos always need dealers."

"Do they have casinos in Montana?" asked Alice.

"They must," said Pepper, whose face looked puzzled.

"You dropped Rasmus off at the resort on Thursday, right?"

"Yes. He wanted to talk to this guy and catch up. I don't know if they met up. Wayne said he might have to do some arm-twisting. I went to a motel along the interstate. I told the police officer he could check up on me if he needed to. When I came back on Saturday, I learned Wayne had been murdered. The guy he met must've killed him. I told that to the police."

She took a gulp from her glass. Her cheeks flushed.

"Where were you two on Monday?"

"Dingle Grove. It's not far from here. Cute town. But . . . I don't know, Wayne hated the town. He said he felt watched."

"Did you know someone saw Wayne at the resort on Monday?"

"Then somebody made a big mistake or is lying. He went for a haircut on Monday."

"I assume the car is yours," said Alice. "Because he only got out of jail a few weeks ago."

"Yeah."

"Did he drive to the barber to get a haircut?"

"Yeah. He said he'd be careful. He planned to pick up a license in Montana."

170

Pepper thought Monday was a perfect day to have her own hair touched up at the beauty shop, and Wayne set off to get his haircut. He reported back on time to pick her up. Alice asked which colorist she used in Dingle Grove, and Pepper named the shop. Alice smiled brightly and complimented her choice before identifying the owner as going to school with her daughter. Pepper seemed to relax.

"I know I must look a wreck," said Pepper, rubbing one eye with her fist before she took a huge swallow from her glass. "This is for my nerves. For the rest of my life, I got nobody to dress up for. The cop wanted to see me again first thing this morning. Did I know this or that? I'm not letting him pin this murder on me."

"I'm sorry they're making this hard," said Alice, putting a whisper of empathy in her voice. "I imagine you're their only lead for information about Wayne. He never gave you any clue of who this buddy was or why he felt like he was being watched?"

Pepper shrugged. "The police seem to think Wayne came here to do something bad, but he wasn't really. He said he had to give this guy a heads up about the danger. Wayne worried his watcher was also after his old friend. He kinda thought they could team up like the last time and save each other."

"Any idea what kind of danger?" asked Alice. "They were friends but Wayne was willing to do some arm twisting?"

"It was war. Wayne said back then he had the guy's back, but he wasn't sure of how grateful the guy would be." Her eyes flashed. "He was going to tell him about their watcher. He said the guy was a killer. That pal of his should have protected Wayne."

"You never had a chance to learn about the meeting."

"No. I never expected Wayne to get murdered." Pepper slugged down the last of her drink and wiped her mouth with her hand. When she looked up at Alice, her eyes were glassy.

"Maybe he wanted to meet an old friend from prison," asked Alice, "one he's been writing to all these years?"

"The police asked that. No. Wayne didn't even know where the guy lived until I contacted his sister."

"So, you do have a name?" asked Alice.

Rasmus's fiancé's mouth twisted as if she had made a bad mistake, but just as quickly her instincts took control.

"Wayne remembered the guy had a sister named Megan Killian Warbee. Wayne thought it was a funny name, so he remembered it all these years and asked me to look her up. I Googled her and asked how I might find her brother. It wasn't hard. Not too many Warbees around, and she turned out to be very friendly."

"Wayne's friend's name was . . .?

Pepper closed the space between them and tucked into Alice's shoulder. Her breath smelled sour. "Angelo Killian."

"He works here," said Alice.

"I know." Pepper backed up and leaned against the wall. "Megan said her brother is something of a loner, and she was happy that an old friend was looking him up. Angelo apparently doesn't have much contact with family, but he always let her know when he moved. He used to send a Christmas card to her children."

"While Wayne was in prison, you contacted Megan and got Angelo's address. Very thoughtful," said Alice. "Then Wayne wrote to his old friend and told him of his planned visit."

Pepper shook her head. "He thought it was best if I wrote. In prison they read everything that comes in and out. Wayne told me what to say." Pepper turned secretive again and shielded her mouth. "Wayne told him they had a stalker."

"You told this to the police?"

Pepper's head waffled, neither a yes or no.

"You dropped Wayne off on Thursday, left, came back Saturday morning, only to find out someone killed him."

"I told the police it was probably Angelo. No one else knew Wayne. Unless it was the stalker."

"Did Wayne mention he felt the presence of someone watching him at the inn?" asked Alice.

"He never had a chance. He was sure Angelo was in trouble too. I gotta go get me another drink." Pepper looked around and whispered, "Wayne said Angelo did some crazy shit in Vietnam."

"Really?"

Pepper nodded. "Wayne wanted him to know it was about to catch up with both of them."

Alice felt her face contort. *Could that be right? Was Wayne killed because he was warning Frosty? But any warning had to come on Monday. If Frosty felt his apple orchard hideout had been compromised, surely the logical thing would have been to leave right away. Why did he hang around?*

"Please, Pepper, just a couple more questions: Could the information about the threat to either Wayne or Angelo have come from Wayne's jail friends?"

"I don't know. I doubt it. But Wayne had lots of women friends who wrote him letters and came to visit. Someone warned him that once Wayne got out of prison, he wouldn't be able to see his old pal Angelo ever again. That's why we visited the inn. Maybe he wanted to say goodbye."

Alice let Pepper's phrasing bounce around in her head. Was Rasmus the original target? Or just a lure for Frosty? Or did he need Rasmus to flush him out? Did it make any difference which one died first? Of course, if the killer knew where Frosty lived, why not kill him four years ago when he first arrived at the resort property? But then why not kill Rasmus the day he got out of prison? Alice found it all too confusing unless the slayer needed Rasmus to lead him to Frosty. He wanted them together in the same place.

"And you've no idea of their past history in Vietnam?" asked Alice.

"Nothing."

"Where are you staying?"

"Here at the resort. They gave me a different room. Smaller, but I got—my things out of our room. You won't tell?"

"Tell what?"

"That I went back into Wayne's room after forensics left. I got a key on Thursday when Wayne checked in. After the police finished, I had to get our credit cards, or I couldn't even pay for the food here."

"The police would have returned his personal effects," said Alice.

Pepper shook her head. "I couldn't risk it. We weren't married yet, and he kept his money in gift cards." Her body twitched, and she turned to check for other guests in the hallway.

"Wayne had gift cards?"

"Yeah. They were his, not mine. But anyone can cash a gift card, even the cops. That's why I had to get them back." Her voice whined and one shoulder rose to touch her jaw.

"Forgive me for asking, but he just got out of prison. How'd he obtain gift cards?"

"They were . . . bank gift cards that his . . . friends sent him on account of him finally getting out of prison. A little something to start a new life." Her eyes challenged.

None of this made any sense to Alice. Who were Wayne's friends that they would send him gift cards upon being released from prison? Pepper must have seen Alice's doubt in her face because she began an explanation.

"Wayne loved *me*," said Pepper. "But I'm not stupid. A man in prison has a lot of time on his hands, and Wayne got lonely. He wrote to . . . many pen pals over the years. Women can be . . . lonely too. And it's encouraging to receive a handwritten letter. You wouldn't think a man in prison could write lovely letters, but he did. He . . . um . . . asked them to write to his mother and gave them my name and address. For about six months gift cards arrived. He trusted me to save them for him and to write a thank you to each person. Look, it was our start."

"I'm not judging. May I ask how many he received?" asked Alice. She recalled television news that reported scams by prisoners.

"Um . . . close to fifty, I guess. Most are for a hundred dollars, but many are two-fifty. After Wayne died, I had to get the cards out of our room. I snuck in, found Wayne's hiding place, and got out of there as fast as I could. I didn't want any cop stealing them. As I ran toward the door to leave, however, I knocked over a fake plant stuck in white glass pebbles. Made so much noise on the ceramic floor that I thought for sure the cops would catch me."

Chapter 27

After a steamy shower loosened Alice's muscles, after a dinner of Tran's chicken for Audrey, and after room service delivered a roasted pork burrito with hot cinnamon apples on the side for Alice, the dog lay at the bottom of the bed and snored into her dog blanket.

"We've had a big day," whispered Alice. Not to disturb her bloodhound, she turned on the television to watch a muted late show. The warmth of the blanket and pillows propping up her body did little to keep her ankle from swelling, her knee from puffing, or her spine from feeling thick. Alice watched television neither thinking of the day nor wondering what the comedian said.

A text came in from Lieutenant Unzicker:

"We need to square stories. With certain provisions, Gilly Chapel plans to represent Frosty. We're keeping him under wraps for a few days for his safety, but I want you and the others to be safe too. Let us finish this. Go home. I'll be at the inn at 6:30 a.m. tomorrow. Need to talk. If it weren't for Gilly, we'd have a confession from this guy."

Alice felt her heartbeat increase.

Alice to Unzicker: *"By under wraps do you mean in a cell?"*

Unzicker: *"Of course not. Gilly moved him in with her Arsenic and Old Lace Ladies."*

Alice: *"Her grandmother and grand-aunt?"*

Unzicker: *"Yes. If he cooperates, he'll be pampered. If not, he'll be dead. What is it with elderly women and shotguns?"*

Alice: "*Easier to strike a target, I guess. At least Frosty's safe.*"

When they stopped messaging, Alice thought Gilly had made a good call. Her grandmother and aunt had run a country-western bar off the interstate for years. They were savvy old birds as tough as nails. Frosty would be both protected and confined.

A second text message arrived from Lena:

"*I found the memorial for a West Point graduate who died in Vietnam. Jack McKiddie. He was shot in camp by enemy sniper fire. I'll give you a printed copy of the memorial tomorrow if I have difficulty sending it now. The inn's Wi-Fi is making me nuts. McKiddie sounds like a nice guy. Wanted to be in the Olympics. Hero worshiped a previous West Point lieutenant who went to the Olympics and then to Vietnam. One more thing, a bullet from friendly fire was found lodged in McKiddie's hip.*"

Alice to Lena: "*I'm up and awake. Do you have a moment to talk?*"

Lena: "*Julian's in the shower. I read him the riot act about keeping secrets from me and not being in our room the first two nights with me before our wedding. This is not a good time for me to cut out on him.*"

Alice: "*Tomorrow then. I'm having breakfast with Lieutenant Unzicker at 6:30. Want to join us?*"

Lena: "*Are you crazy? No. I'll meet you at 10:00. Sending a download of memorial. Maybe.*"

The attachment came through. But after she read it, Alice had more questions. It described Jack McKiddie's high school achievements, an A-student, track star. Besides being handsome and athletic, he grew up in a small town outside of Nashville, Tennessee. His father, a barber who decorated his shop with news articles of Olympic athletes. His mother, a stay-at-home mom. When he graduated from West Point, he went to Vietnam. Two months after his arrival, he was struck down by multiple shots from an enemy sniper and one shot of friendly fire to his hip.

Alice watched Audrey breathe. Her side went up and down. Occasionally, her tail thumped against the bed with a good dream of play. If Audrey hadn't been so deep in sleep, Alice might have gotten out of bed for mindless busy work like rechecking her backpack or re-sorting the dirty laundry or counting packages of Audrey's food. Work usually soothed and focused her mind. Stories weren't sitting right.

Frosty might have seen Rasmus shoot the lieutenant, but of course, he didn't identify the victim by name. If Jack McKiddie were shot by enemy fire like the government report stated, was Rasmus responsible for the one friendly-fire bullet to hit him in the hip? Alice couldn't picture Rasmus shifting rifles. No matter how fast he tried to be, his technique had to be too slow to compete with soldiers responding to gun fire. Everything seemed to point to two shooters aiming at McKiddie.

Alice looked again at the text attachment of the memorial. It had been posted online by the McKiddie family.

Alice was convinced Frosty hadn't murdered Rasmus. He was too short, and Rasmus too tall, too heavy, too prison shrewd. For Frosty to kill Rasmus, he'd have to convince him to sit in a chair.

Elizabeth and Unzicker mentioned the tight pool of blood on the floor. Alice pictured a tall killer surprising Rasmus as he stood behind him, the strike fast, allowing Rasmus to crumple to the floor and bleed out. Rasmus had no chance to fight back.

How did the killer get into the room? Pepper still had her key af-ter the murder. That's how she opened the door to retrieve the credit cards. Rasmus had the other. Had he used it to wheedle his way into Rasmus's room?

At the thought of safety, Alice had a sick feeling in the pit of her stomach. Francis said his clerical collar gave him a new aura of trust. Had Francis worn the collar when he first arrived on the property? Is that how he fenagled his way into Rasmus's room?

Her heart beat faster. Francis was tall enough and strong enough, but he struck Alice as someone who delighted in being disrespectful, not someone who planned murder. Yet, he liked the idea of being a fixer.

Surely Julian would have said something, thought Alice. *Wouldn't he?*

Both Julian and Francis said one of them had kept an eye on Frosty the night before the wedding. They were more concerned that he might flee—not murder Rasmus.

Let's say Frosty was truthful when he said he witnessed Rasmus shooting and killing Jack McKiddie. That would mean that the enemy gun had to be in Rasmus's possession. An easy thing since Frosty mentioned trading contraband for drugs. The military, however, went with the information they had. An enemy bullet meant an enemy kill. But they were wrong. For his own reason to manipulate Frosty or to feed his own hatred of officers, Rasmus murdered the new lieutenant. So, if Rasmus was the murderer, what had wounded Frosty's spirit?

Logic and imagination told Alice Frosty was the friendly fire that lodged a bullet in McKiddie's hip. She guessed Rasmus maybe thought he needed to anchor Frosty to his black-market scheme. Make Frosty a little dirtier with the workings during a chaotic war. Keep him obligated. So maybe he urged Frosty to shoot when he was stoned, his mind was pliable to anger or a cruel joke. Frosty shot the lieutenant first. Rasmus in a hail of bullets finished him.

Alice checked her watch. It was too late to call Unzicker who had a family of his own. His two boys and a wife doted on him. She concluded her sketchy conclusions and questions could wait until morning. Let Unzicker get a good night sleep. Let Audrey rest after a grueling day. Alice punched up a pillow and closed her eyes, but sleep, along with a body stiffness, came in fits and starts. Once she awoke to her knee throbbing.

Her wicked side hoped Frosty suffered the same aches and pains she did.

Chapter 28

Standing in the lobby of the inn at 6:30 a.m., Lieutenant Unzicker sipped steaming coffee from a russet-colored mug. He didn't say anything as Alice entered but motioned to a small sitting room with glass window-paned doors just off the lobby. His eyes seemed swollen as if he'd little sleep. He dressed in street clothing that didn't hide his handgun. His badge, normally tucked into a pocket, was prominently clipped to his belt. He made no mention of Alice's awkward stiff movements.

Audrey did her happy-to-see-you wiggle, and Unzicker's hand rubbed the top of her head before they entered the sitting room, before Unzicker closed the doors behind them, and before he turned professional. He sat down on a chair that allowed him to watch the lobby. Alice moved a chair closer to him and sat. She also wanted to view the lobby. If it was important to him, it was important to her.

Outside the closed glass doorway, Cyril pushed his walker into the lobby and took a seat near the coffee urn. Although Alice couldn't hear his conversation with the inn staff, the woman nodded and smiled before heading to the kitchen.

"What did Frosty tell you?" asked Alice, keeping her voice low.

Unzicker gave a sad grin. "You aren't going home, are you?"

"Give me a reason," Alice looked at Unzicker, her voice pleading. "Were you able to talk to Frosty without Gilly?"

He shook his head. "I might have to take in someone, and you and your tribe of snoopers might consider it distasteful. I want to do it quietly and quickly. No one involved in this case needs to amp up emotions. I'm asking you to take everyone and go home." His statement sounded like a command. "Now, tell me if he told you about a lieutenant in Vietnam."

"He did," answered Alice. "We agree that Frosty couldn't have killed Rasmus, but do you think he played a role . . . in the shooting of a lieutenant in Vietnam?"

"We have him in *custody*, for his own safety," said Unzicker, "The ladies got him up at five this morning."

"Ah," was all Alice could think to comment. "Who do you suspect killed Rasmus?"

"We only want an individual to come in for questioning."

"What did Frosty tell you?"

Unzicker drained his coffee mug. "He told us about Rasmus killing a lieutenant in Vietnam. By his behavior, I'm thinking he played a role in that. Why else is he so protective of the story?"

"There is something he is hiding, but he never told me he also fired a gun that night." Knowing that Unzicker inched toward the same conclusion she had, Alice felt a sense of relief. "The government reported they found two different types of bullets in the body. One friendly fire in his hip—I'm guessing Frosty did that. Many other bullets from an enemy gun—I'm guessing that was Rasmus using contraband. So, are you going to arrest Frosty for his role in the death of Lieutenant McKiddie?"

Unzicker's eyes instantly narrowed, and Alice swallowed hard. This early in the morning, she had forgotten she hadn't yet told Unzicker the name Lena found doing research on memorial sites.

"Who told you the Vietnam victim was Lieutenant McKiddie because Frosty never gave us a name."

"I'm sorry. I learned late last night from Lena after you texted me.

I planned to tell you this morning. May I ask who called for towels to be delivered to Rasmus's room the morning of the murder?"

Still peeved, Unzicker asked, "What is it with you? You open your mouth with a question, and people blab what they know?"

"I have that kind of face," said Alice, hoping Unzicker would smile.

"We'll assess the situation with this new information," said Unzicker as he sat back in his chair, took out his phone, and punched in a text message.

Really peeved this time, concluded Alice.

"Frosty believes someone is after him because Rasmus told him so," said Unzicker. "How'd Lena come up with the name McKiddie?"

"Newspaper archives and funeral memorials," answered Alice. "His name is Jack McKiddie, to be precise. When I talked to Frosty at the rest stop, he gave me a description of the soldier who died. West Point. Ambitions to racewalk at the Olympics. Lena took those details and found McKiddie's name. The date of the murder and the description of the lieutenant match—apparently not too many West Point grads dream of going to the Olympics for racewalking. Lena only found one other who became a hero to McKiddie."

A kitchen worker carried a tray out to Cyril and placed it on the ornate table next to him. An egg sat in an egg cup, two pieces of toast stacked on a plate, and two tiny jelly jars (Alice guessed apple butter and apple jelly) set up near the knife. Cyril proceeded to crack the egg with the back of a spoon. Francis wheeled the old man in the wheelchair into the lobby and positioned him near Cyril before leaving.

"What do you make of him?" said Unzicker, nodding his head in Francis's direction.

"Francis?" said Alice with some surprise in her voice. "He couldn't have been anywhere near the killing of Jack McKiddie."

"Of course not. He was in Laos during the war. But for Rasmus? Francis is Frosty's alibi and Frosty is Francis's alibi for the night of Rasmus's murder. Friends have been known to develop a pact. I can see Frosty feels his life is threatened. He has a tall friend ready to get rid of the menace."

"And Artie?" asked Alice. "And Julian? Do you think they're covering for Francis?"

"I've nothing to say at this time."

"Pact. You see friendship as his motive?" challenged Alice.

"Wouldn't be the first time a buddy helps a buddy. Do you have any history on Francis?" Unzicker's tone closed in on a conclusion: Francis was the killer.

"No history. He's a little surly and not much of a sharer about the war. Majorly sarcastic. He strikes me as living in a testosterone world of fishing. Crusty, a bit raw, no panache."

Unzicker read whatever text appeared on his phone. In a faraway voice he said, "No panache."

Alice felt stunned by Unzicker's conclusions and mentally kicked herself for not giving him McKiddie's name as soon as Lena sent it to her. He could have run the name through whatever search engines the police used and maybe found some connection to the killer.

But what if Francis cut out while Frosty and Julian slept? Of course, the night before she too had considered Francis's height and strength. While he was an Internet clergyman, he took too much pleasure in wearing the clerical collar of a minister. No one seemed to mind as he bragged about his confirmation online. Was that due to Halloween being around the corner and adults enjoying dress-up? Had she been lulled into Julian's explanation of Francis the fisherman?

"Answer me this: Who plunged a kitchen knife into the scarecrow?" asked Alice. "Because if it were Francis, he'd be pointing you in the direction of Frosty. Why would he do that?"

"It's why we need to talk to Francis at the station. Have you noticed he seems to be all over this resort, usually with the old guy in the wheelchair? Why is that? They don't seem to be related. Escorting an old guy in a chair does provide a picture of innocence and probably allows him to go anywhere. Do anything. Stop by a kitchen. Light fingers could swipe a knife when backs are turned. Takes only a moment to plunge a knife into a scarecrow. Remember he came to us with a holstered blade. He suggested we could test it for the murder weapon. He said he learned of the weapon from housekeeping."

"You said the ankle knife wasn't the murder weapon," said Alice.

"It wasn't, but I get suspicious when people overshare." Unzicker's eyes were particularly narrow, his lips thin.

"I don't know Francis," said Alice. "I see your point, but I can't get past that Artie and Julian would have to know . . ."

"And that's why I want you to go home. Let us untangle this—now that we have another name to check out."

Alice closed her eyes slowly as she realized where the police investigation could go. "Lena and Julian plan to leave for Hawaii."

"I'm well aware." Unzicker looked at Alice with hard eyes. "There may be a delay."

"You can't . . . they have plans."

Unzicker stood to leave the sitting room. "I'm going back to the station. Leave this investigation behind, Alice. Go home. If I arrest Francis, you don't want to be culpable. What will that do to your friendship with Julian, and ultimately with Lena if they think you were complicit and never gave them a heads up?"

With that said, Unzicker left before Alice could argue. Alice struggled with the thread of the investigation Unzicker followed. But then Francis did seem closer to Frosty than Julian did. His experience at the Laos border probably mirrored Frosty's encounters down a tunnel, killing men as fast as a hand grenade in the dark. After all these years, perhaps Francis thought life was unfair to put Rasmus with his threats and warnings in Frosty's path. But was he willing to do more than a foolish stunt of strapping a knife to his ankle? Was he willing to become a fixer and kill this new enemy?

Alice might have believed Francis could be the killer except for

Housekeeping delivering the towels. Why would Francis make the call for clean towels to be sent to Rasmus's room? He'd gain nothing by the discovery. The killer, however, absolutely wanted the body to be found. In Alice's mind that didn't fit with Francis's infuriating superior style of making a joke of things. To Alice, Francis seemed like the kind of guy who'd snicker in the corner because he knew the irony of a body waiting to be discovered.

She watched Unzicker walk to the sideboard in the lobby with tall glass urns filled with Halloween candy corn and licorice cats. As he spoke to Cyril, Unzicker's hand scooped pieces of black licorice before he left the building.

Alice gathered Audrey's leash and left the sitting room for the lobby. She looked forward to a long walk with Audrey to clear her thinking. Why had Francis wheeled out the older gentleman slumped in a wheelchair? What did his attention to the older man give Francis? Access to what? Or access to whom?

Chapter 29

Alice greeted Cyril and the man in the wheelchair. Giving Audrey the down command, Alice watched as her dog surprisingly complied, settling near the feet of Cyril's companion. The hound's eyes told Alice that lovely smells emanated from feet, almost as good as a crotch.

The man in the chair was Lester.

"Lester Myron Livingston. I live at 4130 Bruce Road, in Tawney, Kentucky. Can I go home now?"

He was dressed in gray sweatpants, a white T-shirt, and a gray, zippered sweat jacket with red piping trim. Everything about his skin was loose and spotted. Sunspots appeared through his thin white hair. Alice's heart sank.

"Do you want breakfast?" she asked. "Would you like me to pour you some coffee?"

"Lester Myron Livingston," he repeated and gave his address again.

Alice looked at Cyril who flashed a knowing look. He buttered a small piece of toast and added a dollop of apple butter.

"Put it near his mouth," he instructed.

Alice placed the piece near Lester's trembling lip. His mouth worked as if he were chewing even before the toast passed into his mouth. "Would you like another?" asked Alice, even though Cyril shook his head.

"Lester Myron Livingston," he repeated, followed by his address, followed by his desire to go home.

Alice felt tears gather in her eyes as Bernadette rushed into the lobby.

This morning Bernadette looked like a used-up woman in her six-ties. Her face carried a pink excitement, her movements were jerky, almost like a kid caught with a hand in the cookie jar. Muddy colors of not-quite-green or not-quite-brown replaced her normal bright col-ored clothing of lime green and tangerine. On her feet she wore Keds without socks. The hollows in her cheeks exaggerated as her breathing accelerated into quick puffs.

"There you are, darling," she sang and looked embarrassed. No recognition crossed Lester's eyes. Instead, he looked startled, almost fearful. "Time for breakfast." She grabbed the handles of the chair and pulled him back from Alice and Cyril. "Thank you for sitting with him. We have a big day." She whisked Lester Myron Livingston toward the dining room. "We're going to see the minister again. You like him. He's asked for you to join him for oatmeal."

"I never paid any attention to him," said Alice. "Lena thought Bernadette must be setting up a secret persona to write about the resort. I never noticed Lester . . . I . . ."

"Don't beat yourself up about it," said Cyril. "That one," he nodded in the direction of Bernadette, "is no reporter or any kind of writ-er. But I can't believe she's any kind of loving wife either. Mark my words, she probably feels trapped in her marriage. When he does say something more than his name, he mentions his wife from long ago. If this one could, she'd park Lester at the curb and skedaddle. No doubt about it, you marry an older gent, you got your hands full. Did you at least notice that Bernadette and that attendant, Gavin, are having an affair?"

"What? No. I haven't been paying attention."

Before she knew about Lester, Alice had thought the attendant was

Bernadette's husband. He was more her age and seemed distantly attentive to her love of miniature golf. He rolled his eyes the way a long-time husband might. To Alice, Gavin didn't seem like a lover. His body language was all wrong. But maybe that could be his act in public to hide an affair.

Cyril explained how Gavin wasn't careful with Lester, not abusive, but abrupt and tentative as he took care of him. Gavin's eyes follow Bernadette about the room. And the looks that passed between Bernadette and Gavin spoke of a secret language between them.

"They're whispering all the time," said Cyril. "Either Gavin is new to being an attendant or he's playing the role as an excuse to be with Bernadette. No one the wiser. But I'll give that Gavin some credit. Lester does have a beautiful close shave every morning. Wish I had that kind of shave." Cyril's hand went to his chin.

"Do they both ignore Lester?" asked Alice as Audrey's face came to her knees.

"If Francis is around, yes. They dump him on Francis—probably believe he's a real minister. Lester's lonely and neither of them two pay the least bit of attention. Push him here. Push him there. No wonder Lester asks to go home. Gotta admit, I never thought Francis would get himself roped into a scheme of being a nursemaid. You wait and see. In that dining room, it won't be her sitting with him. Francis or some other guest will be feeding oatmeal to Lester. She'll be off with Gavin. It's not easy when you lose your marbles."

Alice reached out and put her hand on Cyril's.

"I'm not talking about *me!*" Cyril flicked his hand away from Alice's. "Lester needs better company than those two. Tell you something else: Gavin doesn't have a room of his own. Housekeeping told me they make up the room with two double beds and a pull-out couch—in the registered name of Lester Myron Livingston, of course. Strange sleeping arrangement, I say. Which one's on the couch?"

"How do you know this?" asked Alice.

"You're not the only one with snooping skills. Who's gonna pay attention to a man in his nineties with a walker? I go where I want. People are only sensitive if you fall down and threaten a lawsuit."

Another impossible situation, thought Alice. *Lester estranged from this world, yearning to go home to something familiar. But really, why is he even here? Why would Bernadette bring him along if her purpose were a fling? Why not drop him off with other family or at a nursing home that offers respite for a caregiver?*

For a second, Alice's mind went back to Lena's theory that Lester was cover for the rumored reporter story. But Lester definitely wasn't playing the role of an elderly man with dementia. She had to agree with Cyril. Bringing him to a resort smacked of callous cruelty.

Audrey rose from the floor and gave Alice an insistent nudge with her nose. Time for a walk, a welcome activity that allowed Alice to think. After the murderer was caught, Alice intended to help Lester any way she could. But first she needed to think about the murderer and Unzicker's questions about Francis.

Do the police really think Francis is using Lester and his clerical collar to blend into crowds? And do what?

"I'll see you later?" asked Alice. "Maybe it's time for all of us to go home. Lieutenant Unzicker thinks the murder investigation will wrap up today or tomorrow."

"Who did it?" asked Cyril with a sniff.

"Well, the police have a man in custody. So, I guess we'll hear about it, but maybe we shouldn't stay."

"I like the food," said Cyril, signaling his determination not to leave. "You don't want to be here for the final take-down of the killer?"

"Not really," said Alice. "Arrests are always sad."

Audrey grumbled a gargle, and Alice picked up her backpack and gathered the leash to begin their morning walk.

"Don't you get tired of lugging that thing around?" asked Cyril.

"What? The backpack?" Cyril nodded. "Maybe at first but having it with me has saved my butt a number of times. Extra dog clean-up supplies," said Alice with an eyeroll. Then she was off, desiring to be well away from the inn and the apple orchard. Maybe today she'd avoid the busy apple pickers and walk toward the stream Audrey enjoyed. They headed north toward the cider house and the worn path behind the building. This particular morning, Audrey twisted more than usual to glance right, left, and behind.

As she rounded the corner of the russet-painted cider house toward the backside with no windows, the barrel of a gun came up behind Alice and pressed under her jaw. A man's fingers removed her phone from her back pocket and turned it off.

"Hold still," said Gavin. He stood slightly behind her and to her right, his left hand circled around her back and gripped Alice's left arm. Right hand pushed against her jaw with more force, causing her face to tilt to the left. How many times had Alice been grateful for Audrey being docile, in her own dog world of enjoyment? Not a bit of teeth-baring German shepherd in her or Rottweiler or Doberman. In fact, Audrey wagged her tail as her nose slammed into Gavin's crotch. Of course, he swore and threatened to kick Audrey, but the dog's moment of affection did bring the gun down from Alice's jaw, and Alice angled her body, ready to block Gavin's retaliation. Instead, he dropped the gun to jam it into her ribs. Alice bit her lip and chose not to attempt a yell for help.

A few resort workers were still parking their cars in the distant lot, too far away to hear her. No day guests would arrive for another couple of hours. No joggers. No dog walkers. No one within ear shot.

Gavin was a slim man, a hair shorter than Alice's six-foot height. He was dressed in jeans, a blue plaid shirt over a T-shirt. He could easily be taken for a man going out to change the oil of his truck. Despite anger at Audrey, he appeared efficient, determined, and quiet. He raised the gun again and pressed it harder against Alice's jaw. She stood stock-still, eyes darting to catch a glimpse of help, hardly taking a breath despite a drumming heart.

Bernadette walked around Alice to face her. "We're taking a walk."

A man's handkerchief came out of her pocket. Bernadette shook it before wadding it up and stuffing it in Alice's mouth. "We need to make a swap, and we think you're the perfect temptation."

Chapter 30

Heavy clouds raced across the blue sky, and the air turned chilly. Bernadette had zip-tied Alice's hands in front of her and had taken control of Audrey's leash. The hound didn't seem to mind that Bernadette paid no attention to her, instead, she sniffed smells along the path and squatted for quick relief. Bernadette gave impatient jiggles of the leash to move Audrey along, but she quickly learned that in a pulling contest with a bloodhound, the dog won, particularly when she needed a private moment.

"I have a plastic bag for pick up," said Alice but her words came out as a series of muffled, nonsensical sounds.

Bernadette glared at her for a moment and tugged Audrey forward.

Alice could tell Bernadette wanted to be loud and insistent with Audrey. But being forceful and noisy? Not a good idea during an abduction. Their escape from the apple resort was instead filled with eyerolls and heavy breaths of frustration from the woman dressed in murky colors.

When Audrey stopped, stared, and wagged her tail, Alice caught a quick movement out of the corner of her eye. Someone with a backpack well-away from the resort disappeared behind a farm wagon. There a second and then gone. Alice's eyes scanned for a yellow bus. She remembered the young boy who'd requested that Mrs. Penrose paint a snake on his arm because he spied the priest with one. Children watched. Would they be brave enough to tell the police or be unaware and head for school? Alice faked a sneeze and pushed a portion of the hanky through her lips. Bernadette came forward to stand in front of her and removed the gag.

"What's the matter with you?"

"Sinus drainage," said Alice.

The gag went back, and they continued to walk. Alice didn't believe either kidnapper noticed a witness to their stunt. Hopefully, it was Maia.

Alice grabbed onto the thought that the young girl could be a monkey wrench to their plans. As her chin rose, a cool wind lifted Alice's tangled gray curls.

The first drops of rain sent them toward a stand of big trees. When Alice saw the old farmhouse with the tall, white phlox elbowing thistles, her shoulders relaxed. Alice stomped her foot for attention and nodded her head toward the ramshackle house. They all scurried for shelter before the clouds let loose with a downpour. She pushed down fear that threatened to make her giddy. Their abduction of her was absurd on so many levels, but she needed to think clearly and stop imagining comic kidnappers dashing for cover while holding colorful umbrellas over her, a bloodhound, and a gun.

The front door opened with a shove.

"Too early for this kind of weather. Feels like November," said Gavin.

The wind whipped trees and made the framing of the structure strain and pop. As quickly as the rain started, it stopped. Golden leaves hanging onto branches glimmered in the newly released sun.

Bernadette and Gavin seemed to think the house an appropriate hideout and that a trade wouldn't take long. They were new to abduction and hadn't scouted out the house with rotted wood and little roofing. Alice stopped herself from smiling. They hadn't hurt Audrey or released her to explore the world on her own. Alice bet they had no idea of the possessed, stubborn, needy nature of her dog. No this wouldn't take long. All she had to do was protect Audrey when the couple's frustration turned to violence.

Audrey enjoyed a good-girl ear scratch from Alice's bound arms.

Bernadette's hand leaned on Alice's shoulder to encourage her to sit on the floor, and she pulled the handkerchief from Alice's mouth. The backpack slid down Alice's shoulders and rested at the small of her back. Unfortunately, the pack straps trapped Alice's elbows and restricted what little mobility she had with tied wrists.

"No screaming. We don't want to hurt you, but we will," said Bernadette.

"No one to hear me," mumbled the practical Alice. The giddiness hadn't quite left her. She caught Audrey's eye and wanted to beg, *"No howling from you, either."* She glanced around the room. If Audrey chose to bark or howl, no one could stop her. Alice tried to assess the couple's cruelty. She knew of the gun and guessed at a very sharp knife. How was she to protect Audrey?

Alice leaned back against the wall, her spine arching, conforming to adapt to the backpack behind her. The coolness of the wall awakened her awareness of her aging body, still stiff from a search for Frosty. The position of the backpack pinched the muscle next to her spine. If she had to fight one of these two, there'd be no upper cuts or kidney jabs. Maybe she could stomp on Bernadette's foot.

Audrey's nose checked her out with a good sniff that left drool on Alice's midriff.

"This house is as good as any," said Bernadette. "Not much of a walk back to the inn. People probably forgot this place long ago."

The rain might have stopped, but big drops of water plopped from the ceiling and rafters, open to the sky.

"We can move her quickly to a swap site," said Bernadette. "You're more familiar with this area than I am. When you visit your grand-daughter, what's a busy site we can use for the exchange?"

Gavin shrugged.

"Come on, Gavin. When you visited your daughter, where do you two go?"

"Bernie, we never planned for this," said Gavin. "I don't know what to suggest. We never go west of Dingle Grove, and we only go there because the town has a main street that my daughter loves."

"The Graybill Bend Hospital's pretty busy," offered Alice. "At any given time, the emergency room has lots of commotion. People focus on their own misery. They might not notice an exchange. The loading dock area for supply delivery is usually quiet. They never notice Audrey when we visit."

"How far is it from here?" asked Bernadette.

"Less than ten miles. Check your phone or my phone for directions if you don't believe me. Of course, we'll need a car."

"We're not turning on any phone," said Gavin. "We aren't idiots."

"The hospital could work," said Bernadette. "I have to go back for the car anyway. First I'll tell the police that you left me a note before you took her. Of course, we'll have to add that you want me to drive Frosty to the hospital for the exchange."

"I don't like it," said Gavin.

"I'll be the crazy, contrite woman. So far they've believed hysterical. How could I know that the man I hired to care for my dear husband was . . . was . . ." Her next words couldn't come out. She stared at Gavin and bit her lips.

"The police won't allow you to become another hostage," said Alice.

Gavin and Bernadette gave her a curious look as they moved to the opposite wall and whispered. Alice continued to sit on the floor and felt water seep into the backside of her jeans. She leaned forward to keep her vest from soaking in the trickle that fell down the wall.

Alice looked to relocate her place in the room, but the house was as dilapidated as she thought. Pieces of flowery wallpaper hung in strips, but much of the wall covering was missing. Water-damaged floorboards appeared to be rickety and unsafe. From her spot on the floor next to the wall, Alice could see the sky through a space that once held a windowpane. She imagined she heard one of Rikki's drones hovering above the house and taking pictures of her sitting on the floor. If only it were true.

For all its damage, Alice felt the warmth that once occupied the old farmhouse. Two pictures still hung on the wall. One a drawing of an old man praying before helping himself to bread. The other a faded black and white photograph of a child dressed in clothing of the 1920s with high-top black shoes, laced around the ankles. Audrey parked her butt on Alice's thigh. Alice's tied hands and trapped arms tried to loop around her dog's neck to pull her close. But the hound was fidgety.

"I know," said Alice. "After a walk, you always get fed. I'm sorry, babe."

Gavin and Bernadette stared in Alice's direction as she talked to her dog.

"Now what?" asked Alice as she struggled for a more comfortable position. "The floor's wet, the wind's picked up. We're going to get cold."

She felt like a prop in Bernadette's drama.

"Now I go back," said Bernadette. "Tell the police I saw you taken. Tell them I found a ransom note."

Bernadette pulled a piece of wrinkled paper and pen from her jacket pocket. To Gavin she said, "You're right. We'll keep this note short." To Alice she said, "Write: *I've got Alice. Willing to swap her for Frosty. Will be in touch.*"

Alice raised her bound hands a couple of inches and wiggled her fingers.

Bernadette's anger flared. "I'm not untying you. Write. Nobody's concerned about your penmanship." She kicked the bottom of Alice's foot.

"Bernie, I don't know. Kidnapping was never in our plan," said Gavin.

"Frosty went into hiding. It's not my fault. Don't blame me for taking Rasmus at his word that Frosty was a friend. We were supposed to find him working in the kitchen with the other staff members."

Gavin's brow wrinkled as he looked at Alice. "What supplies do you have in that backpack?"

"Water, energy bars, emergency medical, a sweatshirt."

"Gimme the sweatshirt," order Gavin.

Alice wiggled and pushed the backpack to her side, but other than being double-jointed, no effort allowed her to unzip the backpack while her wrists were together. She gave up when a sharp pain shot across her spine—that and the interference of a big dog poking her nose into Alice's ribs for a treat.

"No funny business," said an impatient Bernadette as she came forward and kneeled. She wrenched the sweatshirt from the pouch. "We don't need a note. This is good. It will convince them I know what I'm talking about. I can say she dropped it when she saw me. Her eyes pleaded with me to go back and tell the police what had happened." With a flair for hyping panic in her voice, Bernadette added, "I ran as fast as I could . . . but of course, I'll take my time. Someone should miss her. Let them stew in their own juice."

Bernadette's confidence changed to a nervous bravado. She bragged about the house being a good hideout. She mentioned Alice's snacks and water could hold them for the next several hours until she could convince others to allow her to make the swap.

"It's a good plan," said Bernadette with determination. "We don't want to spend another thirty years waiting or searching for Frosty like we did with Rasmus. We have our promise to Dad."

"I know," said Gavin. "I don't have thirty more years."

Alice felt doom in his statement.

"It's now or never," said Bernadette. "Gavin, we are so close.

Time for me to go back to play scatterbrained." She moved close to Gavin and put her arms around him. "I love you. This is for Mom and Dad." She caressed his cheek, then said, "Watch her. I hear she's tricky."

Chapter 31

Bernadette left the farmhouse. On watch for the unexpected, Gavin made the floor squeak as he slowly paced between one glassless window frame and one protected by broken, weathered boards. Audrey found a shriveled, petrified orange, as hard as a baseball, and swatted it about like a ball. Her brow wrinkled with curiosity, her mouth picking it up and spitting it out. The orange grew a thin layer of icky dust as it rolled through a pool of water and across the dry old floor. Alice imagined children coming to this ghost house to play.

"How does this plan of yours work?" asked Alice. "You know Bernadette's going to tell the police that you kidnapped me," said Alice. "How do you think that will go over? Sure, it puts her in the clear until Lieutenant Unzicker confirms you two are brother and sister. Then you both become bad guys." Alice shook her head and winced before she repeated, "Her own brother."

"Bernie knows what's she's doing." His voice was resigned.

Gavin took a seat on the floor, ten feet across from her. His face, blank, but he rocked his ankles and allowed his toes to tap the floor.

You think she knows, but do you? Bad plan, thought Alice. *You have no idea who you're dealing with. Unzicker won't take this well. You're picturing a couple rural cops, but you're about to unleash a battalion: county police were sure to join in with local Limekiln officers. Small towns have Internet sites for breaking news. Television crews won't be far behind. If they get wind of a spectacle, curious townspeople will make the drive with phone cameras in hand.* Alice thought of Maia. *Maybe even apple pickers.*

"May I ask if your last name's McKiddie?" To Alice, the conclusion was obvious, but now was the time for him to make the big reveal. She and Unzicker once talked about hostage taking. *"One side needs to control the dialogue,"* he said. *"With luck, it's the good guys."*

Alice jettisoned the idea of standing near Gavin and twisting at tornado speed to allow the backpack to swing away from her body and knock the kidnapper into next Sunday. First, she wasn't sure of her speed at sixty-four years old. Second, she needed days to heal her back with a toasty heating pad called Audrey.

Gavin's face flushed. "What if my name is McKiddie? What have you heard?"

"I once heard a story about a Jack McKiddie. Are you related?"

"My older brother." Gavin brought up the gun and rested it on his knee but pointed the barrel at Alice. "Where did you hear about Jack?"

Alice ignored the question. "Can I ask if you served in Vietnam? I know Jack did."

"I did serve—after Jack."

"Must have been in the Seventies. Toward the end of the war?"

Gavin nodded. "The government was in negotiations for peace while bombing the hell out of Hanoi."

They talked about Gavin's experience serving in the military, even as the war showed signs of collapsing. His day after day mission: building a schoolhouse. By day he and other soldiers built, by night the enemy or villagers or bad luck destroyed the new structure. Rumor said higher-ups knew the war would end badly and that efforts in rebuilding villages were useless. If true, someone along the chain of command held up the cancelation of orders to stop building the schoolhouse. So, Gavin and his team continued day after day.

"We all knew building the schoolhouse was pointless work. But at least we weren't out there burning villages or getting blown up. Even now I can't get the smell of plywood out of my nose, and my arms still ache at the thought of sandbags."

"Kind of like Sisyphus," said Alice unable to stop being a teacher. "In Greek mythology a man's punishment by the gods is to continually roll a boulder up the hill only to watch it roll back down. But he embraced the judgment of doing fruitless work, as absurd as it was."

Gavin gave a small smile. "I like that. Maybe he saw the joke. After a while, we all thought of the war as a bad joke. When the schoolhouse got shot up, supplies stolen, burned down, we had to laugh. So stupid."

"I heard about Jack from Frosty," said Alice. She wanted to test Gavin's anger. "He said your brother was an upbeat kind of guy. In the mess of war, he tried to cheer up people."

"Then why did he kill him?" Gavin sat straight, his shoulders squared. His jaw tightened. Toes stopped tapping.

"How do you know he did?" asked Alice.

Gavin stood up and paced again. "Look. You don't know. This isn't your fight."

"We have time, and I don't seem to be doing anything." Alice tilted her wrist and checked her watch as Audrey batted the orange across the floor then bounded after it. "Can't hurt to give me Jack's story. Everyone at the inn knows I take long walks with Audrey. It will take Bernadette a while to convince them I was taken. Let's face it, she has laid a few whoppers on them. They aren't going to snap-to just because she said so. Remember the police didn't believe her when she first told them about hearing marbles rolling across the floor."

"We both heard something drop and roll across the tile. She thought Frosty might be hiding up there. Police had searched the room." Gavin shrugged his shoulders. "If the guy wanted to hide, perfect spot."

"Funny thing—turned out someone knocked over a fake planter with glass pebbles. But Bernadette is a good actress. Her act of fear annoyed the police and convinced the inn staff that she might be a writer, here to do a magazine story. They might take her new information about a kidnapping as hype for a magazine article."

"I told her the magazine thing might attract too much attention. But she's good at reading people. It was her idea to send an anonymous letter announcing a writer was inspecting safety for handicapped guests. She said we needed all the confusion we could muster."

"Where'd she find Lester?"

Sitting back down on the floor near the glassless window, Gavin said. "I told her we didn't need Lester." His hand waved the thought of Lester away. He placed the gun on the floor as he turned his shoulder toward Alice. Still, his hand lingered above the gun with a loose grip on the handle.

"Then tell me about your family and Jack when you were all kids. It will pass the time."

Gavin wiped his mouth with the back of his hand and leaned against the lathe wall. The story began with, "You should have known my dad."

Finn McKiddie was a proud Irish father who displayed pictures of his son Jack on the walls of his barber shop: Jack the scholar. Jack the football player. Jack the track star. Everyone knew he was headed to West Point years before any special recommendation was written. It was all Finn talked about as he snipped hair or shaved faces. He rarely uttered Jack's name but referred to him as *that boy of mine*. Soon the identity embedded in Bernadette's and Gavin's mind as well. *Our brother* replaced Jack's name. A barbering future was good enough for Gavin, but Jack was going to be somebody. He was the family's ticket to something wonderful.

Jack graduated from West Point and begged an assignment in Vietnam. His personal hero, a fellow speed-walker, had graduated before him from the academy and had been to the Olympics in Japan. Combat in Vietnam took his life. Jack was determined to pick up the challenge, go to Vietnam, and when he returned—the Olympics.

"Except it didn't happen," said Gavin. "Rasmus and Frosty killed my brother and my mom and dad. Dad and I got home from the barber shop when two soldiers walked to the door. You never think it's real."

Ursula McKiddie, Jack's mother, a no-nonsense, sturdy woman of German heritage, was the first to take to her bed, with no energy for life. In nine months, she died. Pneumonia, the doctor said. Finn followed ten years later after Bernadette and Gavin promised on the soul of their mother that they'd get justice for Jack.

"I guess from our mother we inherited stubbornness and from Dad . . . from Dad, focus and patience. Bernie wanted to find out what happened. Maybe there had been a mistake in identifying the body. Jack dying wasn't in our family plan. You have to understand Dad wouldn't hire other barbers—just me. With only me and Dad working in the barber shop, we didn't make enough income for any of us to go to college. West Point had been an answer to dad's dream. Once Jack got home, he was supposed to help me go to college. Then both of us would help Bernie. We are family."

Alice took a deep breath and felt the sadness—tight family bonds that didn't allow the brother and sister to consider options or to move forward—except for revenge.

"How'd you find out what really happened to Jack? As I remember 1971 and 72, accurate information was sketchy."

"It took a long time. Bernie harassed everyone she could think of for a report. When it finally came through years later, we saw he had been shot several times by an enemy weapon, but one bullet in the hip came from friendly fire. That's what they called it. By then, I had been over there and felt the heat. Friendly fire made sense to me, but not to Bernie. She insisted we exhume his body. Man, that was hard. We filed the paperwork and scraped the money together to pay a specialist to examine Jack's wounds. He thought the friendly fire came first. Because of the angles of other wounds, he concluded the kill shots came after Jack fell."

"You assumed what?" asked Alice.

"It wasn't the war. It was murder. That's when Bernie got the idea to read through sympathy cards and letters . . . some even came a couple years after Jack's death. She wanted to find someone who might have been there or at least knew Jack. How could it be that friendly fire came first?"

From three sympathy notes from men who served with Jack to her sit-down discussions with them about the incident, Bernadette pieced together questions and concluded Jack had been murdered. The names Wayne Rasmus and Angelo Killian emerged. No one knew for sure, but three men agreed that if funny business went on with Jack's death, those two—who were dodgy at best—might know something. Angelo, the guy called Frosty, was a loner and a scary dude. He had a drug habit.

"Killian disappeared after the war. We couldn't find him in any records. But Rasmus was in constant trouble. It didn't take much to keep tabs on him. Mostly, he was in jail." Gavin's face deadened and his voice reflected defeat.

"How'd you even know when Rasmus got out of jail?"

"Bernie's really smart." He shook his head as if amazed. "With Rasmus in jail, she had a lot of time to find a way to get to him. She almost took a job as a guard, but some do-good groups run pen-pal programs for prisoners. Beats me as to why, but Bernie saw it as an opportunity. She's been writing to him for the past six years by using the ID of one of our cousins. He wanted her to visit him in prison, but she strung him along until this year—her first visit. He even asked her for money to help him make the transition into civilian life. Gave her an address to send bank gift cards to his mother. How stupid did he think she was? She didn't do it, but toward the end of his imprisonment, that's when she met with him one-on-one and learned the date for his release.

"He said he planned to visit his old pal Frosty. That's when I wrote to him while he was still in prison. Not with in-your-face threats because that would've attracted the authorities. But I asked him about a debt that needed to be settled. Asked if he remembered his old pal Jack. Bernie said when she saw Rasmus a second time, he worried about where he'd go to be safe. He told her about Frosty living the high life at a resort."

"He knew where Frosty lived?" asked Alice even as she recalled Pepper's story of contacting Frosty's sister for information about him.

Gavin nodded.

"How?" asked Alice.

"Don't know. I guess they've been in touch all this time." Gavin's face turned sour.

He described Bernadette's dippy act extending into a last meeting with Rasmus a couple weeks before his release. She told him of being approached by a tall, threatening man. She had managed tears coming to her eyes for effect. She pleaded with Rasmus to tell her who his enemy was. Who could it be that was after Rasmus? And by association, after her. Was his enemy tailing her? Watching her every move? Was she in danger?

"I told her the story didn't make sense. But she knew best. Rasmus said he didn't have a beef with anyone tall, but he named Angelo 'Frosty' Killian and the Elizabeth Madtree Apple Orchard Resort. He wasn't sure if Frosty would be willing to help him disappear to Montana. He hinted, however, that Frosty might hold a grudge and be ready to take him out. He told Bernadette that Frosty once shot a soldier in Vietnam. Gave the guy's name—Lieutenant Jack McKiddie."

"I still don't get it," said Alice as she rolled a shoulder for comfort. "Why did Frosty go into hiding if they were writing all these years? Were they friends or not? You see what I'm saying? Bernadette may have gotten something wrong," said Alice.

"All I know, Rasmus knew about the resort. If he hadn't been writing to him, someone must have given him Frosty's address at the resort."

Memories of Pepper's loyalty as well as other female pen pals, slipped through Alice's mind. Rasmus remembered Frosty's sister because her married name was Warbee, and it made him laugh. Pepper contacted the sister and received Frosty's address—Madtree's Apple Orchard Resort. Once he had passed that information on to Bernadette, the showdown for all the players locked into place.

Alice wondered how Bernadette managed to stay out of Rasmus' view once they both were on the property. Afterall, he knew her by sight. But, of course, she knew he was there. Use Lester as an excuse to have meal delivered to the room. Be watchful until . . .

"I take it you killed Rasmus." Alice kept her voice matter of fact. He nodded as if she had asked, *Do you like orange juice?*

Then he began his story.

"There's a small alcove on the third floor where I could wait. Once I knew Rasmus moved into the room, I took up the position. Watched him go into and out of his room, always swinging the door wide until it banged against the wall inside the room. As it swung back to close, the door hesitated before the final click. I knew I only had that moment to grab it."

Gavin's target had a strut as he left the room, and since he never took time to watch the door close or even to stay in the hallway to listen for the click as it locked, Gavin poised for the right moment to catch the door. Of course, Rasmus had hurried down the hallway and turned the corner to the elevator. He never noticed Gavin in the hallway. Entering the room, Gavin took a position on the tile floor and waited for hours in the dark, ready.

When Rasmus returned after two a.m., he was drunk. He grabbed the remote and turned on the television for room light. Against the blue lit screen, Rasmus had no distinguishable features. An inhuman dark mass, staggering, while attempting to find the button to activate programming.

"Rasmus never saw me. Never heard me. I came up from behind

him. A straightedge has a weight to it. It lies in your hand willing to do its work. I've shaved thousands of necks and watched each little pop up and down of a pulse. Men know the familiar angle of their neck as they shave. It's a habit like riding a bicycle. With one hand, I tilted Rasmus's head back and made the skin of his neck taut. Just so. Zip. And it was done. Deep—so deep there was no panic or hope. Just the blissful darkness of death. I'm sure he barely felt anything more than a paper cut. I let him drop into a heap."

Gavin's face glowed with appreciation of his work. Unzicker's evaluation of the crime was correct. Gavin was practiced with cold efficiency. An old description came to Alice's mind about the meaning of a barber pole outside the barber shop. The red signifying bloodletting.

He had used his dad's favorite straight-edge razor, the one without any kind of skin guard. He kept it in pristine condition for the perfect moment. Gavin wanted the years of searching and plotting to be over. He knew Bernadette preferred a different end filled with pain, panic, and remorse from Rasmus. Gavin just wanted him dead. Afterwards, he invented a colorful story for her of how he ended Rasmus's life with a dance of agony.

If Alice felt like a prop for Bernadette, with Gavin she felt like a witness, the accurate historian for his side of the story. Her mouth went dry.

"You're a barber like your dad," she said with softness. Her sentence felt pointless.

"I maintained dad's barber shop, but my heart wasn't into cutting hair like my dad's was. Bernie held maybe twenty different jobs over the years. Lately, she became an aide at a nursing home."

At the mention of the nursing home, Alice asked, "How did Bernadette manage to bring Lester along to the inn?"

"He has no family other than a grand-nephew who is stationed in Korea. Lester doesn't like the nursing home much, and he's always asking to go home. Bernie contacted the nephew and got his permission to take the old man out for a few days. Let him see more than four walls. And that gave us Lester Myron Livingston for the resort reservations. Mr. and Mrs. Livingston."

"Lots of paperwork in that," said Alice, but she thought, *Documents can be traced and verified.*

"You bet," said Gavin.

"But people trust Bernie because she plays the role of an innocent. Right?" commented Alice.

"Told you, she's smart. She knows people won't ask too many questions about some old dude. Reminds them of their own mortality."

"You realize we could walk out of here together and back to the inn. You could turn yourself over to the police and tell this story," said Alice. "People will then know about Angelo Killian, and the police can bring charges. Isn't that what you want?"

"Do you really think any government cares about what happened in 'Nam? Anyway, turning myself in will implicate Bernie. No. I'm willing to take the heat. When this is over, I want her to walk away clean."

Alice felt overwhelmed and her kneecaps twitched with fear. For a moment, she could have been in an icy slide toward a ditch, one where pumping the brakes did no good. She swallowed hard to maintain control.

"Gavin, this could end badly. Please, stop this madness. The police aren't going to make a trade for me and give you Frosty. Bernadette may be smart, but she isn't aware of how the police operate."

"Then this will end as it is supposed to." He twirled the gun in his hand as if he were a gunslinger and pointed the barrel to his temple. "I got me a bum ticker. Two heart attacks. For me, it's now or never. It doesn't matter how I go."

So this is Stockholm syndrome, thought Alice. *Learn the perpetrator's sad story and feel bad for crazy decisions made in the past.*

But people Alice loved could soon be outside the door. With all the Chicken Little stories Bernadette told regarding the murder, Alice couldn't imagine Unzicker taking her storytelling seriously. Besides, she hoped one person had the courage to go to the police—Maia.

Alice had been in scrapes before, but most of the time she wasn't alone with a killer. Most of the time, others united in a band to protect each other. With Alice's imagination working out dreadful endings to the drama Bernadette created, Audrey left her belly-crawl of stalking her orange and sprang to her feet. Her tail whipped back and forth with joy before bellowing a howl followed by intense barking.

Alice knew her rescuers were outside.

Chapter 32

Insistent, rapid barking and howls answered Audrey's. She danced to the door and continued barking, throwing herself at Alice and Gavin, then dashing back to the door. The chorus outside thundered back with more barking and howling.

"Shut that dog up," ordered Gavin. He seemed agitated by a force he couldn't control.

Alice was on her feet. "My guess—James Kennedy and his hounds followed our trail," said Alice over the barking. "You'd like Jim. He was a dog handler in Vietnam. Nice guy. You two could have hit it off."

"I don't care who he is. Make her stop this noise."

Alice held up her wrists, still tied with a piece of plastic. "I'm hampered."

"That's not coming off."

He took a step toward Audrey, and Alice took a step toward him. The weight of the hanging backpack dragged down her arms and caused the plastic ties to cut into her wrists as she moved to place her body between Audrey and Gavin.

Gavin shouted at Audrey who took a second to give him a dirty look of disappointment before going back to barking at the door. Maybe it was Alice's body language screaming that she was ready to take a bullet for her dog, but Gavin backed away.

"Sweetie? Soon. It's okay." Audrey went to Alice for ear caresses. She stopped barking but made low grumbly sounds in her throat.

"They didn't trust the story Bernie told, did they?" said Gavin. His voice was loud enough to be heard over the bloodhound woofing coming from outside, but he sounded reasonable. His eyes narrowed. "Here we go." He checked the gun.

"Doesn't have to be the end," said Alice, her heart hammering.

Gavin said nothing but angled near a window to peer out.

Alice rolled her neck and blinked to keep tears of fear from filling her eyes. People she cared about waited outside to protect her. She didn't want them hurt. Nor did she want to see Gavin blasted out of existence by officers charging into the house.

Gavin glared at her but didn't respond. She leaned against the wall to take some of the backpack weight from her arms and tried to keep Audrey next to her. The hound wiggled away and gave every indication of wanting to go outside, dancing, pawing the door, followed by her body slamming against Gavin. She almost toppled him on the second go-round. Gavin raised the handle of the gun to take a swing at the dog.

"Hey!" yelled Alice, crippled by the awkward backpack. She stood as tall and as menacing as a sixty-four-year-old could. "You hit that dog, and I swear I'll send you out that open window. Let the cops play target practice with you."

"Alice, you okay?" Above noise of the outside bloodhounds wanting to play with Audrey, the question came from Unzicker using a blowhorn.

"Wet with rain," yelled Alice, "but so far okay."

"Mr. McKiddie, are you keeping Alice as a hostage, or is she free to leave the house?"

Gavin grew more confused but also annoyed with Audrey, who began scratching at the door. Thin shavings of the old wood's surface fell with each scrape of Audrey's nails. Gavin reached over the dog and opened the door. Audrey bounded outside.

"That won't work," said Alice with dismissive authority in her voice. "You ever own a dog?"

Gavin shook his head. Seconds of freedom convinced Audrey she wanted back in the house. She bellowed and barked, threw herself against the door and tried to claw her way back inside. Gavin opened the door, and Audrey dashed in, throwing herself at Alice.

"Not quite the hostage situation you imagined, is it?" said Alice.

"I didn't imagine a hostage situation at all. This wasn't our plan. Okay, take your dog and leave. I wouldn't have shot you or your dog." He went to Alice, pulled a gleaming straight-edge razor from his pocket and cut the plastic binding. Alice shrugged the backpack to the floor.

"I apologize," said Alice. "But you should know, if you had struck her, I'd have done my level best to chuck you out that window."

"Truce?" asked Gavin.

"You never truly imagined a seige?"

"No."

"Then, I'm staying until we both walk out of here. Put the gun down, and we both squeeze through the door at the same time."

Gavin looked shaken, as though he wanted to throttle Alice and her dog.

"Mr. McKiddie?" called Unzicker. "What will it be? We can talk if you'd like. Turn on Alice's cell phone and I'll give you a call."

Despite appearing shaken, Gavin removed Alice's phone from his pocket and turned it on. Within seconds, her phone rang, but Gavin showed no sign of answering.

"Oh, for pity's sake, answer the damn phone," said Alice as she walked to Gavin and grappled with removing it from his hand. He took two steps back and pointed the gun at Alice's head.

"What the hell?" said Gavin. "Are you trying to get shot?"

"Are you?" asked Alice as she responded to the incoming call. "Bobby, I'm fine. You saw that Audrey's fine. This may take us a few minutes before we come out. I got a couple things I need to settle."

Alice evil-eyed Gavin and hoped the pounding pulse in her throat wasn't visible.

"Yes, he has a gun. No, I'll be okay. That's right. That's right. Not yet."

"Put the phone on speaker," demanded Gavin.

"Bobby, he wants our conversation on speaker."

The lieutenant's voice sounded canned as it fleetingly cut in and out. "Mr. McKiddie, I'm willing to give you some time because Alice asked me to. Do you need any food?"

"No," said Gavin. Alice raised her hand for his attention. "What?"

"Bobby, we're all pretty wet," said Alice. "After the rain stopped, water caught on the roof keeps dripping on us. I could use a warm, dry towel."

"No." Gavin glared at Alice and twisted toward the glassless window to study outside.

"Alice, do you also need some hot coffee?" asked Unzicker. "I can call for a hot thermos."

"It'd be nice, black no sugar, but give me a few minutes."

"Put down the phone," demanded Gavin. "What do you think this is? A picnic? We don't have to set up housekeeping." Gavin's voice squeaked and then broke as he spoke. Once the call ended, and Alice put the phone on the floor between them, Gavin paced and watched for a storm of officers charging the house.

"Will he let Bernie go?" asked Gavin. "She didn't really have anything to do with this. I could tell the police that I made her play a game called kidnap." He made impotent gestures with his hands as though he played a phantom game of dodgeball.

At least for now Gavin was thinking of being alive when the police won. Alice tipped her palms up and said, "It's possible."

"Bernie can't go to jail," said Gavin. He grabbed the phone, dialed three numbers, but canceled the call.

"Give the lieutenant your set of demands."

"I wasn't calling the lieutenant."

Alice stood framed by a glassless window and gave a small wave to the police outside. She wanted the officers to see her even if her knee-caps trembled. Two police cars angled to protect gathering officers. Jim and his hounds had pulled back from the police line. In addition to Unzicker, six other officers with guns drawn waited behind cars.

"What the hell do you think you're doing?" said Gavin. "You could get shot. They might mistake you for me."

"I've known most of those officers since they were in school. If they feel the need to shoot, I assure you, it will be at you, and they won't miss." Alice hoped her voice was confident and calm. She grabbed Audrey's collar and embraced her in a hug. The hound's steady heart-beat calmed her own up-and-down emotions.

Gavin dropped back into the room and away from windows.

"The longer you wait, more police will arrive. Limekiln's police are out there, and I saw a volunteer from Grindstone. The county po-lice are probably on their way. I've always thought they strictly follow the manual, see the world as black and white. I know you don't see yourself as a bad man, but county police will. I'll be disappointed if anyone is hurt—even you."

It was a tactic and tone Alice had used on misbehaving students many times. Most caved and apologized because they had crossed a line and once caught, didn't want to *disappoint* Mrs. T. Alice wondered if she and Gavin had shared enough for him to back down from a gun fight.

"Are you all right?" asked Alice.

Gavin stood with his back to the far wall. His voice rock steady, he said, "I promise this situation isn't going to be death by cop. I wouldn't do that to anyone or their family."

"Tell the police what you want."

"I want an exchange. You for Frosty."

"Won't happen," said Alice. "By this time, Unzicker knows that

Frosty shot your brother. You said yourself that forensics revealed the bullet to Jack's hip came from a friendly gun. Frosty's gun."

Alice had no idea if her pep talk was factually true. Was there actual proof Frosty shot Jack or did truth depend on Frosty's confession? War records declared friendly fire. With a hard-fought war ending badly, probably no one took time to match guns or imagined what the details were telling them. However, any forensic truth probably lay in the cool hand of bureaucracy, probably buried in a warehouse somewhere—if it existed at all.

"Gavin, if someone shoots a soldier, the military will care. I think they will keep Frosty in lockup." *Liar, liar, pants on fire* echoed through Alice's head.

Audrey was back at the door, scratching to go out.

"Then I want to know about Bernie." He almost pleaded with Alice. "Can't you make her stop that? She'll hurt her paws, won't she?"

Alice's heart skipped. She bit down hard on her back teeth. His concern for Audrey sounded like a goodbye. She picked up her phone from the floor and punched in Unzicker's number. "Bobby, Gavin wants to know about his sister. What has happened to her?" Alice took a breath, "You're on speaker."

That moment felt like she had given the lieutenant permission to join in her lie. The kind of *tell-him-what-you-need-to lying. Keep-him-calm-and-patient lying.*

She could have walked out of the house with Audrey, but she felt as soon as she did that, Gavin would turn the gun on himself. Although Gavin had murdered Rasmus, there was a simple, mad decency about him. He killed Rasmus without torture. He worried about Audrey's paws. Or was that her Stockholm syndrome speaking again?

Alice was grateful Unzicker chose patience over action in a hostage situation. In their first phone call when they spoke off-speaker, he had asked her if McKiddie had a daughter in Dingle Grove. Her answer, "That's right." Then he asked, "He's not intent on killing you, just Frosty?" Her answer again was "That's right." Last question from Unzicker, "Is he suicidal?" Alice answered, "Not yet."

If Unzicker knew about the daughter, concluded Alice, *Bernadette talked. Did she tell the complete truth or spin another set of foolish lies?*

As if reading her thoughts, Unzicker said, "Mr. McKiddie, Bernadette is back at the inn. She told us about Rasmus stringing her along with stories about your brother Jack McKiddie and how you stepped in to save her from . . . humiliation. Rasmus's other girlfriend, Pepper, told us he was the kind of bad guy who used women. I have the records from the prison of phone calls and letters between Bernadette and Rasmus and those from at least twenty other women. Mr. McKiddie, we need to talk about Rasmus, but we think the files we've gathered will help explain Bernadette's history with that man. It wasn't her fault. And since we're waiting, there is someone who wants to talk to you."

"Bernie?"

"No, someone else." Unzicker's voice encouraged. "Think of it as a surprise."

His folksy style made his words sound like he was offering a free puppy, but Alice knew his spin on the facts wasn't the happy ending Gavin and Bernadette wanted. No way was there enough time to gather prison records specifically for Bernadette's letters to Rasmus. Bobby had talked to Pepper many times during the investigation and was now spinning her story to include Bernadette.

"Give us some time to consider this, Bobby," said Alice and she canceled the call.

Gavin looked agitated. He repeated for Alice the facts of tracking down Rasmus and killing him. Only this time, he cast Bernadette as a follower not as the brains behind the plan. Minutes of waiting moved to an hour. Alice knew Unzicker's playbook. Keep everyone calm. Build rapport. Offer support. Get him to put the gun down and walk out.

"Bernie talked to the police . . . to protect me. When I gave up searching for Rasmus, Bernie never did. She never married. Never had a life. But she could never have killed Rasmus despite worshiping Jack. She's not like that."

Audrey went back to Alice, and they wrestled as Alice kneeled and tried to trap her dog on her lap. "Time to behave," whispered Alice into her dog's ear. Clearly miffed when there were other hounds outside, Audrey walked to the door, lay down, and pressed her nose to the crack above the threshold.

"Tell the police the story of Bernadette, the one they already believe is true. Rasmus was trying to use her even though he had shot your brother."

"And Frosty?"

"You thought he was in on it," said Alice, mentally punching herself. "Now you realize he had nothing to do with Bernadette. You know Frosty was a witness to the killing of your brother. You don't need personal revenge. Let the government handle this."

"That's not happening. He put a bullet into Jack's hip. That alone would have destroyed his Olympic ambitions . . . and Dad's. With Jack down, Rasmus murdered him."

The phone rang again.

"Mr. McKiddie, it's been over an hour. Bernadette is worried about you. She's still back at the inn and concerned that you'll catch a cold because of this rain. She asked if you want French toast. Can you believe that? Just like a sister to worry. Are you coming out? My men could also use a lunch break about now. We can pick up something for you. I'm not so sure about French toast, though."

Gavin's face paled. "Cinnamon French toast with soft butter," he whispered to no one. His eyes glistened. "Christmas morning. Bernie's sending me a message. She wants me alive at Christmas." To Unzicker he said in a strong, confident voice, "I think it's time for Alice to leave."

"Bobby, when we come out, we come out together. The door's narrow, but we'll exit side by side."

"No," said Gavin. "We won't. Lieutenant, Alice will come out with her dog. I need a minute to myself."

"Well, I got to tell you," said Unzicker, his voice both rapid and strange in a goofy way. "Alice, your coffee just arrived, and Mr. McKiddie, your surprise is here."

Audrey stood by the door and barked her demand to be let out. Alice stayed stark-still, hoping two officers with guns wouldn't bust through the back door.

"We're about to knock his socks off, Alice," said Unzicker.

"Make that damn dog stop barking. What's he talking about?" asked Gavin.

"Don't know," said Alice. She felt a shiver.

"Dad?" said a troubled woman's voice over the blowhorn.

Gavin shot a look of panic at Alice.

A young, thin, scared voice of a teenage girl followed. "Grampy?"

Chapter 33

Audrey sideswiped through the doorway as soon as Alice opened it a crack and bounded past the police cars and into the paws and mouths of the two rescue hounds held by Jim Kennedy and his wife, Donna.

"You don't want your granddaughter to see anything ugly," said Alice. "She sounds like a nice kid."

Gavin put the gun on the floor next to Alice's backpack.

"Come on," Alice said, "we go out doing the wave." She raised her arms and wiggled her fingers. "None of that ladies-first business. It's together."

Since Gavin heard his granddaughter call him again from outside, his chin dropped, and he made no eye contact. He took a breath of resignation and moved to the doorway. As they walked down the broken front step, officers were already coming forward. Of course, an excited Audrey surged back and beat them to Alice and Gavin. Alice noticed a scared fifteen-year-old girl huddled next to a woman, probably her mother.

The silence as Alice and Gavin walked away from the house broke with a din of chatter, clapping, and barking. Alice soon found a crowd of people around her and lost track of Audrey until a nose attacked from behind and wedged between her knees, almost toppling her. At that point, a sea of blue crowded Gavin and he disappeared.

Lena and Julian came to her side as well as Elizabeth and Artie. Curious guests of the inn collected at the back of the crowd. Pepper Finwall, Rasmus's lady friend, also stood in the back of the group, crying.

With her leash flapping, Audrey blasted away from Alice in the direction of Jim and Donna who corralled their two rollicking bloodhounds. As Alice attempted to follow her dog, Audrey disappeared again into the crowd. Bloodhounds were notorious for catching a curious scent and impulsively hunting. Where had her girl gone? With several apologies, Alice tore through the crowd to get to Jim. As she approached, she finally saw other friends sitting on the bumper of a pickup, feeding Audrey, who swallowed chunks of dog food whole.

"Hope you don't mind," said Virgil. "Me and Francis thought this girl might be hungry."

Alice relaxed. Of course, her dog was hungry. After a morning walk, Audrey usually had breakfast, but the few treats Alice had in her pocket weren't enough for her eating machine. How long had the siege in the broken house delayed her nourishment?

After Audrey consumed traditional dog food from Francis's fingers, Virgil shared a package of weenies with his old pal Audrey one-for-me, one-for-you style. Audrey appeared to be in heaven.

"Are you sure these aren't meant for humans?" asked Virgil. "Sure are good."

"Quieter back here," said Sylvie as she put her arm around Alice's back.

"Your dog seems to like me," said Francis. "I think I impress her with *my* dog collar." He touched the white clerical collar he had worn for the last several days.

"You go along and do what you have to," said Sylvie. "Police will have questions. We got this. But we want the full story after you shower."

"And food," said Alice. "I'm starving."

"Want a weenie?" asked Virgil while shaking a bag of Tran's dog treats.

Unable to take in all the questions coming from people in the crowd and feeling rattled by attention, Alice looked for escape before she sat down for a long talk with Unzicker. One grandmother with her hands on her granddaughter's shoulders stood off to the side. Maia looked frightened, but when she caught Alice's eye, she flashed a confident thumbs-up. Alice went to Maia and wrapped her arms around her.

"Thank you."

Chapter 34

Alice spent all day Wednesday sitting with the police and telling and retelling the story of the abduction, only stealing breaks to run off for necessary walks with Audrey.

By Thursday, breakfast at the inn was both lavish and welcoming. Scrambled eggs and cottage fries were dwarfed by baked apple pancakes, apple-cinnamon kugel, turkey-apple sausage, applewood smoked bacon, apple muffins and pastries. For the brave, Artie created his version of an appletini: a bright green drink of hard cider and green apple schnapps garnished with a slice of Golden Delicious. The gathering was Elizabeth's thank-you to the police, Alice and her friends who poked around, and the inn guests who'd endured the crime scene.

Guests regretted not having a magazine writer on the scene, but once the standoff at the ghost house cropped up, several guests had their own personal moment talking with the media. Many easily adapted to television interviews. A news microphone shoved into faces didn't hinder them at all. Boredom broke for two teenage boys who set up their own live streaming of their experiences and managed to snag older adults to join them.

"I was scared, but not terrified. You know what I mean. Like when you see a bug in the bathroom, and your heart jumps, but you're not too timid to pick up a shoe."

"Yes, I'll return to the inn next year. Lots to do, and this was so exciting. I heard the abandoned house is being made into a stage for ghost stories. Ya gotta know I'll be back for that."

"I thought it was part of their Halloween program. I wasn't scared at all until we heard a woman had been abducted for real. My husband and I had to see what the police would do. It was so intense that I almost peed my pants."

With the breakfast over, Lieutenant Unzicker called Alice's army of snoopers into the gathering room at the inn and closed the glass door.

"Thank you for not getting yourselves killed," began Unzicker with a teasing grin. "We've talked to all of you individually, but I thought I should get you together to answer your questions. Do it in one fell swoop."

"What happens to the killer and his sister?" asked Francis.

"That's in the hands of the county prosecutor's office. All I can do is present evidence. If they go to trial, some of you may be asked to testify." He looked at Alice.

"And Angelo Killian?" asked Julian, his voice low. "What's gonna happen to him?"

Unzicker made a face. "That one is complicated. We had a long night last night. Look, we don't have any evidence that he did anything wrong while he lived on resort property or in this county."

He looked beyond the closed doors and at Elizabeth and Artie who continued to cater to guests lingering at tables over drinks.

"Against his lawyer's advice, Angelo, err . . . Frosty confirmed taking a shot in Jack McKiddie's direction while he was in Vietnam. My guess—that shot may have struck McKiddie in the hip. If that is true, it wasn't a kill shot as far as we know. And it's also true that at the sounds of their shots, other soldiers and officers added to the confusion when they came out of buildings and fired at McKiddie's general direction."

"Friendly fire from the officers could have struck McKiddie," stated Francis for once shedding his callous tone.

"We have no way of knowing. Frosty also has confessed to seeing Rasmus use an enemy gun to kill McKiddie. But that's not my jurisdiction, and other than his unrecorded verbal account, I have no evidence of what went on in Vietnam. My concern is here. I will file a report on the murder and the abduction and send it to the county prosecutor. And I'll check with the prosecutor to see if he wants to pursue anything else. After Frosty began to share small details, Gilly pulled rank as his lawyer and has muzzled him for good. The prosecutor has worked with her before and may have opinions about how the evidence against Frosty, or lack thereof, stacks up."

To Alice, Unzicker's explanation sounded spongy.

"What if Bernadette and Gavin stir up publicity for their trial?" asked Julian. "What if they blame Frosty for their brother's death to create sympathy for their situation?"

"At this point they don't seem to want publicity," answered Unzicker. "But if they do tell their story to the media, maybe the feds will investigate Frosty more in depth. It's out of my hands. The county will deal with the murder of Wayne Rasmus and the abduction of Alice." Unzicker shook his head. "I can't imagine much sympathy for a pair that kidnapped a woman to get leverage. There was no reason to do that. And, like I said, the county may or may not send a report to the feds. In the meantime, if the resort wants him back, Frosty might return tomorrow."

All eyes went to Elizabeth who entered on Unzicker's last four words. *Frosty might return tomorrow.*

"Thank God," said Elizabeth. "Our busy season goes through January, and we have two sides of beef coming in the beginning of next week from a local farmer."

There was a soft gasp from several people in the room, and Elizabeth's face flushed before she continued her explanation. "The children love him, and I'm not happy with the substitute tram driver who needs to get back to accounting. We have so much to do for Halloween, and the beekeepers are coming. I want the resort back to normal."

Artie slipped into the room and stood behind his sister, holding his phone in his hand. "I just booked mystery writers who want to workshop here," said Artie, "and a blog writer emailed us and wants to do a story about managing an inn alongside a farming business."

Unzicker took a call and the gathering broke up.

As they walked out of the room, Francis came to Alice's side.

"Well, you'll be busy next year if they prepare for the McKiddie trial."

"If there is a trial," said Alice who wondered how bad Gavin's heart was. "Are you worried about Frosty?"

"Frosty, nah. Thanks for putting him in touch with a bearcat of a lawyer. Besides, we're talking federal government. What have they got to gain? How many manhours do they want to invest in an old case where one soldier wounded another? Do they really want to dredge up memories of chaos or dig through evidence that they have already deemed as friendly fire? Nah. He's good. Sometimes inertia is a beautiful thing."

Even though everyone planned to pack cars and trucks with luggage, friends and guests milled about the parking lot. They patted shoulders and gave hugs. Lena happily became a general with commands for packing their trunk with suitcases and garment bags. Audrey pulled in the direction of Virgil and Cyril, who sat on the sidelines. Sylvie sought out Alice.

"Wish you could've seen Lieutenant Unzicker before Bernadette found him," said Sylvie. "That child Maia, Francis, and Cyril tripleteamed him with information. It was like a hen-house warning the farmer about a fox."

"Cyril?"

"Don't tell him I complimented him, but turns out for his age, he's really sharp. Believe it or not, Cyril looked up Lester Myron Livingston's address. It's a memory care facility. Cyril had found Francis in the breakfast room with Lester in his wheelchair. He then clumped along while Francis pushed Lester until the three of them tracked down your police lieutenant." Sylvie shook her head and cackled. "The old boy has still got it. He pointed his finger at the lieutenant and began his spiel with 'See here.' In the meantime, Francis had made a call to the home to untangle what's been going on and promised to escort Lester home. I hope they bring charges against Bernadette for neglecting Lester. She wasn't his wife at all."

"I don't know about charges," said Alice. "That's for the county to decide and for Lester's family and nursing home to consider."

Sylvie gave a sly smile. "At least Lester had the best shave of his life, don't you think?"

Alice felt her own wicked smile grow with irony. "He certainly did."

"That child Maia is another smart one," said Sylvie. "She said you were in trouble, and Unzicker listened but with all that was happening, in one ear out the other. You know how they sometimes do. But, let's face it, Alice, you're a big girl. It is hard for any of us to imagine someone kidnapping you. It wasn't until Maia told of a woman taking control of Audrey that any of us took the child seriously. That and Cyril stomping on the lieutenant's foot with his walker. He said, 'Listen to the kid.'"

"By the time Bernadette found Unzicker," continued Sylvie, "he had already called for that guy Jim and his hounds. Bernadette had no story to tell. Everything she said fell flat. Putting the cuffs on her and describing how the abduction could end nasty made her open-up. Not so tough after all. To save her brother's life, she told about his family nearby.

"Whew! We had a dandy time." Sylvie's eyes sparkled. "Don't forget to give us a holler for your next murder investigation." Sylvie gave Alice a quick handshake that turned into a strong hug. "Francis has taken charge of Lester Myron Livingston, and after our last trip with Audrey to the Inn, your car is too cramped. Virgil, Cyril, and I are hitching a ride back to your house in the resort limo. We are leaving in style."

Then Sylvie was gone.

Lena slipped her arm around Alice's waist, and Alice's arm went around her best friend's shoulders.

"We'll be off in a few minutes. I'll see you before Julian and I leave for our proper, long-awaited honeymoon in Hawaii, away from murders. You going to be okay? You've been awfully quiet."

"I'm okay," said Alice.

Lena's eyes turned naughty. "I wonder what Baer would say if he were alive to see you abducted?"

Alice felt a warm glow at the mention of Baer. "He did his best to control his inner cave man."

"He certainly loved you."

Both grinned. "When away on a job, he'd call to make sure I closed windows against the rain. At home, he hovered around the children and me. His eyes would worry. He'd get those creases above his nose. He'd insist I drink a glass of chocolate milk for electrolytes to keep up my strength. For an artist, he wanted things just so."

"I envied you," said Lena.

"How's Julian handling new truths about friends?" asked Alice.

"Ach." Lena sounded like she was clearing her throat. "We all deal with old wounds all the time, don't we?" Both women gazed in Audrey's direction. "Alice, did you ever imagine that when we retired, we'd become detectives, and I'd have my ribs broken or Julian have broken hands and hyperthermia?" Lena's eyes opened wider. "Oh God, that you'd get grazed by a bullet and then in less than a year be abducted? Or that the three of us could have been shot dead in a vineyard? Of course, I wasn't scared, but it is amazing. We have exciting lives."

Alice squeezed her friend's shoulder. "We live in interesting times. I think we'll be snooping until we're ninety because we've been the very best of friends for decades. If Cyril can continue to prowl around in people's lives, so can we."

Lena's chin came up. "I promise to push your wheelchair to the crime scene."

"No," said Alice. "I thought I'd haul your hospital bed. That way you won't get all sweaty and your hair will still be curled and pretty."

"I like your way better," said Lena with a wide grin. "Remember, I want a sexy bed jacket to throw around my shoulders, and you be sure to mount my computer to the side of the bed. That way I can investigate as we roll down hospital hallways."

The absurd descriptions went on until both watched Audrey sit near Virgil, who willingly shared the last two bites from a package of Tran's Keep Me Happy dog treats.

The two women continued to hold onto each other in silence, unable to say goodbye to the orchard. Alice felt her unease with unanswered questions slip away and the blessings of friendships grow.

As cars drove away from the inn, Alice said to Lena, "You're the absolute best."

"No, I'm the prettiest, but you're the best," said Lena.

"No, you."

"You."

"Damn," said Julian, ripping off his bandana, his voice pitching higher. "If you two keep yapping, I'm never getting to Hawaii."

Alice and Lena looked at each other and laughed, but it was Audrey who had the last word. Her baritone howl answered Julian's concern. Then her muscular shake sent slobber in all directions and convinced the two honeymooners to run for their car. Left alone in the parking lot, Alice watched Audrey pick up a find.

"No! What's in your mouth?"

Audrey turned her head away from Alice in a gesture that said "*Nothing.*"

"Don't you swallow that." The tussle began as Alice wrestled a slimy golf ball from the bloodhound's mouth.

"I'm not angry. You're such a big, beautiful, complicated girl. We couldn't have solved the murder without you. But with Lena and Julian away, I think it's time for you and me to spend many days lollygagging. Soon it will be too cool for chasing bubbles in the yard, but we'll find something. Like visiting Josh to pick up Frosty's knives. Like playing keep-away with Cooper. Would you like to visit Jim's bloodhounds?"

Alice opened the door to the dowager Lincoln. Audrey willingly leaped in and gave Alice the look. *"Are you coming or what?"*

Acknowledgments

In the 1960s my father worked with a man who lost his oldest son to combat in Vietnam. I think for Dad the moment triggered memories of his loss of a brother and cousins in World War II. My dad's perspective touched my heart.

Even in writing a mystery, researching wartime has its own path. I researched the impact of war on my family through genealogy, even for those in the Civil War. I want to thank the men who were willing to share stories from World War II, Korea, and Vietnam, as well as former students who served in Fallujah. Thank you, everyone for your service and insight.

On Pinterest, I have a collection of bloodhound photos that continue to inspire descriptions of Audrey. On Facebook, I follow people like Maria, who own bloodhounds. What a joy. I continue to do research on bloodhounds by reading every page of *Bonckers* and *The Daily Drool*, newsletters from Bloodhounds West, Northern Chapter. In the spring of 2020, our plans to visit Cindy, Pat, and Pam had to be canceled because of the virus, but I still follow their postings. Thanks to all who love this breed and share. And thanks to new friends who post experiences and questions about trailing dogs.

Rachel edited *Murder Comes to Madtree*, and her insight helped me flesh out scenes. Thank you, Rachel.

Thanks to Rich, who agreed to be an early reader of a *Madtree* draft and shared his Air Force experiences in the 1960s.

Thank you to my cousin Nancy, who through her postings, showed me the fun of face painting.

Thanks to friends who continue to support my efforts: Carolyn, Peg, Carol, Joyce, Nancy, Christine, Dave, Dianne, Linda, Charlotte, and the Karens.

The Barrington Writers continue to share their reactions to my early drafts. Thanks for being patient. Chicago Writers Association provides suggestions on development and publicity. Sisters in Crime helps to tweak my enthusiasm.

As always, Al is my first reader, driver to book fairs, photographer, coffee maker. Thank you for being supportive and patient even during this time of virus. Thank you, my quarantine partner.

Thanks to everyone who has helped with information and suggestions. Thanks for lifting me up. The mystery feels done, but some cringe-worthy fact or comma placement may have alluded me. Sorry for that. As I proofread, my brain has a way of inserting what should be, without the correction ever getting to the paper. Alas, the errors are mine. Absolutely maddening!

Other Writings by
Georgann Prochaska

Fiction: Mysteries

The Case of the Girl Who Didn't Smile (2015)
What fate awaited the little girl accused of arson that took a life?
Named to Lascaux Top Ten 2015

The Case of the Hound Who Didn't Stay (2016)
Disappearances of people in Dingle Grove are carefully tucked away
in memory until Audrey the bloodhound finds two graves.

The Case of the Ex Who Plotted Revenge (2017)
What information from Internet does an ex-con dredge up to take
revenge on Limekiln?
Winner of Second Place for mysteries, Royal Dragonfly Awards

Murder Comes to the Vineyard (2018)
After a woman is murdered, Alice persists in fulfilling her promise. Is
Cade buried in the vineyard or did he simply run away from secrets?

Murder Comes to Grindstone (2019)
When a tornado struck Grindstone, why were two little girls found
in the Tuthill basement? Why did they disappear afterwards?

Nonfiction: Memoir

On Little Cat Feet: Alzheimer's Disease: Subtle, Meddlesome, Sinister (2014)
Alzheimer's enters lives slowly. A caregiver constantly battles to
remember the disease is the enemy, not a loved one.

CPSIA information can be obtained
at www.ICGtesting.com
Printed in the USA
FSHW020948120521
81310FS